OXFORD WORLD'S CLASSICS

JUST SO STORIES

RUDYARD KIPLING (1865–1936) was born in Bombay in December 1865. He returned to India from England in the autumn of 1882, shortly before his seventeenth birthday, to work as a journalist first on the *Civil and Military Gazette* in Lahore, then on the *Pioneer* at Allahabad. The poems and stories he wrote over the next seven years laid the foundation of his literary reputation, and soon after his return to London in 1889 he found himself world-famous. Throughout his life his works enjoyed great acclaim and popularity, but he came to seem increasingly controversial because of his political opinions, and it has been difficult to reach literary judgements unclouded by partisan feeling. The Oxford World's Classics series provides the opportunity for reconsidering his remarkable achievement.

LISA LEWIS is a freelance writer and researcher. She is currently working on an anthology of Kipling's writings on literature. She is a former Chairman of the Kipling Society and has made a special study of his manuscripts.

OXFORD WORLD'S CLASSICS

For over 100 years Oxford World's Classics have brought readers closer to the world's great literature. Now with over 700 titles—from the 4,000-year-old myths of Mesopotamia to the twentieth century's greatest novels—the series makes available lesser-known as well as celebrated writing.

The pocket-sized hardbacks of the early years contained introductions by Virginia Woolf, T. S. Eliot, Graham Greene, and other literary figures which enriched the experience of reading. Today the series is recognized for its fine scholarship and reliability in texts that span world literature, drama and poetry, religion, philosophy and politics. Each edition includes perceptive commentary and essential background information to meet the changing needs of readers.

OXFORD WORLD'S CLASSICS

RUDYARD KIPLING

Just So Stories
for Little Children

WITH ILLUSTRATIONS BY THE AUTHOR

Edited with an Introduction and Notes by
LISA LEWIS

OXFORD
UNIVERSITY PRESS

OXFORD

UNIVERSITY PRESS

Great Clarendon Street, Oxford OX2 6DP

Oxford University Press is a department of the University of Oxford.
It furthers the University's objective of excellence in research, scholarship,
and education by publishing worldwide in

Oxford New York

Athens Auckland Bangkok Bogotá Buenos Aires Calcutta
Cape Town Chennai Dar es Salaam Delhi Florence Hong Kong Istanbul
Karachi Kuala Lumpur Madrid Melbourne Mexico City Mumbai
Nairobi Paris São Paulo Singapore Taipei Tokyo Toronto Warsaw

with associated companies in Berlin Ibadan

Oxford is a registered trade mark of Oxford University Press
in the UK and in certain other countries

Published in the United States
by Oxford University Press Inc., New York

Introduction, Note on the Text, Explanatory Notes © L:isa Lewis, 1995
Preface, Bibliography, Chronology © Andrew Rutherford 1987
Updated Bibliography © Andrew Rutherford 1996

The moral rights of the author have been asserted

Database right Oxford University Press (maker)

First published as a World's Classics paperback 1995
Reissued as an Oxford World's Classics paperback 1998

British Library Cataloguing in Publication Data

Data available

Library of Congress Cataloging in Publication Data
Kipling, Rudyard, 1865–1936.
Just so stories, for little children / Rudyard Kipling; with
illustrations by the author; edited with an introduction by
Lisa Lewis.
p. cm.—(Oxford world's classics)
Includes bibliographical references.
1. Children's stories, English. 2. Animals—Juvenile fiction.
[1. Animals—Fiction. 2. Short stories.] I. Lewis, Lisa.
II. Title. III. Series.
PR4854.J83 1995 823'.8—dc20 94–31326

ISBN–13: 978–0–19–283436–2
ISBN–10: 0–19–283436–3

7

Printed in Great Britain by
Clays Ltd, St Ives plc

CONTENTS

GENERAL PREFACE

RUDYARD KIPLING (1865–1936) was for the last decade
of the nineteenth century and at least the first two decades
of the twentieth the most popular writer in English, in
both verse and prose, throughout the English-speaking
world. Widely regarded as the greatest living English poet
and story-teller, winner of the Nobel Prize for Literature,
recipient of honorary degrees from the Universities of Oxford, Cambridge, Edinburgh, Durham, McGill, Strasbourg,
and the Sorbonne, he also enjoyed popular acclaim that
extended far beyond academic and literary circles.

He stood, it can be argued, in a special relation to the age
in which he lived. He was primarily an artist, with his
individual vision and techniques, but his was also a pro-
foundly representative consciousness. He seems to give
expression to a whole phase of national experience, sym-
bolizing in appropriate forms (as Lascelles Abercrombie
said the epic poet must do) the 'sense of the significance of
life he [felt] acting as the unconscious metaphysic of the
time'.[1] He is in important ways a spokesman for his age,
with its sense of imperial destiny, its fascinated contempla-
tion of the unfamiliar world of soldiering, its confidence in
engineering and technology, its respect for craftsmanship,
and its dedication to Carlyle's gospel of work. That age is
one about which many Britons—and to a lesser extent

[1] Cited in E. M. W. Tillyard, *The Epic Strain in the English Novel*
(London, 1958), 15.

Americans and West Europeans—now feel an exaggerated
sense of guilt; and insofar as Kipling was its spokesman,
he has become our scapegoat. Hence, in part at least, the
tendency in recent decades to dismiss him so contemptu-
ously, so unthinkingly, and so mistakenly. Whereas if we
approach him more historically, less hysterically, we shall
find in this very relation to his age a cultural phenomenon
of absorbing interest.

Here, after all, we have the last English author to appeal
to readers of all social classes and all cultural groups, from
lowbrow to highbrow; and the last poet to command a
mass audience. He was an author who could speak directly
to the man in the street, or for that matter in the barrack-
room or factory, more effectively than any left-wing writer
of the 'thirties or the present day, but who spoke just as
directly and effectively to literary men like Edmund Gosse
and Andrew Lang; to academics like David Masson, George
Saintsbury, and Charles Eliot Norton; to the professional
and service classes (officers and other ranks alike) who took
him to their hearts; and to creative writers of the stature of
Henry James, who had some important reservations to
record, but who declared in 1892 that 'Kipling strikes me
personally as the most complete man of genius (as distinct
from fine intelligence) that I have ever known', and who
wrote an enthusiastic introduction to *Mine Own People* in
which he stressed Kipling's remarkable appeal to the sophisticated critic as well as to the common reader.[2]

An innovator and a virtuoso in the art of the short story,
Kipling does more than any of his predecessors to establish

---

[2] See *Kipling: The Critical Heritage*, ed. Roger Lancelyn Green (London, 1971), 159–60. *Mine Own People*, published in New York in 1891,
was a collection of stories nearly all of which were to be subsumed in
Life's Handicap later that year.

it as a major genre. But within it he moves confidently between the poles of sophisticated simplicity (in his earliest tales) and the complex, closely organized, elliptical and symbolic mode of his later works which reveal him as an unexpected contributor to modernism.

He is a writer who extends the range of English literature in both subject-matter and technique. He plunges readers into new realms of imaginative experience which then become part of our shared inheritance. His anthropological but warmly human interest in mankind in all its varieties produces, for example, sensitive, sympathetic vignettes of Indian life and character which culminate in *Kim*. His sociolinguistic experiments with proletarian speech as an artistic medium in *Barrack-Room Ballads* and his rendering of the life of private soldiers in all their unregenerate humanity gave a new dimension to war literature. His portrayal of Anglo-Indian life ranges from cynical triviality in some of the *Plain Tales from the Hills* to the stoical nobility of the best things in *Life's Handicap* and *The Day's Work*. Indeed Mrs Hauksbee's Simla, Mulvaney's barrack-rooms, Dravot and Carnehan's search for a kingdom in Kafiristan, Holden's illicit, star-crossed love, Stalky's apprenticeship, Kim's Grand Trunk Road, 'William''s famine relief expedition, and the Maltese Cat's game at Umballa, establish the vanished world of Empire for us (as they established the unknown world of Empire for an earlier generation), in all its pettiness and grandeur, its variety and energy, its miseries, its hardships, and its heroism.

In a completely different vein Kipling's genius for the animal fable as a means of inculcating human truths opens up a whole new world of joyous imagining in the two *Jungle Books*. In another vein again are the stories in which he records his delighted discovery of the English countryside, its people and traditions, after he had settled at Bateman's in Sussex: England, he told Rider Haggard in 1902, 'is the most wonderful foreign land I have ever been in';[3] and he made it peculiarly his own. Its past gripped his imagination as strongly as its present, and the two books of Puck stories show what Eliot describes as 'the development of the imperial . . . into the historical imagination'.[4] In another vein again he figures as the bard of engineering and technology. From the standpoint of world history, two of Britain's most important areas of activity in the nineteenth century were those of industrialism and imperialism, both of which had been neglected by literature prior to Kipling's advent. There is a substantial body of work on the Condition of England Question and the socio-economic effects of the Industrial Revolution; but there is comparatively little imaginative response in literature (as opposed to painting) to the extraordinary inventive energy, the dynamic creative power, which manifests itself in (say) the work of engineers like Telford, Rennie, Brunel, and the brothers Stephenson—men who revolutionized communications within Britain by their road, rail and harbour systems, producing in the process masterpieces of industrial art, and who went on to revolutionize ocean travel as well. Such achievements are acknowledged on a sub-literary level by Samuel Smiles in his best-selling *Lives of the Engineers* (1861–2). They are acknowledged also by Carlyle, who celebrates the positive as well as denouncing the malign aspects of the transition from the feudal to the industrial world, insisting as he does that the true modern epic must be technological, not military: 'For we are to bethink us that the Epic verily is not

[3] *Rudyard Kipling to Rider Haggard*, ed. Morton Cohen (London, 1965), 51.

[4] T. S. Eliot, *On Poetry and Poets* (London, 1957), 247.

Arms and the Man, but *Tools and the Man*,—an infinitely
wider kind of Epic.'[5] That epic has never been written in its
entirety, but Kipling came nearest to achieving its aims in
verses like 'McAndrew's Hymn' (*The Seven Seas*) and stories like 'The Ship that Found Herself' and 'Bread upon the
Waters' (*The Day's Work*) in which he shows imaginative
sympathy with the machines themselves as well as sympathy
with the men who serve them. He comes nearer, indeed,
than any other author to fulfilling Wordsworth's prophecy
that

If the labours of men of Science should ever create any material
revolution, direct or indirect, in our condition, and in the impres-
sions which we habitually receive, the Poet will sleep then no
more than at present, but he will be ready to follow the steps of
the Man of Science, not only in those general indirect effects, but
he will be at his side, carrying sensation into the midst of the
objects of the Science itself.[6]

This is one aspect of Kipling's commitment to the world
of work, which, as C. S. Lewis observes, 'imaginative literature in the eighteenth and nineteenth centuries had [with
a few exceptions] quietly omitted, or at least thrust into the
background', though it occupies most of the waking hours
of most men:

And this did not merely mean that certain technical aspects of
life were unrepresented. A whole range of strong sentiments
and emotions—for many men, the strongest of all—went with
them. . . . It was Kipling who first reclaimed for literature this
enormous territory.[7]

[5] *Past and Present* (1843), Book iv, ch. 1. Cf. ibid., Book iii, ch. 5.
[6] *Lyrical Ballads*, ed. R. L. Brett and A. R. Jones (London, 1963), 253–
4.
[7] 'Kipling's World', *Literature and Life: Addresses to the English Association* (London, 1948), 59–60.

He repudiates the unspoken assumption of most novelists that the really interesting part of life takes place outside working hours: men at work or talking about their work are among his favourite subjects. The qualities men show in their work, and the achievements that result from it (bridges built, ships salvaged, pictures painted, famines relieved) are the very stuff of much of Kipling's fiction. Yet there also runs through his *œuvre*, like a figure in the carpet, a darker, more pessimistic vision of the impermanence, the transience—but not the worthlessness—of all achievement. This underlies his delighted engagement with contemporary reality and gives a deeper resonance to his finest work, in which human endeavour is celebrated none the less because it must ultimately yield to death and mutability.

ANDREW RUTHERFORD

ACKNOWLEDGEMENTS

WARMEST thanks to Fiona Campbell, Peter Lewis, and Donald Mackenzie for help with the Introduction; to Terry Barringer, Margaret Campbell, Douglas Gray, Sara Johnson, and Rosalind Meyer for advice on research; and, for information on specific points, to Margaret Bain, Tessa Chester (Bethnal Green Museum of Childhood), Jeremy Coote (Pitt Rivers Museum), Fiona Easton (the Hakluyt Society), Rosalind Kennedy (President, Melbourne Branch, the Kipling Society), Peggy Leo (Brattleboro Museum and Art Center), John McGivering, and Laurence Smith. Thanks also to the ever-friendly and helpful staff of the Bodleian Library.

INTRODUCTION

SEVERAL stories of fantasy animals published near the beginning of the twentieth century have become well-loved children's classics: Beatrix Potter's *The Tale of Peter Rabbit* (1902), Kenneth Grahame's *The Wind in the Willows* (1908), as well as Kipling's *The Jungle Book* (1894) and its sequel (1895). These were followed in 1902 by his *Just So Stories for Little Children*. All three writers invent for their creatures imaginary worlds of great lyrical charm, as if to compensate for their own lonely or unhappy childhoods. Potter and Grahame dreamed of escape into the country-side, she to holidays in Scotland or the Lake District, he to his grandmother's home on the Thames. Kipling's earthly paradise was both wilder and more varied: an Indian jungle, the Arctic seas, and in *Just So Stories* prehistoric caves, as well as deserts, rivers, and uninhabited islands scattered about the world.

Kipling was a man without deep roots in any country. Born in India of a Yorkshire father and a mother of Scottish descent, he was sent back to England to board with a foster-family at Southsea in Hampshire, near the naval base of Portsmouth. Most of his formal education came from four years at boarding-school in Devonshire, after which, aged 16, he returned to India to work. At the time of his first success he was living in London; he then moved, on his marriage, to Vermont in New England. But by 1902 he was permanently settled in Sussex. Though he identified strongly with, and used in his writing, aspects of all these places—even the much-hated Southsea left him with a permanent interest in ships and the sea—he could never be said to belong to any of them in the sense that (say) Hardy belonged to Wessex.

Just So Stories was begun during the American years. It is unique among Kipling's works, if only because it is the one book that he would illustrate himself. All his novels and prose collections include at least some verse, but here he uses four different modes: stories, poems, drawings, and explanatory captions to the full-page illustrations, giving suggested answers (such as the names of the animals) to questions a child might ask.

Moreover the book is 'for little children', a younger group than any he had previously addressed. Though it includes material (like the picture-map 'Ye Manie Mouthes of ye Amazons River') more likely to interest an older reader, the first three stories at least are designed for reading aloud to the pre-school age-group. *Just So Stories* was also the first of Kipling's works to involve his own children, whose comments he actively sought: his daughter Elsie wrote that the stories were read to herself and her brother 'for such suggestions as could be expected from small children'.[1]

Most of these tales had a long oral life before they were written down. The series was at least eight and possibly ten years in gestation, during a period that would prove eventful for the writer and his American wife. They moved between countries, living first among her relations, then close to his. Their three children were born and one would die. These were also the years when Kipling became rich, and his reputation grew from critical success to international

[1] From a memoir in C. E. Carrington, *Rudyard Kipling: His Life and Work* (London: Macmillan, 1955), 511.

celebrity. Then, as the new century began, the intellectual climate changed and seemed to leave him behind—a writer of fables for children, whom adults (it was claimed) no longer took seriously.[2]

What seems to be the first mention of a Just So story can be found just before Kipling's eldest child Josephine was born. In November 1892 he was toying with the idea of some children's stories about animals, to be rooted in the legends of India that he had loved when he was a little boy in Bombay, and in the folk-tales of many lands that he continued to collect and enjoy. In a letter to the editor of the children's magazine *St Nicholas*, Mrs Mary Mapes Dodge,[3] he listed some proposed titles: of these 'Toomai of the Elephants', 'Tiger! Tiger!', and 'Mowgli's Brothers' went into *The Jungle Book*, which dominated his prose writing for the next three years. But he also mentioned a 'camel tale', though no such tale appeared in *St Nicholas* (or any-where else) until 'How the Camel got his Hump'.

In the summer of 1893, Kipling's father John Lockwood Kipling visited the young family at their new home 'Naulakha', near Brattleboro, where they had settled in order to be near Carrie Kipling's mother. Lockwood had just retired after twenty-eight years' service as art teacher and museum curator in Bombay and Lahore, and his wife Alice, Kipling's mother, was busy house-hunting in England. During this visit 'Rikki-Tikki-Tavi' was finished, the story about an Indian mongoose which was the first of the

[2] See T. S. Eliot, *The Athenaeum* (9 May 1919), 297–8; E. M. Forster, *Daily Herald* (9 June 1920); Virginia Woolf, 'Mr Kipling's Notebook', *The Athenaeum* (16 July 1920). See also Edward Shanks on comments by his parents' generation soon after the Boer War, *Kipling Journal* (Dec. 1941), 7.
[3] Thomas Pinney (ed.), *The Letters of Rudyard Kipling* (London: Macmillan, 1990), 71–2.

Jungle Book series to be published in *St Nicholas*. Lockwood himself had recently published his collection of essays *Beast and Man in India*. In the chapter on the camel is this passage:

It was on his back that the body of Shah Ali Shah was laid after death, and he was sent into the wilderness till the Angel Gabriel met him and, taking the rope, led him no man knew whither. Before that ghostly funeral the camel resembled a horse, but the Angel Gabriel gave him a hump like the mountains into which he disappeared . . .[4]

The following summer, father and son met again and discussed the animal series. Then, according to Mrs Kipling's diary, 'The Camel' was begun.

Baby Josephine was still a little young for it, but another potential child listener was available at this early stage: her 3-year-old cousin Marjorie Balestier. Marjorie's father was Carrie Kipling's brother Beatty, a charming, generous ne'er-do-weel with whom the Kiplings were at first intimate, but with whom they quarrelled disastrously in 1896. The much-publicized court case that followed, combined with some Anglo-American ill-feeling caused by a dispute over Venezuela, drove the family (by then including 6-month-old Elsie) to take permanent refuge in England.

There they settled at Rottingdean in Sussex, where their son John was born. They found a house near Kipling's uncle and maternal aunt, Sir Edward and Lady Burne-Jones; various cousins and friends also lived in or visited the neighbourhood. At this time at least one other child began to listen to the stories. Angela Thirkell, daughter of Kipling's cousin Margaret Mackail (*née* Burne-Jones), remembered:

[4] John Lockwood Kipling, *Beast and Man in India* (London: Macmillan, 1892), 245.

During those long warm summers Cousin Ruddy used to try out the *Just So Stories* on a nursery audience. Sometimes Josephine and I would be invited into his study, a pleasant bow-windowed room, where Cousin Ruddy sat at his work-table...

The *Just So Stories* are a poor thing in print compared with the fun of hearing them told in Cousin Ruddy's deep unhesitating voice. There was a ritual about them, each phrase having its special intonation which had to be exactly the same each time and without which the stories are dried husks. There was an inimitable cadence, a kind of intoning here and there which made his telling unforgettable.[5]

Kipling describes how this ritual began in a preface that also explains the series' title (see p. 1): they were bedtime stories that had to be told 'just so', without variation, if they were to lull the listener to sleep. This preface was published with the first story in *St Nicholas* in December 1897, when Josephine was 5 years old. (It seems a pity that it was never reprinted: but it is to some extent traduced by the captions to the book's illustrations, which encourage not slumber but questions.) Earlier that year Kipling may have had an idea for another tale in the series. In January 1897 he wrote in a letter to his aunt Louisa Baldwin[6] that Josephine was nearly ready to read, but that they were trying 'to keep her back'. Her portrait in 'The Tabu Tale' combines with some contemporary evidence to suggest a highly strung, over-active child; they may have worried about stimulating her further. In any case, it seems likely that the oral version of 'How the First Letter was Written' began not long after this time.

To that story and its sequel, 'How the Alphabet was

---

[5] Angela Thirkell, *Three Houses* (1931); quoted, Roger Lancelyn Green, *Kipling and the Children* (London: Elek Books, 1965), 170–1.

[6] Unpublished letter, 7 Jan. 1897 (Kipling Papers, Sussex University).

Made', Kipling would add the poem 'Merrow Down', ex-
pressing his grief for his 'Best Beloved', the 'daughter who
was all to him'. Josephine died of pneumonia in March
1899, during the family's last visit to New York, three
months after her sixth birthday. The loss devastated her
father, who had himself been desperately ill with the same
malady. His recovery was slow, and for about five months
he was unable to write. In August they were lent a house
in Scotland by the millionaire Andrew Carnegie, and it was
there that he began to write again: the first mention of
creative activity in his wife's diary was 'The Elephant's
Child', told to his two younger children, and at least one
other Just So story. According to Roger Lancelyn Green
(p. 176), 'The Beginning of the Armadilloes' and 'The Sing-
Song of Old Man Kangaroo' were also drafted at this time.
The family had spent a winter holiday in Africa the previous year, during which Kipling had travelled up country
along the route taken by the little elephant; Green plaus-
ibly suggests (p. 171) that the elephant and leopard stories
had had their oral beginnings soon afterwards.

Besides this African visit, the two latter stories may have
been inspired by a small boy's letter. Kipling's American
publisher, F. N. Doubleday, had become a close friend,
whose support had been invaluable to them during their
New York ordeal. Doubleday's son Nelson said in an
article in the *Saturday Review of Literature* (1948) that
after reading 'How the Whale got his Throat' in *St Nicholas*,
he wrote to Kipling asking for more stories of the same
kind which his father could publish as a book. Nelson
claimed to have suggested as subjects, 'how the leopard got
his spots, how the elephant got his trunk, about the crocodile and so on'.[7] He also said that he had asked for, and

---

[7] Quoted, *Kipling Journal* (Apr. 1949), 10.

received, a royalty from his father after the book came out, of 'a penny for every copy sold', less five cents advanced for the stamp to England. While the details of this account may be inaccurate after so many years, there is something convincing about that penny royalty.

In October 1899, while the stories begun in Scotland were being revised, the South African War broke out. Kipling became much involved in welfare work for the troops and their dependants. He visited hospitals, travelled on troop trains, and wrote articles to keep up public support. His poem 'The Absent-Minded Beggar' launched a fund that raised a quarter of a million pounds, as well as a publicity campaign that led to the founding both of the Soldiers' and Sailors' Families Association, and of the Absent-Minded Beggar (later Treloar) Hospital in Hampshire.[8] By special request of the Commander-in-Chief, he also spent two weeks working on a newspaper for the troops at Bloemfontein. During this time he, who had written so much about the trials of a soldier's life, saw his first battlefield: a skirmish at Kari Siding. This followed the ambush of British troops at Sanna's Post, some of whose fleeing survivors he met.[9]

The war was unpopular with many people, and Kipling's patriotic writings at this time lost him much sympathy. His over-exposure was summed up by Jerome K. Jerome in his column 'Idle Ideas': 'I'm getting just a little wee bit tired of Mr Kipling. . . . Since this war began he appears to have dominated the universe to the exclusion of all other beliefs. Kipling day by day has grown into a sort of nightmare . . .'[10]

If it seemed to the public that he was entirely taken up

[8] *Kipling Journal* (Mar. 1993), 38–9 (letter and references).
[9] See 'The Uses of Reading', *A Book of Words* (1928).
[10] *The Sun* (7 May 1900; quoted, *Kipling Journal* (July 1942), 16).

with war writings, both prose and verse, his private muse—
or Daemon as he liked to call it—was busy on other things.
It was during this time that he finally finished *Kim*. This,
his greatest novel, was his last and most loving statement
on India. Its composition had stretched over many years—
indeed, *Kim* and *Just So Stories* are more or less coeval
(oddly enough, Potter wrote her *Peter Rabbit* over this
same period). Kipling now published a further Just So
series: the Armadilloes, the Elephant, the Leopard, the
Kangaroo, the First Letter, the Cat, and the Butterfly all
appeared in the American *Ladies' Home Journal* in 1900–
2. The public muse went on to work at a new series of
soldier poems, and some military and naval stories, that
would be collected respectively in *The Five Nations* (1903)
and *Traffics and Discoveries* (1904). Many of these de-
nounced the unnecessary waste of lives and suggested ways
in which Kipling thought, or his friends told him, that
future imperial wars might be shortened or avoided—including some form of universal military training. Conan
Doyle in *The Great Boer War* (1900, p. 529), and George
Bernard Shaw in the pamphlet *Fabianism and the Empire*
(1900, pp. 40–1), had both supported such a measure.
Kipling's version can be found in 'The Army of a Dream';
in a letter to his old friend Edmonia Hill,[11] he called this
story 'a political pamphlet' which *Traffics and Discoveries*
was 'intended to carry'. Though the book also includes
two famous stories from the private Daemon, '"They"'
and 'Mrs Bathurst', it remains his final retrospective on the
war.

The Kipling family spent the last months before peace
came at the 'Woolsack', a house built by Cecil Rhodes in

---

[11] 8 Mar. 1905 (copy in Kipling Papers).

the grounds of Groote Schuur, his estate near Cape Town, especially to be lent to writers and artists. It was made available to the Kiplings for as long as they should want it. They all loved the place, which was set in beautiful gardens on the slopes below Table Mountain, including a private zoo where the exact coat colours of giraffes, zebras, and elands could be checked against the living animal. In May 1902, as peace talks began, they returned to England. Next month Kipling was putting *Just So Stories* in order and writing the poems for it.

A number of sources have been suggested for the series: Aesop, Darwin, Joel Chandler Harris's *Uncle Remus*, all of which Kipling is known to have read. The animals in the leopard story learn to survive by protective coloration. The tactics of the prey animals in the armadillo story, begging their enemy not to do the one thing that will save their lives, have been used in many folk tales—but they also recall Brer Rabbit's tactics with Brer Fox. Another possible source is mentioned in the first chapter of Kipling's autobiography, where he says that at school he wrote parodies of Margaret Gatty's *Parables from Nature* (which imitates Aesop).

While the illustrations most obviously recall Aubrey Beardsley and *The Yellow Book*, the influence of Burne-Jones and the Arts and Crafts Movement—which did so much to form Kipling's personal taste—should not be forgotten. Besides Italian art before Raphael, the members of that circle greatly admired Albrecht Dürer and William Blake (both mentioned approvingly in *The Light that Failed*, Kipling's 1891 novel with an artist-hero). Hokusai and other Japanese artists were also important to them (Kipling visited Japan in 1889 and 1892). Total book design was one of the Movement's preoccupations in the 1890s. Burne-Jones was a principal illustrator for the luxury editions produced by William Morris's Kelmscott Press; meanwhile artists such as Walter Crane were working on more commercial ventures that aimed at raising the general standard. In the study at Bateman's, besides Ruskin's *Elements of Drawing* (1857; 1892 edition), there is a copy of Crane's *Of the Decorative Illustration of Books Old and New* (1896). Another formative influence on Kipling was his father's wide knowledge of the arts and crafts of India. All these sources, and folk-art from many lands, contributed to the styles of drawing in *Just So Stories*. Apparently Kipling was somewhat defensive about this venture into an art beyond his own: his wife is quoted as saying that he never minded criticism of his writings, but 'did not take at all kindly to those who criticised his *drawings*'.[12]

The individual stories have their origins in many cultures. If the first inspiration for the camel was a Muslim legend, another ingredient in the story comes from the Bible and the Protestant work ethic: Kipling's camel is not given his hump as a reward for piety, but as a punishment because he will not work. On the brick surround to the fireplace in the study at Naulakha, Lockwood Kipling had carved during that first visit the second (italicized) part of this verse from the Gospel of St John:

I must work the works of him that sent me, while it is day: *the night cometh, when no man can work.*

The substitution of a Djinn for the Angel Gabriel, together with the style of the illustrations to this story, recall E. W. Lane's *Arabian Nights*. This book had acquired cult status

---

[12] Cecily Nicholson, *Kipling Journal* (Sept. 1981), 37.

in Kipling's family. His Aunt Georgie Burne-Jones had
read it to him at an emotive moment in his childhood. His
young cousin has written that it was a long-running family
joke to talk in a parody of Lane's exotic style.[13] Some of
the parody has crept into *Just So Stories*: 'O Best Beloved',
'O Enemy and wife of my Enemy', 'O Queen, be lovely
for ever'.

Not all the stories' sources are so easy to trace, given the
wide and random variety of Kipling's reading. Some probable or possible origins are suggested in the notes. But we
may be reasonably certain of these three influences on the
camel tale, two of which are connected to Kipling's father,
and the third a book that is known to have had special
significance for him.

The mixing of Christian and Asian traditions occurs in
Kipling's autobiographical story '"Baa Baa Black Sheep"',
describing his unhappy life in Southsea when he was 6
years old. Punch, like the young Kipling, is born in Bombay, where he loves to hear local folk-tales told by the
Indian servants; but is then sent home with his younger
sister to live with strangers in England. Introduced by his
foster-mother to the Bible (of which he has never previously heard), Punch

welded the story of the Creation on to what he could recollect of
his Indian fairy tales, and scandalized Aunty Rosa by repeating
the result to Judy. It was a sin, a grievous sin, and Punch was
talked to for a quarter of an hour. He could not understand where
the iniquity came in, but was careful not to repeat the offence,
because Aunty Rosa told him that God had heard every word he
had said and was very angry . . .

[13] Lady Lorna Howard, *Kipling Journal* (Sept. 1985), 69.

Mrs Sara Holloway, original of 'Aunty Rosa', put Kipling off fundamentalist Christianity for life. But by making him (as punishment for various 'sins') learn chapters of the Bible by heart, she gave him a lasting passion for its language. She did not manage to kill his love of folk-stories and fables from other lands, or his fondness for working them into his fiction. In his poem 'Jobson's Amen' (*A Diversity of Creatures*) he engages in a dialogue with someone very like her:

> 'Blessed be the English and all their ways and works.
> Cursed be the Infidels, Hereticks, and Turks!'
> 'Amen,' quo' Jobson, 'but where I used to lie
> Was neither Candle, Bell nor Book to curse my brethren
>   by . . .'

Jobson goes on to describe exotic scenes he has loved:

> 'But a well-wheel slowly creaking, going round, going round,
> By a water-channel leaking over drowned, warm ground—
> Parrots very busy in the trellised pepper-vine—
> And a high sun over Asia shouting: "Rise and shine!" . . .'

The incurious scorn of the English for other folks and their ways was always offensive to Kipling.

Like the Elephant's Child, he himself had an insatiable curiosity which led him to cross-examine everyone he met. A French writer called Joseph-Renaud met Kipling in old age and commented:

this little dark man with the blinding gold spectacles and the enormous eyebrows, came up and shot a rapid fire of questions at me . . . 'Are the duels in Dumas correct in detail? Are there any such Bretons as those described by Pierre Loti? Is it true that Madame Bovary was a real person? Tell me about this Colette whose animal stories are so much better than mine!' And so on and so on. . . . When he had drained me dry he turned abruptly away with a quick 'good-night'. I had never met so tenacious an interviewer.[14]

And wherever he went he collected folk-tales, ballads, and proverbial sayings. The list of books in his study includes such material from French, Indian, Persian, Arab, ancient Greek, old Norse, Chinese, African, and native American sources, as well as English, Irish, and Scots. His unique skill lies in selecting from what he saw, heard, and read, so as to blend from incongruous material a new and different experience for the reader.

One such unexpected source is Freemasonry. It is a little startling to find Masonic signs and symbols in a children's book, yet the initial letter to 'The Butterfly that Stamped' shows Solomon wearing Masonic insignia (see note to p. 169). In 1886, as a young journalist in Lahore, Kipling joined a lodge that included (as he would write) 'Muslims, Hindus, Sikhs, members of the Araya and Brahmo Samaj'[15] as well as a Parsee, a Jew, and a Roman Catholic of mixed European and Asian descent. If he exaggerates the numbers of these (it was more like one of each), this was neverthe-less a valuable opportunity for him. Few other venues al-lowed a young Englishman to meet such a variety of castes and creeds. He writes of their evenings in 'The Mother-Lodge':

> For monthly, after Labour,
> We'd all sit down and smoke
> (We dursn't give no banquets
> Lest a Brother's caste be broke)

[14] Quoted, Philip Mason, *Kipling: The Glass, the Shadow and the Fire* (London: Cape, 1973), 229–30.
[15] Hindu reform movements.

An' man on man got talkin'
Religion an' the rest,
An' every man comparin'
Of the God 'e knew the best.

So man on man got talkin'
An' not a Brother stirred
Till mornin' waked the parrots
An' that dam' brain-fever bird;
We'd say 'twas 'ighly curious,
An' we'd all ride 'ome to bed,
With Mo'ammed, God, an' Shiva
Changin' pickets in our 'ead...

In this friendly atmosphere he collected oral tales, as he
collected written ones through his father's Museum library.

Fables have always been easily exported. The Arabic
Sindibad collection (some of which can be found in *Arabian Nights*) included a story adapted from the Hindu
Panchatantra, 'The Faithful Mongoose'—which probably
also fathered Kipling's 'Rikki-Tikki-Tavi' (*The Jungle
Book*). A Brahmin goes out, leaving a pet mongoose to
look after his baby. A snake comes and is killed by the
mongoose. When the Brahmin returns it runs to meet him,
and he, seeing blood on its muzzle, believes it has attacked
his son and kills it in his rage. Too late he finds the baby
asleep and the dead snake lying by the cradle. The mongoose became first a weasel, then a dog as the tale worked
its way through the Arabic and Hebrew. Only aristocrats
kept dogs, so the child's father was no longer a Brahmin
but a Sheikh. The Sheikh became a knight as the story
travelled across Europe. In fourteenth-century Wales the
child's attacker was still a snake, but this was seen as im-
probable and tradition made it a wolf. Meanwhile the knight
who killed the faithful guardian became Prince Llewellyn.

In 1800 this version was repeated to the visiting English poet W. R. Spencer, whose ballad on the subject 'Beth Gelert' is still to be found in anthologies.[16] But it is not this darker, masculine-heroic part of the story, but the opening situation in which a pet animal saves a boy from a predator, that Kipling uses in 'Rikki-Tikki-Tavi'. Similarly, it is not the heroic theme of a dead Muslim saint but the detail of a humpless and horselike camel that he uses in *Just So Stories*. Nevertheless, such multicultural roots help to give the tales universality. Some of his plot-elements are common to folk- and fairy-tales all over the world: for instance, the Elephant's Child's trip to see the Crocodile is a version of the classic visit to an ogre or a monster's den. Some other examples of this are Odysseus in the cave of Polyphemus (of which there is a version in *Arabian Nights*), the giant's home in *Jack and the Beanstalk*, and Peter Rabbit in Mr McGregor's garden.

Reviewing *Just So Stories* for *The Bookman* in 1902, G. K. Chesterton noticed this aspect of the book. He called the stories

a great chronicle of primal fables, which might have been told by Adam to Cain . . .

For the character of the *Just So Stories* is really unique. They are not fairy-stories, they are legends. A fairy tale is a tale told in a morbid age to the only remaining sane person, a child. A legend is a fairy tale told to men when men were sane . . .

Chesterton went on to add:

the peculiar splendour, as I say, of these new Kipling stories is the fact that they do not read like fairy tales told to children by the

[16] *The Panchatantra*, trans. from the Sanskrit by Franklin Egerton (London: Allen & Unwin, 1965), 16–19, 147–50. William Robert Spencer, *Poems* (London: Cadell, 1811).

modern fireside, so much as like fairy tales told to men in the
morning of the world. They see animals, for instance, as primeval
men saw them; not in types and numbers in an elaborate biologi-
cal scheme of knowledge, but as walking portents . . .[17]

H. W. Boynton in *Atlantic Monthly* saw *Just So Stories* as
'the only recent original book for children'.[18]

The *Times Literary Supplement*'s reviewer also liked the
book, but suggested that old-fashioned readers might be
offended by it, because the stories were written for 'a know-
ing and travelled child', a 'modern tyrant', sceptical of old
beliefs.[19] 'Modern' children were expected to be less dumbly
respectful than their predecessors because, over the previous thirty years, legislation had given them rights of their
own.[20] Also, the spread of contraception meant smaller
families, placing a higher value on the individual child.

A. C. Deane's lampoon in *Punch*, 'A Very-Nearly Story
(Not at all by Mr Rudyard Kipling)',[21] suggested that
Kipling's hypothetical reader was not modern enough:

Once upon a time—not very long ago—an Eminent Writer met
a Modern Child.

'Approach, Best-Beloved,' said the Eminent Writer, 'come
hither, oh 'scruciating idle and pachydermatous phenomenon, and
I will tell you a 'trancing tale!'

The Modern Child regarded him with mild curiosity.

'Feeling a bit chippy?' he asked, 'slight break in the brain-box?
Or why do you talk like that?—No, can't stop now, I'm sorry to
say.' . . .

---

[17] Quoted, Roger Lancelyn Green (ed.), *Kipling: The Critical Heritage*
(London, Routledge & Kegan Paul, 1971), 273–5.
[18] *Atlantic Monthly* (May 1903), 699.   [19] *TLS* (3 Oct. 1902).
[20] Peter Keating, *The Haunted Study* (London: Secker & Warburg,
1989), 153–4.
[21] *Punch* (8 Oct. 1902), 248.

It develops that the tale the author is to tell is 'How the RUDDIKIP got His Great Big Side!'. The child listens reluctantly, while smoking a cigarette, but eventually 'rose and fled'.

More recently, Angus Wilson saw the first seven stories as 'the cream of the collection. . . . They must have been a joy to him and he communicates his joy.' Wilson's analysis of these first seven stories[22] is well worth reading. But of the others he wrote: 'When the stories of private man's advancement begin, we are in the land of Tegumai and Taffy, of Kipling and his own children, and sentimental whimsicality takes over; while the last stories are again too marred by humans, cosy (the Cat that Walked By Himself), or mock-oriental (the Butterfly that Stamped).' It is true that Taffy, and the 'girl-daughter' in the Crab story, seem to be portraits of Josephine and Elsie, while C. E. Carrington (who had read Mrs Kipling's diaries before they were destroyed) thought the Cat tale described the couple's early marriage (see note to p. 149). But Wilson's fine literary judgement is here obscured by his own feelings. Idealized versions of fatherhood and heterosexual marriage were without interest for a man in whose life these things had no place. For a caring father, or a woman reader (or a little girl), the case is different.

From the time of Kipling's first success, some critics have suggested that this was a writer who wrote for *men*; that he was not interested in women, and 'despised' or even hated them.[23] Virginia Woolf in *A Room of One's Own* claimed

[22] Angus Wilson, *The Strange Ride of Rudyard Kipling* (London: Secker & Warburg, 1977), 229.

[23] e.g. Andrew Lang, *Daily News* (2 Nov. 1889); Gilbert Frankau, *Kipling Journal* (Apr. 1931), 5–11; Boris Ford, *Scrutiny*, XI/1 (1942); Martin Seymour-Smith, *Rudyard Kipling* (London: Macdonald, 1989), *passim*.

that the emotions in his works were 'to a woman incom-
prehensible'.[24] Many women readers have none the less
found them rewarding. For instance, Maya Angelou lists
him among writers she 'enjoyed and respected' at school,
and his 'If—' as a favourite poem; later, when she was a
lone black teenage mother in San Francisco, she used to
recite it to her baby.[25]

Few, if any, discussions of gender in Kipling's work have
mentioned *Just So Stories*, yet in this book he places more
emphasis on girls and women than in any of his earlier
children's tales: *The Jungle Book* and its sequel, like *Captains Courageous* and *Stalky & Co.*, are almost entirely
male. So are the first six *Just So Stories*, but in the second
six female characters are variously centred. His attitudes
may be found epitomized in Mother Jaguar, the Cave-
woman, Taffy and the Neolithic Ladies, the girl-daughter,
and super-wife Queen Balkis. Kipling was anti-suffragette,
but he never treats women as stupid or inferior. He was
the type of Victorian for whom motherhood was supreme.
Even the nameless and colourless girl-daughter in 'Crab' is
a sharp-eyed observer with magical gifts of her own. Mother
Jaguar is an example of his Bad Mothers; in encouraging
her cub to attack the two heroes, she is a fabulous version
of Aunty Rosa in '"Baa Baa Black Sheep"', who allowed
her son Harry to bully little Punch. Teshumai Tewindrow
and the Cave-Woman are two of the many Good Mothers
in Kipling's fiction. Here it may be enough to recall that
other magical cave-dweller, Mother Wolf, empowered by

[24] *A Room of One's Own* (London: Hogarth Press, 1929; Panther, 1977),
97.
[25] Maya Angelou, *I Know Why the Caged Bird Sings* (1969; London:
Virago, 1984), 14, 154; *Gather Together in my Name* (1974; London:
Virago, 1985), 48.

maternal love to repel a tiger. Indeed, it is interesting to contrast the nightmarish, child-eating feline of 'Mowgli's Brothers' with the friendly one who plays with a baby. Are they both aspects of Kipling's imagination—as Shere Khan uncontrolled and terrifying—as the Cat that Walked by Himself creatively helpful, but still not wholly domesticated; each shown in tension with a strong female character? In the final story, Balkis and her co-wives could be read as different aspects of such a character, whose love for her man overcomes the male-threatening sides of her personality.

Gender in Kipling is less often discussed than imperialism, his reputation for which has deterred many readers, especially those from once-colonized areas of the world. In the growing number of studies of colonial and post-colonial literature that have followed Edward Said's seminal work *Orientalism* (1979), some critics (including Said himself) have treated Kipling as a key witness for his locus and his time: one who, while identifying with the imperial rulers, is sufficiently sensitive to Indian lives and feelings to make his writings on the subject more ambiguous than he himself may have known. As Said puts it, he was 'blinded by his own insights'.[26] Many of the locations he uses in *Just So Stories* are colonized, but their peoples' traditions are neither devalued nor despised.

One writer from Lahore introduced her recent study of Kipling's Indian writings with this prefatory note: 'It wasn't till the 1970s when I began to read the *Just So Stories* to my sons Taimur and Kamran that I first discovered the rich and ambiguous delight of tales that prepared me for the

[26] Edward Said, *Culture and Imperialism* (London: Chatto & Windus, 1993), 196.

turns and counterturns of Kipling's adult tales.'[27] This ambiguity can often be found, not just within a particular story, but also by comparing and contrasting apparently unrelated tales within a volume, or by looking at the relationship between the stories and the verse. Kipling collections are not, as was once thought, random assemblies of any available texts. While each piece is separate of itself, to read them together will often reveal ongoing themes that link them in a loose, but clearly connected chain. And this is also true of *Just So Stories*.

The *Times Literary Supplement*'s 1902 reviewer suggested that the stories' influence, while failing to promote 'correct and pretty speech', 'will be all in the direction of ... resource, independence, and a desire for knowledge about this wonderful world'. Travel is a continuing theme in the book. Mapping and sea routes can be found in several of the poems, and in the drawing 'Ye Manie Mouthes of ye Amazons River'. Drawings and poems of this type link together stories set in different lands and connect them to English life. But the book begins at sea, in mid-Atlantic—'Fifty North and Forty West'.

Other stories are set in countries that Kipling had visited, or dreamed of visiting. There is local colour, but no attempt at realism; no explanation for a rhinoceros on a rocky island in the Red Sea, or suggestion what (apart from cake) it found to eat there. These are not geography lessons but journeys in the mind.

Kipling loved travelling. He began involuntarily at the age of 2, taken from his natal-shore in Bombay in a paddle-steamer, across the Suez isthmus by train, and then again

---

[27] Zohreh T. Sullivan, *Narratives of Empire* (Cambridge University Press, 1993). Quoted by kind permission of the author.

by paddle-steamer to England. As late as 1889 he crossed
the Pacific in a steamer that also carried sails and used
them. All through his lifetime such journeys would become faster and easier, but would never quite lose their
thrill for him. As a young man he several times broke down
from overwork, when his favourite remedy was to get on
a ship and go off to seek adventures. In one such mood he
wrote his poem 'The Long Trail':

> The days are sick and cold, and the skies are grey and old,
>   And the twice-breathed airs blow damp;
> And I'd sell my tired soul for the bucking beam-sea roll
>   Of a black Bilbao tramp . . .

He travelled all round the world, and longed to do so again:

> Fly forward, O my heart, from the Foreland to the Start—
>   We're steaming all too slow,
> And it's twenty thousand mile to our little lazy isle
>   Where the trumpet-orchids blow!
> You have heard the call of the off-shore wind
> And the voice of the deep-sea rain;
> You have heard the song—how long?—how long?
> Pull out on the trail again!

The geography is doubtful (Kipling was not a numerate
man), but the excitement is irresistible. For many years, the
great liners of the period would take him and his family
yearly to find the sun.

Maps and globes were central to his imagination. In a
speech to the Royal Geographical Society in early 1914
(*A Book of Words*), he spoke of his own and other men's
'mental atlas', and the different ways in which journeys are
perceived in the mind. He foretold how the aeroplane would
change our view of the world. He would still be writing
about globes and air routes in the last sentence of his

posthumous autobiography. Something of his joy in such things, in the variety of the world, the discovery of new places and new cultures, is communicated in *Just So Stories*.

Perhaps the most important linking theme in the book is another of his private joys, the use and deliberate misuse of language. A reviewer in the *Athenaeum*, though finding too much 'clever stuff' in the first three tales, praised Kipling's understanding of 'young folk', calling the Taffy stories, the elephant, and the cat 'perfect, told once for all so that other tellers need not hope to compete'. Kipling's word-games were singled out for particular mention: 'the main invention and delightfully easy exposition, with feats of duplicated onomatopoeic adjectives and the odd little details which children love aptly interfused, carry one on triumphantly . . .'.[28]

Throughout the book, Kipling invites us to share his pleasure in word-play. Baby-talk had been fashionable for a time in Victorian child-novels: examples include *Helen's Babies* (1876) by John Habberton, which Kipling is known to have read, and Lewis Carroll's *Sylvie and Bruno* (1889–93). Kipling himself had used it in 'Wee Willie Winkie' and 'His Majesty the King' (*Wee Willie Winkie and other Stories*). In *Just So Stories* he combines this by-then-outmoded fashion with the more adult wordplay of Carroll's Alice books. The three earliest stories suggest different ways in which spoken language can be used as verbal games. The Mariner's antics in the Whale's 'inside cupboards' are described in a long chain of rhyming monosyllabic verbs. (They also recall a lively child kicking in its mother's womb: at which point one might remember that the baleen from whales' throats was an essential part of the corsets that

[28] *Athenaeum* (4 Oct. 1902).

enclosed a Victorian woman's waist.) The Rhinoceros who 'had no manners then, and he has no manners now, and he never will have any manners' demonstrates the past, present, and future tenses in memorable fashion.

There are graphic coinages: the prey animals are surprised by the leopard 'out of their jumpsome lives'. In the Camel and Leopard stories there are puns on 'hump' and 'spots', while the use of 'play' in the Crab story admits that playing is a serious matter. There is irony, when a crowd excited to lynching-point is described as 'the whole dear, kind, nice, clean, quiet Tribe'. And there are hidden educational messages: the Elephant's Child discovers that a grown-up who talks pompously (the Bi-Coloured-Python-Rock-Snake) may be a truer friend than one who pretends to yield to a child's wishes (the Crocodile). Indeed, the Crocodile proves to be just the sort of stranger to whom you must particularly never speak.

There is rhythm and metre, contrasted in 'The Sing-Song of Old Man Kangaroo'. The story itself is written (though not printed) in free verse; back in 1885, Kipling had written a parody of Walt Whitman for his employers, the *Civil and Military Gazette* of Lahore,[29] with the same long irregular lines and the same repeated endings. This mode, with the mention of a 'Sing-Song' in the story's title, recalls the fact that Aborigine legends, like the two that inspired the story (see its headnote), were traditionally told in chants. The concluding poem tells the tale again in another type of verse, also unrhymed, but with a metre based on three regular stresses, as Anglo-Saxon verse was classically based on four. This was a style that Kipling would use again,

[29] Thomas Pinney (ed.), *Kipling's India* (London: Macmillan, 1986), 64–5.

notably in *Puck of Pook's Hill* (1906), which includes his
most successful imitations of Anglo-Saxon verse: 'The Runes
on Weland's Sword' and 'Harp Song of the Dane Women'.
Here its use suggests a different, Australian-settler folk
tradition. In the Armadillo story that follows 'Kangaroo',
a formal, rhymed quatrain serves a practical purpose. The
young Jaguar, confused by his prey's deliberate mixing
of nouns and verbs ('when you water a Hedgehog you
must drop him into your paw'), takes refuge in a verse
mnemonic.

Various signs address different kinds of reader. The several ways of writing 'Baviaan' in the drawing, using alien
scripts to make what looks like a word in our own familiar
alphabet, can be seen by a sharp-eyed child. An interested
adult can try to decipher the other inscriptions in the drawings. Epithets like 'the great grey-green, greasy Limpopo
River' recall to the classically minded Homer's rosy-fingered
dawn and wine-dark sea.

Further layers of meaning can be found in other games
that are played with words, recalling Alice's conversation
with Humpty-Dumpty in Carroll's *Through the Looking
Glass*. When Kipling asks his words to do extra work he
(like Humpty) always pays them extra. Misspellings carry
further implications: ''satiable curtiosity' has a hint of conversation with a toddler, who will go on curtly saying
'Why?' until satisfied. Malapropisms also serve a dual purpose. The cake that 'smelt most sentimental' not only sounds
poetically right with its alliteration and trochaic rhythm, it
raises nostalgic echoes, suggesting a scent that pleases the
mind as well as the nose. (It was one of Kipling's recurring
themes that 'Scents are surer than sounds or sights | To
make your heart-strings crack' ('Lichtenberg').)

In these games grown-ups have few privileges; sometimes

their warnings or advice save a child from its imprudence, but often it is the child who leads the way. Taffy, not her father, first suggests the idea of writing. The little elephant's maddening question 'What does the Crocodile have for dinner?' seems pointless to the grown-up mind, and likely to cause trouble. All his family greet it in 'loud and dretful tones' and spank him soundly to discourage its repetition. His expedition to the Limpopo is both dangerous and naughty—Kipling makes it clear that he is lucky to escape with his life. But he and his ''satiable curtiosity' win a prize (his new trunk) that will be imitated by all elephants everywhere. Sometimes Kipling is seducing the child into sleep or literacy, but at other moments a window is opened on controlling reader and dependent listener: for example, the power shift at the end of 'The Elephant's Child', when he spanks all the relatives who once spanked him, carries the promise that one day the child will be the stronger. And this is just one way in which grown-ups don't necessarily win in *Just So Stories*. The rich and powerful King Solomon is as guilty of pride as the childish Kangaroo—though he ought to know better—and both are made to repent.

In one or two of the captions, however, Kipling shows the fault of which J. R. R. Tolkien accused Andrew Lang: having 'an eye on the faces of other clever people over the heads of the child-audience'.[30] For example, the reader is urged to decipher the runes in the 'First Letter' illustration, but to do so takes specialist knowledge. Such lapses are comparatively few. Most allusions are kept on the level that Tolkien himself used in his works, where runes, maps, and literary echoes can also be found. The *Lord of the*

---

[30] J. R. R. Tolkien, 'On Fairy-Tales', *Tree and Leaf* (London: Allen & Unwin, 1964), 41 (expanded from a talk given in 1938).

Rings cycle can be read without noticing that Gandalf and other names in it come from the Icelandic *Edda*; readers of *Just So Stories* need not recall the Book of Jonah in order to enjoy the Whale.

Some children take to Kipling's book from the beginning; there are families in which it is as much loved as *The Jungle Book*. But, as Kipling himself said, 'little people are not alike'. Some will be offended (though others will be intrigued) by runic messages they see but cannot understand. Some feel excluded by 'O Best Beloved', with its private reference to Kipling's own daughter. Others object to the repetitions intended to lull them to sleep, allowing the reading adult to escape. A mind that is not yet confident in its use of language may be unsettled by the misapplication and distortion of words, reacting as does Alice to Humpty-Dumpty: 'of all the unsatisfactory people I *ever* met . . .'. An unsympathetic adult reader, or one with half a mind elsewhere, may fail to interact with the listener and so lose most of the stories' magic. Of those children who dislike them, many may change their minds as they grow older, accepting the invitation to join in Kipling's word-games; while of those who enjoyed them from the start, many will come to perceive new subtleties.

They may notice (for instance) that ''satiable curtiosity' is a mispronounced and elided version of 'insatiable curiosity'; but that by leaving out the negative prefix Kipling also suggests that the elephant's curiosity *will* be satisfied, although in an unexpected and threatening way. And since, when read aloud, the apostrophe is not heard, was his curiosity really 'satiable' all along? Or they may feel how the shifting emphasis on the repeated phrase '(and he was a Tewara)' subtly changes its meaning: '*and* he was a Tewara' (as well as a stranger); 'and he was a *Tewara*' (not a member of Taffy's own tribe); while putting the stress on 'a' makes mischievous fun of what Kipling is demonstrating. By such methods the relationships between thought, speech, and the written word are called into question. This enabling way with words, treating them not as fixed entities but as 'serving-men' of multiple and often unexpected skills, further develops the games that Carroll had played, and at which Joyce would become champion of the English-speaking world.

Traces of *Just So Stories* have been noticed in *Finnegans Wake*, in the tale of The Mookse and the Gripes. Here Joyce combines Aesop, classic fairy-tales, and legends, stirring in Kipling in a fashion which, though obviously critical, nevertheless pays—by placing him in such company—a kind of backhanded compliment. The Mookse encounters 'the most unconsciously boggy-looking stream he ever locked his eyes with. It looked little and it smelt of brown and it thought in narrows and it talked showshallow...' Anna Livia Plurabelle, who personifies both the river Liffey and Joyce's wife, here has characteristics of the Parsee's cake and the tortoise Slow-Solid. The Just So allusion is confirmed a few lines later when the Mookse meets a creature sitting on a rock: 'Hic sor a stone, singularly illud, and on hoc stone Seter sate which it filled quite preposterously and by acclimation to its fullest justotototoryum...' A further phrase suggests that Joyce had been caught by the word-play in 'the Precession had preceded according to precedent': he echoes this as 'with preprocession and with proprecession'. It seems that the elephant, the great grey-green, greasy Limpopo river, and the Bi-Coloured-Python-Rock-Snake have been absorbed (python-style) into Joyce's own family life and subjected to his prejudices.

Joyce, as a socialist and an Irishman, was unlikely to

agree with Kipling's politics, but it seems he enjoyed at least some of the writing. While completing *Dubliners* he read Kipling's first story-collection *Plain Tales from the Hills*, remarking: 'If I knew Ireland as well as R. K. seems to know India, I fancy I could write something good.'[31] Later he is said to have joined Kipling with Yeats and Emily Brontë as writers who had 'pure imagination'. In another conversation, Joyce apparently commented:

Plain Tales from the Hills shows more promise, I believe, than any other contemporary writer's youthful work. But he did not fulfil that promise. I believe that the three writers of the nineteenth century who had the greatest natural talents were D'Annunzio, Kipling and Tolstoy—it's strange that all three had semi-fanatic ideas about religion or about patriotism.[32]

Joyce, of course, could himself be semi-fanatic in rejecting both religion and patriotism. But for him to parody the Just So word-play so effectively suggests that this element at least from Kipling's later work had made a lasting impression.

It is widely accepted that in his short story 'Mrs Bathurst' (1904) Kipling foreshadowed the narrative experiments of High Modernism. His influence on T. S. Eliot's poetry has been acknowledged.[33] It could also be argued that a generation raised on *Just So Stories* was at least partly prepared for the verbal complexities of Joyce.

[31] Richard Ellman (ed.), *Selected Letters of James Joyce* (London: Faber & Faber, 1975), 142.

[32] This and 'pure imagination' are from Ellman, *James Joyce* (New York: Oxford University Press), 673 n.

[33] Cf. Lisa Lewis, 'T. S. Eliot and Kipling', *Kipling Journal* (Mar. 1993).

NOTE ON THE TEXT

THE text and illustrations are taken from the first edition of 1902. Additional material is attributed in the notes. There too can be found details of original magazine publications, with important variants in the wording.

Not included is 'My Personal Experience with a Lion', published with the series in the *Ladies' Home Journal*, January 1902, since this was not fiction but autobiography (summarized in *Something of Myself*, pp. 171–3; reprinted *Kipling Journal*, March 1989). Part of 'The Enemies to each Other' (*Debits and Credits*, 1926) may originally, on the evidence of its manuscript (Durham University Library), have belonged with the series.

The first edition, printed by R. & R. Clark of Edinburgh, was a sturdy quarto volume with a decorated cover, reproducing the elephant-and-crocodile drawing in black and white on red. Its very large print was widely spaced on glossy paper (unsuitable, despite Kipling's invitation, for a child to paint on). It came out in September and was reprinted twice before Christmas. There were spin-offs: *Just So Song Book* with musical settings by Edward German came out in 1903, while in 1922 both British and American publishers produced *The Just So Painting Books for Children*.

Of innumerable subsequent editions, many have included illustrations by other hands. None of these can have the same intricate relationship with the text as the author's, without which the stories would be incomplete.

SELECT BIBLIOGRAPHY

THE standard bibliography is J. McG. Stewart's *Rudyard Kipling: A Bibliographical Catalogue*, ed. A. Yeats (1959). Reference may also be made to two earlier works: Flora V. Livingston's *Bibliography of the Works of Rudyard Kipling* (1927) with its *Supplement* (1938), and Lloyd H. Chandler's *Summary of the Work of Rudyard Kipling, Including Items ascribed to Him* (1930). We still await a bibliography which will take account of the findings of modern scholarship over the last quarter-century.

The official biography, authorized by Kipling's daughter Elsie, is Charles Carrington's *Rudyard Kipling: His Life and Work* (1955; 3rd edn., revised 1978). Other full-scale biographies are Lord Birkenhead's *Rudyard Kipling* (1978) and Angus Wilson's *The Strange Ride of Rudyard Kipling* (1977). Briefer, copiously illustrated surveys are provided by Martin Fido's *Rudyard Kipling* (1974) and Kingsley Amis's *Rudyard Kipling and his World* (1975), which combine biography and criticism, as do the contributions to *Rudyard Kipling: the man, his work and his world* (also illustrated), ed. John Gross (1972). Information on particular periods of his life is also to be found in such works as A. W. Baldwin, *The Macdonald Sisters* (1960); Alice Macdonald Fleming (*née* Kipling), 'Some Childhood Memories of Rudyard Kipling' and 'More Childhood Memories of Rudyard Kipling', *Chambers Journal*, 8th series, vol. 8 (1939); L. C. Dunsterville, *Stalky's Reminiscences* (1928); G. C. Beresford, *Schooldays with Kipling* (1936); E. Kay Robinson, 'Kipling in India', *McClure's Magazine*, vol. 7 (1896); Edmonia Hill, 'The Young Kipling', *Atlantic Monthly*, vol. 157 (1936); *Kipling's Japan*, ed. Hugh Cortazzi and George Webb (1988); H. C. Rice, *Rudyard Kipling in New England* (1936); Frederic Van de Water, *Rudyard Kipling's Vermont Feud* (1937); Julian Ralph, *War's Brighter*

Side (1901); Angela Thirkell, *Three Houses* (1931); *Rudyard Kipling to Rider Haggard: The Record of a Friendship*, ed. Morton Cohen (1965); and 'O *Beloved Kids': Rudyard Kipling's Letters to his Children*, ed. Elliott L. Gilbert (1983). Useful background on the India he knew is provided by 'Philip Woodruff' (Philip Mason) in *The Men Who Ruled India* (1954), and by Pat Barr and Ray Desmond in their illustrated *Simla: A Hill Station in British India* (1978). Kipling's own autobiography, *Something of Myself* (1937), is idiosyncratic but indispensable.

The early reception of Kipling's work is usefully documented in *Kipling: The Critical Heritage*, ed. Roger Lancelyn Green (1971). Richard Le Gallienne's *Rudyard Kipling: A Criticism* (1900), Cyril Falls's *Rudyard Kipling: A Critical Study* (1915), André Chevrillon's *Three Studies in English Literature* (1923) and *Rudyard Kipling* (1936), Edward Shanks's *Rudyard Kipling: A Study in Literature and Political Ideas* (1940), and Hilton Brown's *Rudyard Kipling: A New Appreciation* (1945) were all serious attempts at reassessment; while Ann M. Weygandt's study of *Kipling's Reading and Its Influence on His Poetry* (1939), and (in more old-fashioned vein) Ralph Durand's *Handbook to the Poetry of Rudyard Kipling* (1914) remain useful pieces of scholarship.

T. S. Eliot's introduction to *A Choice of Kipling's Verse* (1941; see *On Poetry and Poets*, 1957) began a period of more sophisticated reappraisal. There are influential essays by Edmund Wilson (1941; see *The Wound and the Bow*), George Orwell (1942; see his *Critical Essays*, 1946), Lionel Trilling (1943; see *The Liberal Imagination*, 1951), W. H. Auden (1943; see *New Republic*, vol. 109), and C. S. Lewis (1948; see *They Asked for a Paper*, 1962). These were followed by a series of important book-length studies which include J. M. S. Tompkins, *The Art of Rudyard Kipling* (1959); C. A. Bodelsen, *Aspects of Kipling's Art* (1964); Roger Lancelyn Green, *Kipling and the Children* (1965); Louis L. Cornell, *Kipling in India* (1966); and Bonamy Dobrée, *Rudyard Kipling: Realist and Fabulist* (1967), which follows on from his earlier studies in *The Lamp and the Lute* (1929) and *Rudyard Kipling* (1951). There were also two major collections of critical essays: *Kipling's Mind and Art*, ed. Andrew Rutherford (1964); and *Kipling and the Critics*, ed. Elliot L. Gilbert (1965). Nirad C.

xlvi SELECT BIBLIOGRAPHY

Chaudhuri's essay on *Kim* as 'The Finest Story about India—
in English' (1957) is reprinted in John Gross's collection (see
above). *The Readers' Guide to Rudyard Kipling's Work*, ed. R. E.
Harbord (8 vols., privately printed, 1961–72) is an eccentric
compilation, packed with useful information but by no means
infallible.

Other studies devoted in whole or in part to Kipling include
Richard Faber, *The Vision and the Need: Late Victorian
Imperialist Aims* (1966); T. R. Henn, *Kipling* (1967); Alan
Sandison, *The Wheel of Empire* (1967); Herbert L. Sussman,
Victorians and the Machine: The Literary Response to Technology
(1968); P. J. Keating, *The Working Classes in Victorian Fiction*
(1971); Elliot L. Gilbert, *The Good Kipling: Studies in the Short
Story* (1972); Jeffrey Meyers, *Fiction and the Colonial Experience*
(1972); Shamsul Islam, *Kipling's 'Law'* (1975); J. S. Bratton, *The
Victorian Popular Ballad* (1975); Philip Mason, *Kipling: The
Glass, The Shadow and The Fire* (1975); John Bayley, *The Uses of
Division* (1976); M. Van Wyk Smith, *Drummer Hodge: The Poetry
of the Anglo-Boer War 1899–1902* (1978); Stephen Prickett,
Victorian Fantasy (1979); Martin Green, *Dreams of Adventure,
Deeds of Empire* (1980); J. A. McClure, *Kipling and Conrad*
(1981); R. F. Moss, *Rudyard Kipling and the Fiction of Adolescence*
(1982); S. S. Azfar Husain, *The Indianness of Rudyard Kipling: A
Study in Stylistics* (1983); and Norman Page, *A Kipling
Companion* (1984); B. J. Moore-Gilbert, *Kipling and
'Orientalism'* (1986); Sandra Kemp, *Kipling's Hidden Narratives*
(1988); Nora Crook, *Kipling's Myths of Love and Death* (1989);
and Ann Parry, *The Poetry of Rudyard Kipling* (1992); while
further collections of essays include *Rudyard Kipling*, ed. Harold
Bloom (1987); *Kipling Considered*, ed. Phillip Mallet (1989); and
Critical Essays on Rudyard Kipling, ed. Harold Orel (1989).
Among the most important recent studies are Edward Said,
Culture and Imperialism (1991); Sara Suleri, *The Rhetoric of
English India* (1992); Zohrah T. Sullivan, *Narratives of Empire:
The Fictions of Rudyard Kipling* (1993); and Peter Keating, *Kipling
the Poet* (1994).

Two important additions to the available corpus of Kipling's
writings are *Kipling's India: Uncollected Sketches*, ed. Thomas
Pinney (1986); and *Early Verse by Rudyard Kipling 1879–89:
Unpublished, Uncollected and Rarely Collected Poems*, ed.

Andrew Rutherford (1986). Indispensable is Pinney's edition of *The Letters of Rudyard Kipling*, of which Vols. I and II appeared in 1990, Vol. III in 1995, and Vol. IV in 1998.

A CHRONOLOGY OF KIPLING'S
LIFE AND WORKS

THE dates given here for Kipling's works are those of first authorized publication in volume form, whether this was in India, America, or England. (The dates of subsequent editions are not listed.) It should be noted that individual poems and stories collected in these volumes had in many cases appeared in newspapers or magazines of earlier dates. For full details see James McG. Stewart, *Rudyard Kipling: A Bibliographical Catalogue*, ed. A. W. Yeats, Toronto, 1959; but see also the editors' notes in this World's Classics series.

1865   Rudyard Kipling born at Bombay on 30 December, son of John Lockwood Kipling and Alice Kipling (*née* Macdonald).

1871   In December Rudyard and his sister Alice Macdonald Kipling ('Trix'), who was born in 1868, are left in the charge of Captain and Mrs Holloway at Lorne Lodge, Southsea ('The House of Desolation'), while their parents return to India.

1877   Alice Kipling returns from India in March/April and removes the children from Lorne Lodge, though Trix returns there subsequently.

1878   Kipling is admitted in January to the United Services College at Westward Ho! in Devon. First visit to France with his father that summer. (Many visits later in his life.)

1880   Meets and falls in love with Florence Garrard, a fellow-boarder of Trix's at Southsea and prototype of Maisie in *The Light that Failed*.

1881   Appointed editor of the *United Services College Chronicle*. *Schoolboy Lyrics* privately printed by his parents in Lahore, for limited circulation.

1882   Leaves school at end of summer term. Sails for India on 20 September; arrives Bombay on 18 October. Takes up post as assistant-editor of the *Civil and Military Gazette* in Lahore in the Punjab, where his father is now Principal of the Mayo College of Art and Curator of the Lahore Museum. Annual leaves from 1883 to 1888 are spent at Simla, except in 1884 when the family goes to Dalhousie.

1884   *Echoes* (by Rudyard and Trix, who has now rejoined the family in Lahore).

1885   *Quartette* (a Christmas Annual by Rudyard, Trix, and their parents).

1886   *Departmental Ditties.*

1887   Transferred in the autumn to the staff of the *Pioneer*, the *Civil and Military Gazette*'s sister-paper, in Allahabad in the North-West Provinces. As special correspondent in Rajputana he writes the articles later collected as 'Letters of Marque' in *From Sea to Sea*. Becomes friendly with Professor and Mrs Hill, and shares their bungalow.

1888   *Plain Tales from the Hills.* Takes on the additional responsibility of writing for the *Week's News*, a new publication sponsored by the *Pioneer*.

1888–9   *Soldiers Three; The Story of the Gadsbys; In Black and White; Under the Deodars; The Phantom Rickshaw; Wee Willie Winkie.*

1889   Leaves India on 9 March; travels to San Francisco with Professor and Mrs Hill via Rangoon, Singapore, Hong Kong, and Japan. Crosses the United States on his own, writing the articles later collected in *From Sea to Sea*. Falls in love with Mrs Hill's sister Caroline Taylor. Reaches Liverpool in October, and makes his début in the London literary world.

1890   Enjoys literary success, but suffers breakdown. Visits
           Italy. *The Light that Failed.*

1891   Visits South Africa, Australia, New Zealand, and (for
           the last time) India. Returns to England on hearing of
           the death of his American friend Wolcott Balestier.
           Life's Handicap.

1892   Marries Wolcott's sister Caroline Starr Balestier
           ('Carrie') in January. (The bride is given away by Henry
           James.) Their world tour is cut short by the loss of his
           savings in the collapse of the Oriental Banking Com-
           pany. They establish their home at Brattleboro in Ver-
           mont, on the Balestier family estate. Daughter Josephine
           born in December. *The Naulahka* (written in collabo-
           ration with Wolcott Balestier). *Barrack-Room Ballads.*

1893   *Many Inventions.*

1894   *The Jungle Book.*

1895   *The Second Jungle Book.*

1896   Second daughter Elsie born in February. Quarrel with
           brother-in-law Beatty Balestier and subsequent court
           case end their stay in Brattleboro. Return to England
           (Torquay). *The Seven Seas.*

1897   Settles at Rottingdean in Sussex. Son John born in
           August. *Captains Courageous.*

1898   The first of many winters at Cape Town. Meets Sir
           Alfred Milner and Cecil Rhodes who becomes a close
           friend. Visits Rhodesia. *The Day's Work.*

1899   Disastrous visit to the United States. Nearly dies of
           pneumonia in New York. Death of Josephine. Never
           returns to USA. *Stalky and Co.; From Sea to Sea.*

1900   Helps for a time with army newspaper *The Friend* in
           South Africa during Boer War. Observes minor action
           at Kari Siding.

1901   *Kim.*

1902   Settles at 'Bateman's' at Burwash in Sussex. *Just So
           Stories.*

1903	*The Five Nations.*
1904	*Traffics and Discoveries.*
1906	*Puck of Pook's Hill.*
1907	Nobel Prize for Literature. Visit to Canada. *Collected Verse.*
1909	*Actions and Reactions; Abaft the Funnel.*
1910	*Rewards and Fairies.* Death of Kipling's mother.
1911	Death of Kipling's father.
1913	Visit to Egypt. *Songs from Books.*
1914–18	Visits to the Front and to the Fleet. *The New Army in Training, France at War, Sea Warfare,* and other war pamphlets.
1915	John Kipling reported missing on his first day in action with the Irish Guards in the Battle of Loos on 27 September. His grave was not identified until 1993.
1917	*A Diversity of Creatures.* Kipling becomes a member of the Imperial War Graves Commission.
1919	*The Years Between; Rudyard Kipling's Verse: Inclusive Edition.*
1920	*Letters of Travel.*
1923	*The Irish Guards in the Great War; Land and Sea Tales for Scouts and Guides.*
1924	Daughter Elsie marries Captain George Bambridge, MC.
1926	*Debits and Credits.*
1927	Voyage to Brazil.
1928	*A Book of Words.*
1930	*Thy Servant a Dog.* Visit to the West Indies.
1932	*Limits and Renewals.*
1933	*Souvenirs of France.*
1936	Kipling's death, 18 January.
1937	*Something of Myself For My Friends Known and Unknown.*

1937–9   *The Complete Works of Rudyard Kipling*, Sussex Edition. Prepared by Kipling in the last years of his life, this edition contains some previously uncollected items; but in spite of its title it does not include all his works.

1939   Death of Mrs Kipling.

1940   *The Definitive Edition of Rudyard Kipling's Verse*. This is the last of the series of 'Inclusive Editions' of his verse published in 1919, 1921, 1927, and 1933. In spite of its title the edition is far from definitive in terms of its inclusiveness or textual authority.

1948   Death of Kipling's sister Trix (Mrs John Fleming).

1976   Death of Kipling's daughter Elsie (Mrs George Bambridge).

Just So Stories

CONTENTS

AUTHOR'S PREFACE
(UNCOLLECTED)

SOME stories are meant to be read quietly and some stories are meant to be told aloud. Some stories are only proper for rainy mornings, and some for long, hot afternoons when one is lying in the open, and some stories are bedtime stories. All the Blue Skalallatoot stories* are morning tales (I do not know why, but that is what Effie says). All the stories about Orvin Sylvester Woodsey, the left-over New England fairy who did not think it well-seen to fly, and who used patent labour-saving devices instead of charms, are afternoon stories because they were generally told in the shade of the woods. You could alter and change these tales as much as you pleased; but in the evening there were stories meant to put Effie to sleep, and you were not allowed to alter those by one single little word. They had to be told just so; or Effie would wake up and put back the missing sentence. So at last they came to be like charms, all three of them,—the whale tale, the camel tale, and the rhinoceros tale. Of course little people are not alike, but I think if you catch some Effie rather tired and rather sleepy at the end of the day, and if you begin in a low voice and tell the tales precisely as I have written them down, you will find that that Effie will presently curl up and go to sleep.

Now, this is the first tale, and it tells how the whale got his tiny throat:—

HOW THE WHALE GOT
HIS THROAT

N the sea, once upon a time, O my Best Beloved, there was a Whale, and he ate fishes. He ate the starfish and the garfish, and the crab and the dab, and the plaice and the dace, and the skate and his mate, and the mackereel and the pickereel, and the really truly twirly-whirly eel. All the fishes he could find in all the sea he ate with his mouth—so! Till at last there was only one small fish left in all the sea, and he was a small 'Stute Fish, and he swam a little behind the Whale's right ear, so as to be out of harm's way. Then the Whale stood up on his tail and said, 'I'm hungry.' And the small 'Stute Fish said in a small 'stute voice, 'Noble and generous Cetacean, have you ever tasted Man?'

'No,' said the Whale. 'What is it like?'

'Nice,' said the small 'Stute Fish. 'Nice but nubbly.'

'Then fetch me some,' said the Whale, and he made the sea froth up with his tail.

'One at a time is enough,' said the 'Stute Fish. 'If you swim to latitude Fifty North, longitude Forty West* (that is Magic), you will find, sitting *on* a raft, *in* the middle of the sea, with nothing on but a pair of blue canvas breeches, a pair of suspenders* (you must *not* forget the suspenders, Best Beloved), and a jack-knife, one ship-wrecked Mariner, who, it is only fair to tell you, is a man of infinite-resource-and-sagacity.'*

So the Whale swam and swam to latitude Fifty North, longitude Forty West, as fast as he could swim, and *on* a raft, *in* the middle of the sea, *with* nothing to wear except a pair of blue canvas breeches, a pair of suspenders (you must particularly remember the suspenders, Best Beloved), *and* a jack-knife, he found one single, solitary ship-wrecked Mariner, trailing his toes in the water. (He had his Mummy's leave to paddle, or else he would never have done it, because he was a man of infinite-resource-and-sagacity.)

Then the Whale opened his mouth back and back and back till it nearly touched his tail, and he swallowed the shipwrecked Mariner, and the raft he was sitting on, and his blue canvas breeches, and the suspenders (which you *must* not forget), *and* the jack-knife—He swallowed them all down into his warm, dark, inside cupboards, and then he smacked his lips—so, and turned round three times on his tail.

But as soon as the Mariner, who was a man of infinite-resource-and-sagacity, found himself truly inside the Whale's warm, dark, inside cupboards, he stumped and he jumped and he thumped and he bumped, and he pranced and he danced, and he banged and he clanged, and he hit and he bit, and he leaped and he creeped, and he prowled and he howled, and he hopped and he dropped, and he cried and he sighed, and he crawled and he bawled, and he stepped and he lepped,* and he danced hornpipes where he shouldn't, and the Whale felt most unhappy indeed. (*Have* you forgotten the suspenders?)

So he said to the 'Stute Fish, 'This man is very nubbly, and besides he is making me hiccough. What shall I do?'

'Tell him to come out,' said the 'Stute Fish.

So the Whale called down his own throat to the shipwrecked Mariner, 'Come out and behave yourself. I've got the hiccoughs.'

'Nay, nay!' said the Mariner. 'Not so, but far otherwise. Take me to my natal-shore* and the white-cliffs-of-Albion, and I'll think about it.' And he began to dance more than ever.

'You had better take him home,' said the 'Stute Fish to the Whale. 'I ought to have warned you that he is a man of infinite-resource-and-sagacity.'

THIS is the picture of the Whale* swallowing the Mariner with his infinite-resource-and-sagacity, and the raft and the jack-knife *and* his suspenders, which you must *not* forget. The buttony-things are the Mariner's suspenders, and you can see the knife close by them. He is sitting on the raft, but it has tilted up sideways, so you don't see much of it. The whity thing by the Mariner's left hand is a piece of wood that he was trying to row the raft with when the Whale came along. The piece of wood is called the jaws-of-a-gaff.* The Mariner left it outside when he went in. The Whale's name was Smiler, and the Mariner was called Mr Henry Albert Bivvens, A.B. The little 'Stute Fish is hiding under the Whale's tummy, or else I would have drawn him. The reason that the sea looks so ooshy-skooshy is because the Whale is sucking it all into his mouth so as to suck in Mr Henry Albert Bivvens and the raft and the jack-knife and the suspenders. You must never forget the suspenders.

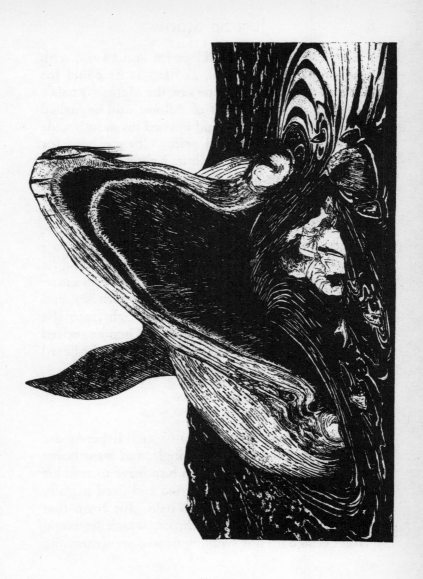

So the Whale swam and swam and swam, with both flippers and his tail, as hard as he could for the hiccoughs; and at last he saw the Mariner's natal-shore and the white-cliffs-of-Albion, and he rushed half-way up the beach,* and opened his mouth wide and wide and wide, and said, 'Change here for Winchester, Ashuelot, Nashua, Keene, and stations on the *Fitch*burg Road';* and just as he said 'Fitch' the Mariner walked out of his mouth. But while the Whale had been swimming, the Mariner, who was indeed a person of infinite-resource-and-sagacity, had taken his jack-knife and cut up the raft into a little square grating all running criss-cross, and he had tied it firm with his suspenders (*now* you know why you were not to forget the suspenders!), and he dragged that grating good and tight into the Whale's throat, and there it stuck!* Then he recited the following *Sloka*,* which, as you have not heard it, I will now proceed to relate—

> By means of a grating
> I have stopped your ating.

For the Mariner he was also an Hi-ber-ni-an. And he stepped out on the shingle, and went home to his Mother, who had given him leave to trail his toes in the water; and he married and lived happily ever afterward. So did the Whale. But from that day on, the grating in his throat, which he could neither cough up nor swallow down, prevented him eating anything except very, very small fish; and that is the reason why whales nowadays never eat men or boys or little girls.

The small 'Stute Fish went and hid himself in the mud under the Door-sills of the Equator. He was afraid that the Whale might be angry with him.

The Sailor took the jack-knife home. He was wearing the blue canvas breeches when he walked out on the shingle. The suspenders were left behind, you see, to tie the grating with; and that is the end of *that* tale.

HERE is the Whale looking for the little 'Stute Fish, who is hiding under the Door-sills of the Equator. The little 'Stute Fish's name was Pingle. He is hiding among the roots of the big seaweed that grows in front of the Doors of the Equator. I have drawn the Doors of the Equator. They are shut. They are always kept shut, because a door ought always to be kept shut. The ropy-thing right across is the Equator itself; and the things that look like rocks are the two giants Moar and Koar, that keep the Equator in order. They drew the shadow-pictures* on the Doors of the Equator, and they carved all those twisty fishes under the Doors. The beaky-fish are called beaked Dolphins, and the other fish with the queer heads are called Hammer-headed Sharks. The Whale never found the little 'Stute Fish till he got over his temper, and then they became good friends again.

WHEN the cabin port-holes are dark and green
   Because of the seas outside;
When the ship goes *wop* (with a wiggle between)
And the steward falls into the soup-tureen,
   And the trunks begin to slide;
When Nursey lies on the floor in a heap,
And Mummy tells you to let her sleep,
And you aren't waked or washed or dressed,
Why, then you will know (if you haven't guessed)
You're 'Fifty North and Forty West!'

HOW THE CAMEL GOT
HIS HUMP

OW this is the next tale, and it tells how the Camel got his big hump.

In the beginning of years, when the world was so new-and-all, and the Animals were just beginning to work for Man, there was a Camel, and he lived in the middle of a Howling Desert because he did not want to work; and besides, he was a Howler himself.* So he ate sticks and thorns and tamarisks and milkweed and prickles, most 'scruciating idle; and when anybody spoke to him he said 'Humph!' Just 'Humph!' and no more.

Presently the Horse came to him on Monday morning, with a saddle on his back and a bit in his mouth, and said, 'Camel, O Camel, come out and trot like the rest of us.'

'Humph!' said the Camel; and the Horse went away and told the Man.

Presently the Dog came to him, with a stick in his mouth, and said, 'Camel, O Camel, come and fetch and carry like the rest of us.'

'Humph!' said the Camel; and the Dog went away and told the Man.

Presently the Ox came to him, with the yoke on his neck, and said, 'Camel, O Camel, come and plough like the rest of us.'

'Humph!' said the Camel; and the Ox went away and told the Man.

At the end of the day the Man called the Horse and the Dog and the Ox together, and said, 'Three, O Three, I'm very sorry for you (with the world so new-and-all); but that Humph-thing in the Desert can't work, or he would have been here by now, so I am going to leave him alone, and you must work double-time to make up for it.'

That made the Three very angry (with the world so new-and-all), and they held a palaver, and an *indaba*, and a *punchayet*,* and a pow-wow on the edge of the Desert; and the Camel came chewing milkweed *most* 'scruciating idle, and laughed at them. Then he said 'Humph!' and went away again.

Presently there came along the Djinn in charge of All Deserts, rolling in a cloud of dust (Djinns always travel that way because it is Magic), and he stopped to palaver and pow-wow with the Three.

'Djinn of All Deserts,' said the Horse, '*is* it right

for any one to be idle, with the world so new-and-all?'

'Certainly not,' said the Djinn.

'Well,' said the Horse, 'there's a thing in the middle of your Howling Desert (and he's a Howler himself) with a long neck and long legs, and he hasn't done a stroke of work since Monday morning. He won't trot.'

'Whew!' said the Djinn, whistling, 'that's my Camel, for all the gold in Arabia! What does he say about it?'

'He says "Humph!"' said the Dog; 'and he won't fetch and carry.'

'Does he say anything else?'

'Only "Humph!"; and he won't plough,' said the Ox.

'Very good,' said the Djinn. 'I'll humph him if you will kindly wait a minute.'

The Djinn rolled himself up in his dust-cloak, and took a bearing across the desert, and found the Camel most 'scruciatingly idle, looking at his own reflection in a pool of water.

'My long and bubbling friend,'* said the Djinn, 'what's this I hear of your doing no work, with the world so new-and-all?'

'Humph!' said the Camel.

The Djinn sat down, with his chin in his hand, and began to think a Great Magic, while the Camel looked at his own reflection in the pool of water.

'You've given the Three extra work ever since

THIS is the picture of the Djinn* making the beginnings of the Magic that brought the Humph to the Camel. First he drew a line in the air with his finger, and it became solid; and then he made a cloud, and then he made an egg—you can see them at the bottom of the picture—and then there was a magic pumpkin that turned into a big white flame. Then the Djinn took his magic fan and fanned that flame till the flame turned into a Magic by itself. It was a good Magic and a very kind Magic really, though it had to give the Camel a Humph because the Camel was lazy. The Djinn in charge of All Deserts was one of the nicest of the Djinns, so he would never do anything really unkind.

Monday morning, all on account of your 'scruciating idleness,' said the Djinn; and he went on thinking Magics, with his chin in his hand.

'Humph!' said the Camel.

'I shouldn't say that again if I were you,' said the Djinn; 'you might say it once too often. Bubbles, I want you to work.'

And the Camel said 'Humph!' again; but no sooner had he said it than he saw his back, that he was so proud of, puffing up and puffing up into a great big lolloping humph.

'Do you see that?' said the Djinn. 'That's your very own humph that you've brought upon your very own self by not working. To-day is Thursday, and you've done no work since Monday, when the work began. Now you are going to work.'

'How can I,' said the Camel, 'with this humph on my back?'

'That's made a-purpose,' said the Djinn, 'all because you missed those three days. You will be able to work now for three days without eating, because you can live on your humph; and don't you ever say I never did anything for you. Come out of the Desert and go to the Three, and behave. Humph yourself!'

And the Camel humphed himself, humph and all, and went away to join the Three. And from that day to this the Camel always wears a humph (we call it 'hump' now, not to hurt his feelings);

but he has never yet caught up with the three days that he missed at the beginning of the world, and he has never yet learned how to behave.

HERE is the picture of the Djinn in charge of All Deserts guiding the Magic with his magic fan. The Camel is eating a twig of acacia, and he has just finished saying 'humph' once too often (the Djinn told him he would), and so the Humph is coming. The long towelly-thing growing out of the thing like an onion is the Magic, and you can see the Humph on its shoulder. The Humph fits on the flat part of the Camel's back. The Camel is too busy looking at his own beautiful self in the pool of water to know what is going to happen to him.

Underneath the truly picture is a picture of the World-so-new-and-all. There are two smoky volcanoes in it, some other mountains and some stones and a lake and a black island and a twisty river and a lot of other things, as well as a Noah's Ark.* I couldn't draw all the deserts that the Djinn was in charge of, so I only drew one, but it is a most deserty desert.

THE Camel's hump is an ugly lump
    Which well you may see at the Zoo;
But uglier yet is the hump we get
    From having too little to do.

Kiddies and grown-ups too-oo-oo,
If we haven't enough to do-oo-oo,
        We get the hump—
        Cameelious hump—
The hump that is black and blue!

We climb out of bed with a frouzly head
    And a snarly-yarly voice.
We shiver and scowl and we grunt and we growl
    At our bath and our boots and our toys;

And there ought to be a corner for me
(And I know there is one for you)
        When we get the hump—
        Cameelious hump—
The hump that is black and blue!

The cure for this ill is not to sit still,
    Or frowst with a book by the fire;
But to take a large hoe and a shovel also,
    And dig till you gently perspire;

And then you will find that the sun and the wind,
And the Djinn of the Garden too,
        Have lifted the hump—
        The horrible hump—
The hump that is black and blue!

I get it as well as you-oo-oo—
If I haven't enough to do-oo-oo!
        We all get hump—
        Cameelious hump—
Kiddies and grown-ups too!

HOW THE RHINOCEROS
GOT HIS SKIN

NCE upon a time, on an un-inhabited island on the shores of the Red Sea, there lived a Parsee* from whose hat the rays of the sun were reflected in more-than-oriental splendour. And the Parsee lived by the Red Sea with nothing but his hat and his knife and a cooking-stove of the kind that you must particularly never touch. And one day he took flour and water and currants and plums and sugar and things, and made himself one cake which was two feet across and three feet thick. It was indeed a Superior Comestible (*that's* Magic), and he put it on the stove because *he* was allowed to cook on that stove, and he baked it and he baked it till it was all done brown and smelt most senti-mental. But just as he was going to eat it there came down to the beach from the Altogether Uninhabited

Interior one Rhinoceros with a horn on his nose, two piggy eyes, and few manners. In those days the Rhinoceros's skin fitted him quite tight. There were no wrinkles in it anywhere. He looked exactly like a Noah's Ark Rhinoceros, but of course much bigger. All the same, he had no manners then, and he has no manners now, and he never will have any manners. He said, 'How!' and the Parsee left that cake and climbed to the top of a palm-tree with nothing on but his hat, from which the rays of the sun were always reflected in more-than-oriental splendour. And the Rhinoceros upset the oil-stove with his nose, and the cake rolled on the sand, and he spiked that cake on the horn of his nose, and he ate it, and he went away, waving his tail, to the desolate and Exclusively Uninhabited Interior which abuts on the islands of Mazanderan, Socotra,* and the Promontories of the Larger Equinox. Then the Parsee came down from his palm-tree and put the stove on its legs and recited the following *Sloka*, which, as you have not heard, I will now proceed to relate:—

> Them that takes cakes
> Which the Parsee-man bakes
> Makes dreadful mistakes.

And there was a great deal more in that than you would think.

Because, five weeks later, there was a heat-wave

in the Red Sea, and everybody took off all the clothes they had. The Parsee took off his hat; but the Rhinoceros took off his skin and carried it over his shoulder as he came down to the beach to bathe. In those days it buttoned underneath with three buttons and looked like a waterproof. He said nothing whatever about the Parsee's cake, because he had eaten it all; and he never had any manners, then, since, or henceforward. He waddled straight into the water and blew bubbles through his nose, leaving his skin on the beach.

Presently the Parsee came by and found the skin, and he smiled one smile that ran all round his face two times. Then he danced three times round the skin and rubbed his hands. Then he went to his camp and filled his hat with cake-crumbs, for the Parsee never ate anything but cake, and never swept out his camp. He took that skin, and he shook that skin, and he scrubbed that skin, and he rubbed that skin just as full of old, dry, stale, tickly cake-crumbs and some burned currants as ever it could *possibly* hold. Then he climbed to the top of his palm-tree and waited for the Rhinoceros to come out of the water and put it on.

And the Rhinoceros did. He buttoned it up with the three buttons, and it tickled like cake-crumbs in bed. Then he wanted to scratch, but that made it worse; and then he lay down on the sands and rolled and rolled and rolled, and every time he rolled the

THIS is the picture of the Parsee beginning to eat his cake on the Uninhabited Island in the Red Sea on a very hot day; and of the Rhinoceros coming down from the Altogether Uninhabited Interior, which, as you can truthfully see, is all rocky. The Rhinoceros's skin is quite smooth, and the three buttons that button it up are underneath, so you can't see them. The squiggly things on the Parsee's hat are the rays of the sun reflected in more-than-oriental splendour, because if I had drawn real rays they would have filled up all the picture. The cake has currants in it; and the wheel-thing lying on the sand in front belonged to one of Pharaoh's chariots* when he tried to cross the Red Sea. The Parsee found it, and kept it to play with. The Parsee's name was Pestonjee Bomonjee,* and the Rhinoceros was called Strorks, because he breathed through his mouth instead of his nose. I wouldn't ask anything about the cooking-stove if *I* were you.

THIS is the Parsee Pestonjee Bomonjee sitting in his palm-tree and watching the Rhinoceros Strorks bathing near the beach of the Altogether Uninhabited Island after Strorks had taken off his skin. The Parsee has rubbed the cake-crumbs into the skin, and he is smiling to think how they will tickle Strorks when Strorks puts it on again. The skin is just under the rocks below the palm-tree in a cool place; that is why you can't see it. The Parsee is wearing a new more-than-oriental-splendour hat of the sort that Parsees wear; and he has a knife in his hand to cut his name on palm-trees. The black things on the islands out at sea are bits of ships that got wrecked going down the Red Sea; but all the passengers were saved and went home.

The black thing in the water close to the shore is not a wreck at all. It is Strorks the Rhinoceros bathing without his skin. He was just as black underneath his skin as he was outside. I wouldn't ask anything about the cooking-stove if *I* were you.

cake-crumbs tickled him worse and worse and worse. Then he ran to the palm-tree and rubbed and rubbed and rubbed himself against it. He rubbed so much and so hard that he rubbed his skin into a great fold over his shoulders, and another fold underneath, where the buttons used to be (but he rubbed the buttons off), and he rubbed some more folds over his legs. And it spoiled his temper, but it didn't make the least difference to the cake-crumbs. They were inside his skin and they tickled. So he went home, very angry indeed and horribly scratchy; and from that day to this every rhinoceros has great folds in his skin and a very bad temper, all on account of the cake-crumbs inside.

But the Parsee came down from his palm-tree, wearing his hat, from which the rays of the sun were reflected in more-than-oriental splendour, packed up his cooking-stove, and went away in the direction of Orotavo, Amygdala, the Upland Meadows of Anantarivo, and the Marshes of Sonaput.*

THIS Uninhabited Island
  Is off Cape Gardafui,*
By the Beaches of Socotra
  And the Pink Arabian Sea:
But it's hot—too hot from Suez
  For the likes of you and me
    Ever to go
    In a P. and O.*
  And call on the Cake-Parsee!

HOW THE LEOPARD
GOT HIS SPOTS

N the days when everybody started fair, Best Beloved, the Leopard lived in a place called the High Veldt.* 'Member it wasn't the Low Veldt, or the Bush Veldt, or the Sour Veldt, but the 'sclusively bare, hot, shiny High Veldt, where there was sand and sandy-coloured rock and 'sclusively tufts of sandy-yellowish grass. The Giraffe and the Zebra and the Eland and the Koodoo and the Hartebeest lived there; and they were 'sclusively sandy-yellow-brownish all over; but the Leopard, he was the 'sclusivest sandiest-yellowest-brownest of them all—a greyish-yellowish catty-shaped kind of beast, and he matched the 'sclusively yellowish-greyish-brownish colour of the High Veldt to one hair. This was very bad for the Giraffe and the Zebra and the rest of them; for he would lie down by a 'sclusively yellowish-greyish-brownish stone or clump of grass, and when the

Giraffe or the Zebra or the Eland or the Koodoo or the Bush-Buck or the Bonte-Buck came by he would surprise them out of their jumpsome lives. He would indeed! And, also, there was an Ethiopian with bows and arrows (a 'sclusively greyish-brownish-yellowish man he was then), who lived on the High Veldt with the Leopard; and the two used to hunt together—the Ethiopian with his bows and arrows, and the Leopard 'sclusively with his teeth and claws—till the Giraffe and the Eland and the Koodoo and the Quagga and all the rest of them didn't know which way to jump, Best Beloved. They didn't indeed!

After a long time—things lived for ever so long in those days—they learned to avoid anything that looked like a Leopard or an Ethiopian; and bit by bit—the Giraffe began it, because his legs were the longest—they went away from the High Veldt. They scuttled for days and days and days till they came to a great forest, 'sclusively full of trees and bushes and stripy, speckly, patchy-blatchy shadows, and there they hid: and after another long time, what with standing half in the shade and half out of it, and what with the slippery-slidy shadows of the trees falling on them, the Giraffe grew blotchy, and the Zebra grew stripy, and the Eland and the Koodoo grew darker, with little wavy grey lines on their backs like bark on a tree trunk; and so, though you could hear them and smell them, you could very seldom see them, and then only when you knew precisely where to look. They had a beautiful time in the 'sclusively speckly-spickly shadows of the forest, while the Leopard and the Ethiopian ran about over the 'sclusively greyish-yellowish-reddish High Veldt outside, wondering where all their breakfasts and their dinners and their teas had gone. At last they were so hungry that they ate rats and beetles and rock-rabbits, the Leopard and the Ethiopian, and then they had the Big Tummy-ache, both together; and then they met Baviaan*—the dog-headed, barking Baboon, who is Quite the Wisest Animal in All South Africa.

Said Leopard to Baviaan (and it was a very hot day), 'Where has all the game gone?'

And Baviaan winked. *He* knew.

Said the Ethiopian to Baviaan, 'Can you tell me the present habitat of the aboriginal Fauna?' (That meant just the same thing, but the Ethiopian always used long words. He was a grown-up.)*

And Baviaan winked. *He* knew.

Then said Baviaan, 'The game has gone into other spots; and my advice to you, Leopard, is to go into other spots as soon as you can.'

And the Ethiopian said, 'That is all very fine, but I wish to know whither the aboriginal Fauna has migrated.'

Then said Baviaan, 'The aboriginal Fauna has joined the aboriginal Flora because it was high time

THIS is Wise Baviaan, the dog-headed Baboon, who is Quite the Wisest Animal in All South Africa. I have drawn him from a statue* that I made up out of my own head, and I have written his name on his belt and on his shoulder and on the thing he is sitting on. I have written it in what is not called Coptic and Hieroglyphic and Cuneiformic and Bengalic and Burmic and Hebric,* all because he is so wise. He is not beautiful, but he is very wise; and I should like to paint him with paint-box colours, but I am not allowed. The umbrella-ish thing about his head is his Conventional Mane.

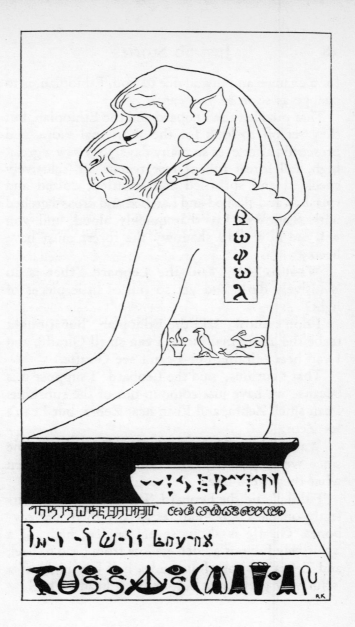

for a change; and my advice to you, Ethiopian, is to change as soon as you can.'

That puzzled the Leopard and the Ethiopian, but they set off to look for the aboriginal Flora, and presently, after ever so many days, they saw a great, high, tall forest full of tree trunks all 'sclusively speckled and sprottled and spotted, dotted and splashed and slashed and hatched and cross-hatched with shadows. (Say that quickly aloud, and you will see how *very* shadowy the forest must have been.)*

'What is this,' said the Leopard, 'that is so 'sclusively dark, and yet so full of little pieces of light?'

'I don't know,' said the Ethiopian, 'but it ought to be the aboriginal Flora. I can smell Giraffe, and I can hear Giraffe, but I can't see Giraffe.'

'That's curious,' said the Leopard. 'I suppose it is because we have just come in out of the sunshine. I can smell Zebra, and I can hear Zebra, but I can't see Zebra.'

'Wait a bit,' said the Ethiopian. 'It's a long time since we've hunted 'em. Perhaps we've forgotten what they were like.'

'Fiddle!' said the Leopard. 'I remember them perfectly on the High Veldt, especially their marrow-bones. Giraffe is about seventeen feet high, of a 'sclusively fulvous golden-yellow from head to heel; and Zebra is about four and a half feet high, of a 'sclusively grey-fawn colour from head to heel.'

'Umm,' said the Ethiopian, looking into the speckly-spickly shadows of the aboriginal Flora-forest. 'Then they ought to show up in this dark place like ripe bananas in a smoke-house.'

But they didn't. The Leopard and the Ethiopian hunted all day; and though they could smell them and hear them, they never saw one of them.

'For goodness' sake,' said the Leopard at tea-time, 'let us wait till it gets dark. This daylight hunting is a perfect scandal.'

So they waited till dark, and then the Leopard heard something breathing sniffily in the starlight that fell all stripy through the branches, and he jumped at the noise, and it smelt like Zebra, and it felt like Zebra, and when he knocked it down it kicked like Zebra, but he couldn't see it. So he said, 'Be quiet, O you person without any form.* I am going to sit on your head till morning, because there is something about you that I don't understand.'

Presently he heard a grunt and a crash and a scramble, and the Ethiopian called out, 'I've caught a thing that I can't see. It smells like Giraffe, and it kicks like Giraffe, but it hasn't any form.'

'Don't you trust it,' said the Leopard. 'Sit on its head till the morning—same as me. They haven't any form—any of 'em.'

So they sat down on them hard till bright morning-time, and then Leopard said, 'What have you at your end of the table, Brother?'

The Ethiopian scratched his head and said, 'It ought to be 'sclusively a rich fulvous orange-tawny from head to heel, and it ought to be Giraffe; but it is covered all over with chestnut blotches. What have you at *your* end of the table, Brother?'

And the Leopard scratched his head and said, 'It ought to be 'sclusively a delicate greyish-fawn, and it ought to be Zebra; but it is covered all over with black and purple stripes. What in the world have you been doing to yourself, Zebra? Don't you know that if you were on the High Veldt I could see you ten miles off? You haven't any form.'

'Yes,' said the Zebra, 'but this isn't the High Veldt. Can't you see?'

'I can now,' said the Leopard. 'But I couldn't all yesterday. How is it done?'

'Let us up,' said the Zebra, 'and we will show you.'

They let the Zebra and the Giraffe get up; and Zebra moved away to some little thorn-bushes where the sunlight fell all stripy, and Giraffe moved off to some tallish trees where the shadows fell all blotchy.

'Now watch,' said the Zebra and the Giraffe. 'This is the way it's done. One—two—three! And where's your breakfast?'

Leopard stared, and Ethiopian stared, but all they could see were stripy shadows and blotched shadows in the forest, but never a sign of Zebra and

Giraffe. They had just walked off and hidden themselves in the shadowy forest.

'Hi! Hi!' said the Ethiopian. 'That's a trick worth learning. Take a lesson by it, Leopard. You show up in this dark place like a bar of soap in a coal-scuttle.'

'Ho! Ho!' said the Leopard. 'Would it surprise you very much to know that you show up in this dark place like a mustard-plaster on a sack of coals?'

'Well, calling names won't catch dinner,' said the Ethiopian. 'The long and the little of it is that we don't match our backgrounds. I'm going to take Baviaan's advice. He told me I ought to change; and as I've nothing to change except my skin I'm going to change that.'

'What to?' said the Leopard, tremendously excited.

'To a nice working blackish-brownish colour, with a little purple in it, and touches of slaty-blue. It will be the very thing for hiding in hollows and behind trees.'

So he changed his skin then and there, and the Leopard was more excited than ever; he had never seen a man change his skin before.

'But what about me?' he said, when the Ethiopian had worked his last little finger into his fine new black skin.

'You take Baviaan's advice too. He told you to go into spots.'

'So I did,' said the Leopard. 'I went into other spots as fast as I could. I went into this spot with you, and a lot of good it has done me.'

'Oh,' said the Ethiopian, 'Baviaan didn't mean spots in South Africa. He meant spots on your skin.'

'What's the use of that?' said the Leopard.

'Think of Giraffe,' said the Ethiopian. 'Or if you prefer stripes, think of Zebra. They find their spots and stripes give them per-fect satisfaction.'

'Umm,' said the Leopard. 'I wouldn't look like Zebra—not for ever so.'

'Well, make up your mind,' said the Ethiopian, 'because I'd hate to go hunting without you, but I must if you insist on looking like a sun-flower against a tarred fence.'

'I'll take spots, then,' said the Leopard; 'but don't make 'em too vulgar-big. I wouldn't look like Giraffe—not for ever so.'

'I'll make 'em with the tips of my fingers,' said the Ethiopian. 'There's plenty of black left on my skin still. Stand over!'

Then the Ethiopian put his five fingers close together (there was plenty of black left on his new skin still) and pressed them all over the Leopard, and wherever the five fingers touched they left five little black marks, all close together. You can see them on any Leopard's skin you like, Best Beloved. Sometimes the fingers slipped and the marks got a little blurred; but if you look closely at any Leopard

now you will see that there are always five spots—
off five fat black finger-tips.

'Now you *are* a beauty!' said the Ethiopian. 'You
can lie out on the bare ground and look like a heap
of pebbles. You can lie out on the naked rocks and
look like a piece of pudding-stone. You can lie out
on a leafy branch and look like sunshine sifting
through the leaves; and you can lie right across the
centre of a path and look like nothing in particular.
Think of that and purr!'

'But if I'm all this,' said the Leopard, 'why didn't
you go spotty too?'

'Oh, plain black's best for a nigger,'* said the
Ethiopian. 'Now come along and we'll see if we
can't get even with Mr One-Two-Three-Where's-
your-Breakfast!'

So they went away and lived happily ever afterward, Best Beloved. That is all.

Oh, now and then you will hear grown-ups say,
'Can the Ethiopian change his skin or the Leopard
his spots?'* I don't think even grown-ups would
keep on saying such a silly thing if the Leopard and
the Ethiopian hadn't done it once—do you? But
they will never do it again, Best Beloved. They are
quite contented as they are.

THIS is the picture of the Leopard and the Ethiopian after they had taken Wise Baviaan's advice and the Leopard had gone into other spots and the Ethiopian had changed his skin. The Ethiopian was really a negro, and so his name was Sambo.* The Leopard was called Spots, and he has been called Spots ever since. They are out hunting in the spickly-speckly forest, and they are looking for Mr One-Two-Three-Where's-your-Breakfast. If you look a little you will see Mr One-Two-Three not far away. The Ethiopian has hidden behind a splotchy-blotchy tree because it matches his skin, and the Leopard is lying beside a spickly-speckly bank of stones because it matches his spots. Mr One-Two-Three-Where's-your-Breakfast is standing up eating leaves from a tall tree. This is really a puzzle-picture like 'Find-the-Cat.'*

I AM the Most Wise Baviaan, saying in most wise tones,
'Let us melt into the landscape—just us two by our lones.'
People have come—in a carriage—calling. But Mummy is
    there. . . .
Yes, I can go if you take me—Nurse says *she* don't care.
Let's go up to the pig-sties and sit on the farmyard rails!
Let's say things to the bunnies, and watch 'em skitter their
    tails!
Let's—oh, *anything*, daddy, so long as it's you and me,
And going truly exploring, and not being in till tea!
Here's your boots (I've brought 'em), and here's your cap
    and stick,
And here's your pipe and tobacco. Oh, come along out of
    it—quick!

THE ELEPHANT'S CHILD

N the High and Far-Off Times the Elephant, O Best Beloved, had no trunk. He had only a blackish, bulgy nose, as big as a boot, that he could wriggle about from side to side; but he couldn't pick up things with it. But there was one Elephant—a new Elephant—an Elephant's Child—who was full of 'satiable curtiosity, and that means he asked ever so many questions. *And* he lived in Africa, and he filled all Africa with his 'satiable curtiosities. He asked his tall aunt, the Ostrich, why her tail-feathers grew just so, and his tall aunt the Ostrich spanked him with her hard, hard claw. He asked his tall uncle, the Giraffe, what made his skin spotty, and his tall uncle, the Giraffe, spanked him with his hard, hard hoof. And still he was full of 'satiable curtiosity! He asked his broad aunt, the Hippopotamus, why her eyes were red, and his broad aunt, the Hippopotamus, spanked him with her broad, broad hoof; and he asked his hairy uncle, the Baboon, why melons tasted just so, and his hairy uncle, the Baboon, spanked him with his hairy, hairy paw. And *still* he was full of 'satiable curtiosity! He asked questions about everything that he saw, or heard, or felt, or smelt, or touched, and all his uncles and his aunts spanked him. And still he was full of 'satiable curtiosity!

One fine morning in the middle of the Precession of the Equinoxes this 'satiable Elephant's Child asked a new fine question that he had never asked before. He asked, 'What does the Crocodile have for dinner?' Then everybody said, 'Hush!' in a loud and dretful tone, and they spanked him immediately and directly, without stopping, for a long time.

By and by, when that was finished, he came upon Kolokolo Bird* sitting in the middle of a wait-a-bit thorn-bush, and he said, 'My father has spanked me, and my mother has spanked me; all my aunts and uncles have spanked me for my 'satiable curtiosity; and *still* I want to know what the Crocodile has for dinner!'

Then Kolokolo Bird said, with a mournful cry, 'Go to the banks of the great grey-green, greasy Limpopo River, all set about with fever-trees,* and find out.'

That very next morning, when there was nothing left of the Equinoxes, because the Precession had preceded according to precedent, this 'satiable

Elephant's Child took a hundred pounds of bananas (the little short red kind),* and a hundred pounds of sugar-cane (the long purple kind), and seventeen melons (the greeny-crackly kind), and said to all his dear families, 'Good-bye. I am going to the great grey-green, greasy Limpopo River, all set about with fever-trees, to find out what the Crocodile has for dinner.' And they all spanked him once more for luck, though he asked them most politely to stop.

Then he went away, a little warm, but not at all astonished, eating melons, and throwing the rind about, because he could not pick it up.

He went from Graham's Town to Kimberley, and from Kimberley to Khama's Country,* and from Khama's Country he went east by north, eating melons all the time, till at last he came to the banks of the great grey-green, greasy Limpopo River, all set about with fever-trees, precisely as Kolokolo Bird had said.

Now you must know and understand, O Best Beloved, that till that very week, and day, and hour, and minute, this 'satiable Elephant's Child had never seen a Crocodile, and did not know what one was like. It was all his 'satiable curtiosity.

The first thing that he found was a Bi-Coloured-Python-Rock-Snake curled round a rock.

''Scuse me,' said the Elephant's Child most politely, 'but have you seen such a thing as a Crocodile in these promiscuous parts?'

'*Have* I seen a Crocodile?' said the Bi-Coloured-Python-Rock-Snake, in a voice of dretful scorn. 'What will you ask me next?'

''Scuse me,' said the Elephant's Child, 'but could you kindly tell me what he has for dinner?'

Then the Bi-Coloured-Python-Rock-Snake uncoiled himself very quickly from the rock, and spanked the Elephant's Child with his scalesome, flailsome tail.

'That is odd,' said the Elephant's Child, 'because my father and my mother, and my uncle and my aunt, not to mention my other aunt, the Hippopotamus, and my other uncle, the Baboon, have all spanked me for my 'satiable curtiosity—and I suppose this is the same thing.'

So he said good-bye very politely to the Bi-Coloured-Python-Rock-Snake, and helped to coil him up on the rock again, and went on, a little warm, but not at all astonished, eating melons, and throwing the rind about, because he could not pick it up, till he trod on what he thought was a log of wood at the very edge of the great grey-green, greasy Limpopo River, all set about with fever-trees.

But it was really the Crocodile, O Best Beloved, and the Crocodile winked one eye—like this!

''Scuse me,' said the Elephant's Child most politely, 'but do you happen to have seen a Crocodile in these promiscuous parts?'

Then the Crocodile winked the other eye, and

lifted half his tail out of the mud; and the Elephant's Child stepped back most politely, because he did not wish to be spanked again.

'Come hither, Little One,' said the Crocodile. 'Why do you ask such things?'

''Scuse me,' said the Elephant's Child most politely, 'but my father has spanked me, my mother has spanked me, not to mention my tall aunt, the Ostrich, and my tall uncle, the Giraffe, who can kick ever so hard, as well as my broad aunt, the Hippopotamus, and my hairy uncle, the Baboon, *and* including the Bi-Coloured-Python-Rock-Snake, with the scalesome, flailsome tail, just up the bank, who spanks harder than any of them; and *so*, if it's quite all the same to you, I don't want to be spanked any more.'

'Come hither, Little One,' said the Crocodile, 'for I am the Crocodile,' and he wept crocodile-tears to show it was quite true.

Then the Elephant's Child grew all breathless, and panted, and kneeled down on the bank and said, 'You are the very person I have been looking for all these long days. Will you please tell me what you have for dinner?'

'Come hither, Little One,' said the Crocodile, 'and I'll whisper.'

Then the Elephant's Child put his head down close to the Crocodile's musky, tusky mouth, and the Crocodile caught him by his little nose, which up to that very week, day, hour, and minute, had been no bigger than a boot, though much more useful.

'I think,' said the Crocodile—and he said it between his teeth, like this—'I think to-day I will begin with Elephant's Child!'

At this, O Best Beloved, the Elephant's Child was much annoyed, and he said, speaking through his nose, like this, 'Led go! You are hurtig be!'

Then the Bi-Coloured-Python-Rock-Snake scuffled down from the bank and said, 'My young friend, if you do not now, immediately and instantly, pull as hard as ever you can, it is my opinion that your acquaintance in the large-pattern leather ulster' (and by this he meant the Crocodile) 'will jerk you into yonder limpid stream before you can say Jack Robinson.'

This is the way Bi-Coloured-Python-Rock-Snakes always talk.

Then the Elephant's Child sat back on his little haunches, and pulled, and pulled, and pulled, and his nose began to stretch. And the Crocodile floundered into the water, making it all creamy with great sweeps of his tail, and *he* pulled, and pulled, and pulled.

And the Elephant's Child's nose kept on stretching; and the Elephant's Child spread all his little four legs and pulled, and pulled, and pulled, and his nose kept on stretching; and the Crocodile threshed his tail like an oar, and *he* pulled, and pulled, and pulled, and at each pull the Elephant's Child's nose grew longer and longer—and it hurt him hijjus!*

Then the Elephant's Child felt his legs slipping, and he said through his nose, which was now nearly five feet long, 'This is too butch for be!'

Then the Bi-Coloured-Python-Rock-Snake came down from the bank, and knotted himself in a double-clove-hitch round the Elephant's Child's hind-legs, and said, 'Rash and inexperienced traveller, we will now seriously devote ourselves to a little high tension, because if we do not, it is my impression that yonder self-propelling man-of-war with the armour-plated upper deck' (and by this, O Best Beloved, he meant the Crocodile) 'will permanently vitiate your future career.'

That is the way all Bi-Coloured-Python-Rock-Snakes always talk.

So he pulled, and the Elephant's Child pulled, and the Crocodile pulled; but the Elephant's Child and the Bi-Coloured-Python-Rock-Snake pulled hardest; and at last the Crocodile let go of the Elephant's Child's nose with a plop that you could hear all up and down the Limpopo.

Then the Elephant's Child sat down most hard and sudden; but first he was careful to say 'Thank you' to the Bi-Coloured-Python-Rock-Snake; and next he was kind to his poor pulled nose, and wrapped it all up in cool banana leaves, and hung it in the great grey-green, greasy Limpopo to cool.

'What are you doing that for?' said the Bi-Coloured-Python-Rock-Snake.

''Scuse me,' said the Elephant's Child, 'but my nose is badly out of shape, and I am waiting for it to shrink.'

'Then you will have to wait a long time,' said the Bi-Coloured-Python-Rock-Snake. 'Some people do not know what is good for them.'

The Elephant's Child sat there for three days waiting for his nose to shrink. But it never grew any shorter, and, besides, it made him squint. For, O Best Beloved, you will see and understand that the Crocodile had pulled it out into a really truly trunk same as all Elephants have to-day.

At the end of the third day a fly came and stung him on the shoulder, and before he knew what he was doing he lifted up his trunk and hit that fly dead with the end of it.

''Vantage number one!' said the Bi-Coloured-Python-Rock-Snake. 'You couldn't have done that with a mere-smear nose. Try and eat a little now.'

Before he thought what he was doing the Elephant's Child put out his trunk and plucked a large bundle of grass, dusted it clean against his forelegs, and stuffed it into his own mouth.

''Vantage number two!' said the Bi-Coloured-Python-Rock-Snake. 'You couldn't have done that with a mere-smear nose. Don't you think the sun is very hot here?'

'It is,' said the Elephant's Child, and before he thought what he was doing he schlooped up a schloop of mud from the banks of the great grey-green, greasy Limpopo, and slapped it on his head, where it made a cool schloopy-sloshy mud-cap all trickly behind his ears.

''Vantage number three!' said the Bi-Coloured-Python-Rock-Snake. 'You couldn't have done that with a mere-smear nose. Now how do you feel about being spanked again?'

''Scuse me,' said the Elephant's Child, 'but I should not like it at all.'

'How would you like to spank somebody?' said the Bi-Coloured-Python-Rock-Snake.

'I should like it very much indeed,' said the Elephant's Child.

'Well,' said the Bi-Coloured-Python-Rock-Snake, 'you will find that new nose of yours very useful to spank people with.'

'Thank you,' said the Elephant's Child, 'I'll remember that; and now I think I'll go home to all my dear families and try.'

So the Elephant's Child went home across Africa frisking and whisking his trunk. When he wanted fruit to eat he pulled fruit down from a tree, instead of waiting for it to fall as he used to do. When he wanted grass he plucked grass up from the ground,

THIS is the Elephant's Child* having his nose pulled by the Crocodile. He is much surprised and astonished and hurt, and he is talking through his nose and saying, 'Led go! You are hurtig be!' He is pulling very hard, and so is the Crocodile; but the Bi-Coloured-Python-Rock-Snake is hurrying through the water to help the Elephant's Child. All that black stuff is the banks of the great grey-green, greasy Limpopo River (but I am not allowed to paint these pictures), and the bottly-tree with the twisty roots and the eight leaves is one of the fever trees that grow there.

Underneath the truly picture are shadows of African animals walking into an African ark. There are two lions, two ostriches, two oxen, two camels, two sheep, and two other things that look like rats, but I think they are rock-rabbits. They don't mean anything. I put them in because I thought they looked pretty. They would look very fine if I were allowed to paint them.

instead of going on his knees as he used to do. When the flies bit him he broke off the branch of a tree and used it as a fly-whisk; and he made himself a new, cool, slushy-squshy mud-cap whenever the sun was hot. When he felt lonely walking through Africa he sang to himself down his trunk, and the noise was louder than several brass bands. He went especially out of his way to find a broad Hippopotamus (she was no relation of his), and he spanked her very hard, to make sure that the Bi-Coloured-Python-Rock-Snake had spoken the truth about his new trunk. The rest of the time he picked up the melon rinds that he had dropped on his way to the Limpopo—for he was a Tidy Pachyderm.

One dark evening he came back to all his dear families, and he coiled up his trunk and said, 'How do you do?' They were very glad to see him, and immediately said, 'Come here and be spanked for your 'satiable curtiosity.'

'Pooh,' said the Elephant's Child. 'I don't think you peoples know anything about spanking; but *I* do, and I'll show you.'

Then he uncurled his trunk and knocked two of his dear brothers head over heels.

'O Bananas!' said they, 'where did you learn that trick, and what have you done to your nose?'

'I got a new one from the Crocodile on the banks of the great grey-green, greasy Limpopo River,' said the Elephant's Child. 'I asked him what he had for dinner, and he gave me this to keep.'

'It looks very ugly,' said his hairy uncle, the Baboon.

'It does,' said the Elephant's Child. 'But it's very useful,' and he picked up his hairy uncle, the Baboon, by one hairy leg, and hove him into a hornet's nest.

Then that bad Elephant's Child spanked all his dear families for a long time, till they were very warm and greatly astonished. He pulled out his tall Ostrich aunt's tail-feathers; and he caught his tall uncle, the Giraffe, by the hind-leg, and dragged him through a thorn-bush; and he shouted at his broad aunt, the Hippopotamus, and blew bubbles into her ear when she was sleeping in the water after meals; but he never let any one touch Kolokolo Bird.

At last things grew so exciting that his dear families went off one by one in a hurry to the banks of the great grey-green, greasy Limpopo River, all set about with fever-trees, to borrow new noses from the Crocodile. When they came back nobody spanked anybody any more;* and ever since that day, O Best Beloved, all the Elephants you will ever see, besides all those that you won't, have trunks precisely like the trunk of the 'satiable Elephant's Child.

THIS is just a picture of the Elephant's Child going to pull bananas off a banana-tree after he had got his fine new long trunk. I don't think it is a very nice picture; but I couldn't make it any better, because elephants and bananas are hard to draw. The streaky things behind the Elephant's Child mean squoggy marshy country somewhere in Africa. The Elephant's Child made most of his mud-cakes out of the mud that he found there. I think it would look better if you painted the banana-tree green and the Elephant's Child red.

I KEEP six honest serving-men*
    (They taught me all I knew);
Their names are What and Why and When
    And How and Where and Who.
I send them over land and sea,
    I send them east and west;
But after they have worked for me,
    I give them all a rest.

I let them rest from nine till five,
    For I am busy then,
As well as breakfast, lunch, and tea,
    For they are hungry men:
But different folk have different views;
    I know a person small—
She keeps ten million serving-men,
    Who get no rest at all!
She sends 'em abroad on her own affairs,
    From the second she opens her eyes—
One million Hows, two million Wheres,
    And seven million Whys!

THE SING-SONG OF
OLD MAN KANGAROO

OT always was the Kanga-
roo as now we do be-
hold him, but a Different
Animal with four short
legs. He was grey and
he was woolly, and his
pride was inordinate: he
danced on an outcrop in
the middle of Australia,
and he went to the Little
God Nqa.*

He went to Nqa at six before breakfast, saying,
'Make me different from all other animals by five
this afternoon.'

Up jumped Nqa from his seat on the sand-flat
and shouted, 'Go away!'

He was grey and he was woolly, and his pride
was inordinate: he danced on a rock-ledge in the
middle of Australia, and he went to the Middle
God Nquing.

He went to Nquing at eight after breakfast,
saying, 'Make me different from all other animals;

make me, also, wonderfully popular by five this
afternoon.'

Up jumped Nquing from his burrow in the
spinifex and shouted, 'Go away!'

He was grey and he was woolly, and his pride
was inordinate: he danced on a sandbank in the
middle of Australia, and he went to the Big God
Nqong.

He went to Nqong at ten before dinner-time,
saying, 'Make me different from all other animals;
make me popular and wonderfully run after by five
this afternoon.'

Up jumped Nqong from his bath in the salt-pan
and shouted, 'Yes, I will!'

Nqong called Dingo—Yellow-Dog Dingo—
always hungry, dusty in the sunshine, and showed
him Kangaroo. Nqong said, 'Dingo! Wake up,
Dingo! Do you see that gentleman dancing on an
ashpit? He wants to be popular and very truly run
after. Dingo, make him so!'

Up jumped Dingo—Yellow-Dog Dingo—and
said, 'What, *that* cat-rabbit?'

Off ran Dingo—Yellow-Dog Dingo—always
hungry, grinning like a coal-scuttle,—ran after
Kangaroo.

Off went the proud Kangaroo on his four little
legs like a bunny.

This, O Beloved of mine, ends the first part of
the tale!

He ran through the desert; he ran through the mountains; he ran through the salt-pans; he ran through the reed-beds; he ran through the blue gums; he ran through the spinifex; he ran till his front legs ached.

He had to!

Still ran Dingo—Yellow-Dog Dingo—always hungry, grinning like a rat-trap, never getting nearer, never getting farther,—ran after Kangaroo.

He had to!

Still ran Kangaroo—Old Man Kangaroo. He ran through the ti-trees;* he ran through the mulga; he ran through the long grass; he ran through the short grass; he ran through the Tropics of Capricorn and Cancer;* he ran till his hind legs ached.

He had to!

Still ran Dingo—Yellow-Dog Dingo—hungrier and hungrier, grinning like a horse-collar, never getting nearer, never getting farther; and they came to the Wollgong River.*

Now, there wasn't any bridge, and there wasn't any ferry-boat, and Kangaroo didn't know how to get over; so he stood on his legs and hopped.

He had to!

He hopped through the Flinders;* he hopped through the Cinders; he hopped through the deserts in the middle of Australia. He hopped like a Kangaroo.

First he hopped one yard; then he hopped three

THIS is a picture of Old Man Kangaroo* when he was the Different Animal with four short legs. I have drawn him grey and woolly, and you can see that he is very proud because he has a wreath of flowers in his hair. He is dancing on an outcrop (that means a ledge of rock) in the middle of Australia at six o'clock before breakfast. You can see that it is six o'clock, because the sun is just getting up. The thing with the ears and the open mouth is Little God Nqa. Nqa is very much surprised, because he has never seen a Kangaroo dance like that before. Little God Nqa is just saying, 'Go away,' but the Kangaroo is so busy dancing that he has not heard him yet.

The Kangaroo hasn't any real name except Boomer. He lost it because he was so proud.

yards; then he hopped five yards; his legs growing stronger; his legs growing longer. He hadn't any time for rest or refreshment, and he wanted them very much.

Still ran Dingo—Yellow-Dog Dingo—very much bewildered, very much hungry, and wondering what in the world or out of it made Old Man Kangaroo hop.

For he hopped like a cricket; like a pea in a saucepan; or a new rubber ball on a nursery floor.

He had to!

He tucked up his front legs; he hopped on his hind legs; he stuck out his tail for a balance-weight behind him; and he hopped through the Darling Downs.*

He had to!

Still ran Dingo—Tired-Dog Dingo—hungrier and hungrier, very much bewildered, and wondering when in the world or out of it would Old Man Kangaroo stop.

Then came Nqong from his bath in the salt-pans, and said, 'It's five o'clock.'

Down sat Dingo—Poor-Dog Dingo—always hungry, dusty in the sunshine; hung out his tongue and howled.

Down sat Kangaroo—Old Man Kangaroo—stuck out his tail like a milking-stool behind him, and said, 'Thank goodness *that's* finished!'

Then said Nqong, who is always a gentleman, 'Why aren't you grateful to Yellow-Dog Dingo? Why don't you thank him for all he has done for you?'

Then said Kangaroo—Tired Old Kangaroo— 'He's chased me out of the homes of my child-hood; he's chased me out of my regular meal-times; he's altered my shape so I'll never get it back; and he's played Old Scratch* with my legs.'

Then said Nqong, 'Perhaps I'm mistaken, but didn't you ask me to make you different from all other animals, as well as to make you very truly sought after? And now it is five o'clock.'

'Yes,' said Kangaroo. 'I wish that I hadn't. I thought you would do it by charms and incantations, but this is a practical joke.'

'Joke!' said Nqong, from his bath in the blue gums. 'Say that again and I'll whistle up Dingo and run your hind legs off.'

'No,' said the Kangaroo. 'I must apologise. Legs are legs, and you needn't alter 'em so far as I am concerned. I only meant to explain to Your Lord-liness that I've had nothing to eat since morning, and I'm very empty indeed.'

'Yes,' said Dingo—Yellow-Dog Dingo,—'I am just in the same situation. I've made him different from all other animals; but what may I have for my tea?'

THIS is the picture of Old Man Kangaroo at five in the afternoon, when he had got his beautiful hind legs just as Big God Nqong had promised. You can see that it is five o'clock, because Big God Nqong's pet tame clock says so. That is Nqong, in his bath, sticking his feet out. Old Man Kangaroo is being rude to Yellow-Dog Dingo. Yellow-Dog Dingo has been trying to catch Kangaroo all across Australia. You can see the marks of Kangaroo's big new feet running ever so far back over the bare hills. Yellow-Dog Dingo is drawn black, because I am not allowed to paint these pictures with real colours out of the paint-box; and besides, Yellow-Dog Dingo got dreadfully black and dusty after running through the Flinders and the Cinders.

I don't know the names of the flowers growing round Nqong's bath. The two little squatty things out in the desert are the other two gods that Old Man Kangaroo spoke to early in the morning. That thing with the letters on it* is Old Man Kangaroo's pouch. He had to have a pouch just as he had to have legs.

Then said Nqong from his bath in the salt-pan, 'Come and ask me about it to-morrow, because I'm going to wash.'

So they were left in the middle of Australia, Old Man Kangaroo and Yellow-Dog Dingo, and each said, 'That's *your* fault.'

THIS is the mouth-filling song
Of the race that was run by a Boomer,
Run in a single burst—only event of its kind—
Started by Big God Nqong from Warrigaborrigarooma,*
Old Man Kangaroo first: Yellow-Dog Dingo behind.

Kangaroo bounded away,
His back-legs working like pistons—
Bounded from morning till dark,
Twenty-five feet to a bound.
Yellow-Dog Dingo lay
Like a yellow cloud in the distance—
Much too busy to bark.
My! but they covered the ground!

Nobody knows where they went,
Or followed the track that they flew in,
For that Continent
Hadn't been given a name.
They ran thirty degrees,
From Torres Straits to the Leeuwin
(Look at the Atlas, please),
And they ran back as they came.

S'posing you could trot
From Adelaide to the Pacific,
For an afternoon's run—
Half what these gentlemen did—
You would feel rather hot,
But your legs would develop terrific—
Yes, my importunate son,
You'd be a Marvellous Kid!

THE BEGINNING OF THE ARMADILLOES

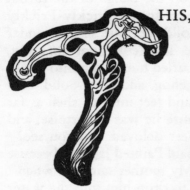

HIS, O Best Beloved, is another story of the High and Far-Off Times. In the very middle of those times was a Stickly-Prickly Hedgehog, and he lived on the banks of the turbid Amazon, eating shelly snails and things. And he had a friend, a Slow-Solid Tortoise, who lived on the banks of the turbid Amazon, eating green lettuces and things. And so *that* was all right, Best Beloved. Do you see?

But also, and at the same time, in those High and Far-Off Times, there was a Painted Jaguar, and he lived on the banks of the turbid Amazon too; and he ate everything that he could catch. When he could not catch deer or monkeys he would eat frogs and beetles; and when he could not catch frogs and beetles he went to his Mother Jaguar, and she told him how to eat hedgehogs and tortoises.

She said to him ever so many times, graciously waving her tail, 'My son, when you find a Hedgehog you must drop him into the water and then he will uncoil, and when you catch a Tortoise you must scoop him out of his shell with your paw.' And so that was all right, Best Beloved.

One beautiful night on the banks of the turbid Amazon, Painted Jaguar found Stickly-Prickly Hedgehog and Slow-Solid Tortoise sitting under the trunk of a fallen tree. They could not run away, and so Stickly-Prickly curled himself up into a ball, because he was a Hedgehog, and Slow-Solid Tortoise drew in his head and feet into his shell as far as they would go, because he was a Tortoise; and so *that* was all right, Best Beloved. Do you see?

'Now attend to me,' said Painted Jaguar, 'because this is very important. My mother said that when I meet a Hedgehog I am to drop him into the water and then he will uncoil, and when I meet a Tortoise I am to scoop him out of his shell with my paw. Now which of you is Hedgehog and which is Tortoise? because, to save my spots, I can't tell.'

'Are you sure of what your Mummy told you?' said Stickly-Prickly Hedgehog. 'Are you quite sure? Perhaps she said that when you uncoil a Tortoise you must shell him out of the water with a scoop, and when you paw a Hedgehog you must drop him on the shell.'

'Are you sure of what your Mummy told you?'

said Slow-and-Solid Tortoise. 'Are you quite sure? Perhaps she said that when you water a Hedgehog you must drop him into your paw, and when you meet a Tortoise you must shell him till he uncoils.'

'I don't think it was at all like that,' said Painted Jaguar, but he felt a little puzzled; 'but, please, say it again more distinctly.'

'When you scoop water with your paw you uncoil it with a Hedgehog,' said Stickly-Prickly. 'Remember that, because it's important.'

'*But*,' said the Tortoise, 'when you paw your meat you drop it into a Tortoise with a scoop. Why can't you understand?'

'You are making my spots ache,' said Painted Jaguar; 'and besides, I didn't want your advice at all. I only wanted to know which of you is Hedgehog and which is Tortoise.'

'I shan't tell you,' said Stickly-Prickly. 'But you can scoop me out of my shell if you like.'

'Aha!' said Painted Jaguar. 'Now I know you're Tortoise. You thought I wouldn't! Now I will.' Painted Jaguar darted out his paddy-paw just as Stickly-Prickly curled himself up, and of course Jaguar's paddy-paw was just filled with prickles. Worse than that, he knocked Stickly-Prickly away and away into the woods and the bushes, where it was too dark to find him. Then he put his paddy-paw into his mouth, and of course the prickles hurt him worse than ever. As soon as he could speak he

THIS is an inciting map of the Turbid Amazon done in Red and Black. It hasn't anything to do with the story except that there are two Armadilloes in it—up by the top. The inciting part are the adventures that happened to the men who went along the road marked in red.* I meant to draw Armadilloes when I began the map, and I meant to draw manatees and spider-tailed monkeys and big snakes and lots of Jaguars, but it was more inciting to do the map and the venturesome adventures in red. You begin at the bottom left-hand corner and follow the little arrows all about, and then you come quite round again to where the adventuresome people went home in a ship called the *Royal Tiger*. This is a most adventuresome picture, and all the adventures are told about in writing,* so you can be quite sure which is an adventure and which is a tree or a boat.

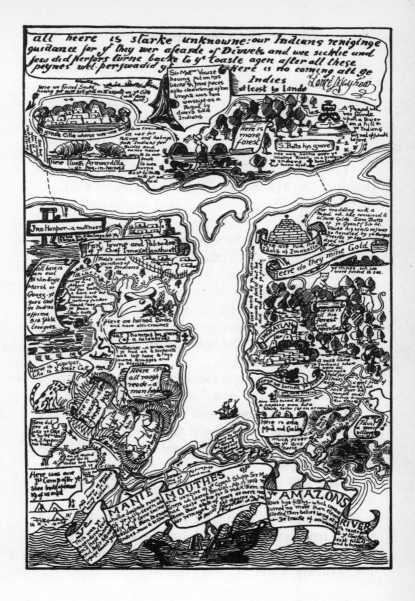

said, 'Now I know he isn't Tortoise at all. But'—
and then he scratched his head with his un-prickly
paw—'how do I know that this other is Tortoise?'

'But I *am* Tortoise,' said Slow-and-Solid. 'Your
mother was quite right. She said that you were to
scoop me out of my shell with your paw. Begin.'

'You didn't say she said that a minute ago,' said
Painted Jaguar, sucking the prickles out of his
paddy-paw. 'You said she said something quite
different.'

'Well, suppose you say that I said that she said
something quite different, I don't see that it makes
any difference; because if she said what you said I
said she said, it's just the same as if I said what she
said she said. On the other hand, if you think
she said that you were to uncoil me with a scoop,
instead of pawing me into drops with a shell, I
can't help that, can I?'

'But you said you wanted to be scooped out of
your shell with my paw,' said Painted Jaguar.

'If you'll think again you'll find that I didn't say
anything of the kind. I said that your mother said
that you were to scoop me out of my shell,' said
Slow-and-Solid.

'What will happen if I do?' said the Jaguar most
sniffily and most cautious.

'I don't know, because I've never been scooped
out of my shell before; but I tell you truly, if you
want to see me swim away you've only got to drop
me into the water.'

'I don't believe it,' said Painted Jaguar. 'You've mixed up all the things my mother told me to do with the things that you asked me whether I was sure that she didn't say, till I don't know whether I'm on my head or my painted tail; and now you come and tell me something I *can* understand, and it makes me more mixy than before. My mother told me that I was to drop one of you two into the water, and as you seem so anxious to be dropped I think you don't want to be dropped. So jump into the turbid Amazon and be quick about it.'

'I warn you that your Mummy won't be pleased. Don't tell her I didn't tell you,' said Slow-Solid.

'If you say another word about what my mother said—' the Jaguar answered, but he had not finished the sentence before Slow-and-Solid quietly dived into the turbid Amazon, swam under water for a long way, and came out on the bank where Stickly-Prickly was waiting for him.

'That was a very narrow escape,' said Stickly-Prickly. 'I don't like Painted Jaguar. What did you tell him that you were?'

'I told him truthfully that I was a truthful Tortoise, but he wouldn't believe it, and he made me jump into the river to see if I was, and I was, and he is surprised. Now he's gone to tell his Mummy. Listen to him!'

They could hear Painted Jaguar roaring up and down among the trees and the bushes by the side of the turbid Amazon, till his Mummy came.

'Son, son!' said his mother ever so many times, graciously waving her tail, 'what have you been doing that you shouldn't have done?'

'I tried to scoop something that said it wanted to be scooped out of its shell with my paw, and my paw is full of per-ickles,' said Painted Jaguar.

'Son, son!' said his mother ever so many times, graciously waving her tail, 'by the prickles in your paddy-paw I see that that must have been a Hedgehog. You should have dropped him into the water.'

'I did that to the other thing; and he said he was a Tortoise, and I didn't believe him, and it was quite true, and he has dived under the turbid Amazon, and he won't come up again, and I haven't anything at all to eat, and I think we had better find lodgings somewhere else. They are too clever on the turbid Amazon for poor me!'

'Son, son!' said his mother ever so many times, graciously waving her tail, 'now attend to me and remember what I say. A Hedgehog curls himself up into a ball and his prickles stick out every which way at once. By this you may know the Hedgehog.'

'I don't like this old lady one little bit,' said Stickly-Prickly, under the shadow of a large leaf. 'I wonder what else she knows?'

'A Tortoise can't curl himself up,' Mother Jaguar went on, ever so many times, graciously waving her tail. 'He only draws his head and legs into his shell. By this you may know the Tortoise.'

'I don't like this old lady at all—at all,' said Slow-and-Solid Tortoise. 'Even Painted Jaguar can't forget those directions. It's a great pity that you can't swim, Stickly-Prickly.'

'Don't talk to me,' said Stickly-Prickly. 'Just think how much better it would be if you could curl up. This *is* a mess! Listen to Painted Jaguar.'

Painted Jaguar was sitting on the banks of the turbid Amazon sucking prickles out of his paws and saying to himself—

> 'Can't curl, but can swim—
> Slow-Solid, that's him!
> Curls up, but can't swim—
> Stickly-Prickly, that's him!'

'He'll never forget that this month of Sundays,' said Stickly-Prickly. 'Hold up my chin, Slow-and-Solid. I'm going to try to learn to swim. It may be useful.'

'Excellent!' said Slow-and-Solid; and he held up Stickly-Prickly's chin, while Stickly-Prickly kicked in the waters of the turbid Amazon.

'You'll make a fine swimmer yet,' said Slow-and-Solid. 'Now, if you can unlace my back-plates a little, I'll see what I can do towards curling up. It may be useful.'

Stickly-Prickly helped to unlace Tortoise's back-plates, so that by twisting and straining Slow-and-Solid actually managed to curl up a tiddy wee bit.

'Excellent!' said Stickly-Prickly; 'but I shouldn't

do any more just now. It's making you black in the face. Kindly lead me into the water once again and I'll practise that side-stroke which you say is so easy.' And so Stickly-Prickly practised, and Slow-Solid swam alongside.

'Excellent!' said Slow-and-Solid. 'A little more practice will make you a regular whale.* Now, if I may trouble you to unlace my back and front plates two holes more, I'll try that fascinating bend that you say is so easy. Won't Painted Jaguar be surprised!'

'Excellent!' said Stickly-Prickly, all wet from the turbid Amazon. 'I declare, I shouldn't know you from one of my own family. Two holes, I think, you said? A little more expression, please, and don't grunt quite so much, or Painted Jaguar may hear us. When you've finished, I want to try that long dive which you say is so easy. Won't Painted Jaguar be surprised!'

And so Stickly-Prickly dived, and Slow-and-Solid dived alongside.

'Excellent!' said Slow-and-Solid. 'A leetle more attention to holding your breath and you will be able to keep house at the bottom of the turbid Amazon. Now I'll try that exercise of wrapping my hind legs round my ears which you say is so peculiarly comfortable. Won't Painted Jaguar be surprised!'

'Excellent!' said Stickly-Prickly. 'But it's straining

your back-plates a little. They are all overlapping now, instead of lying side by side.'

'Oh, that's the result of exercise,' said Slow-and-Solid. 'I've noticed that your prickles seem to be melting into one another, and that you're growing to look rather more like a pine-cone, and less like a chestnut-burr, than you used to.'

'Am I?' said Stickly-Prickly. 'That comes from my soaking in the water. Oh, won't Painted Jaguar be surprised!'

They went on with their exercises, each helping the other, till morning came; and when the sun was high they rested and dried themselves. Then they saw that they were both of them quite different from what they had been.

'Stickly-Prickly,' said Tortoise after breakfast, 'I am not what I was yesterday; but I think that I may yet amuse Painted Jaguar.'

'That was the very thing I was thinking just now,' said Stickly-Prickly. 'I think scales are a tremendous improvement on prickles—to say nothing of being able to swim. Oh, *won't* Painted Jaguar be surprised! Let's go and find him.'

By and by they found Painted Jaguar, still nursing his paddy-paw that had been hurt the night before. He was so astonished that he fell three times backward over his own painted tail without stopping.

'Good morning!' said Stickly-Prickly. 'And how is your dear gracious Mummy this morning?'

'She is quite well, thank you,' said Painted Jaguar; 'but you must forgive me if I do not at this precise moment recall your name.'

'That's unkind of you,' said Stickly-Prickly, 'seeing that this time yesterday you tried to scoop me out of my shell with your paw.'

'But you hadn't any shell. It was all prickles,' said Painted Jaguar. 'I know it was. Just look at my paw!'

'You told me to drop into the turbid Amazon and be drowned,' said Slow-Solid. 'Why are you so rude and forgetful to-day?'

'Don't you remember what your mother told you?' said Stickly-Prickly,—

> 'Can't curl, but can swim—
> Stickly-Prickly, that's him!
> Curls up, but can't swim—
> Slow-Solid, that's him!'

Then they both curled themselves up and rolled round and round Painted Jaguar till his eyes turned truly cart-wheels in his head.

Then he went to fetch his mother.

'Mother,' he said, 'there are two new animals in the woods to-day, and the one that you said couldn't swim, swims, and the one that you said couldn't curl up, curls; and they've gone shares in their prickles, I think, because both of them are scaly all over, instead of one being smooth and the other very prickly; and, besides that, they are rolling round and round in circles, and I don't feel comfy.'

'Son, son!' said Mother Jaguar ever so many times, graciously waving her tail, 'a Hedgehog is a Hedgehog, and can't be anything but a Hedgehog; and a Tortoise is a Tortoise, and can never be anything else.'

'But it isn't a Hedgehog, and it isn't a Tortoise. It's a little bit of both, and I don't know its proper name.'

'Nonsense!' said Mother Jaguar. 'Everything has its proper name. I should call it "Armadillo" till I found out the real one. And I should leave it alone.'

So Painted Jaguar did as he was told, especially about leaving them alone; but the curious thing is that from that day to this, O Best Beloved, no one on the banks of the turbid Amazon has ever called Stickly-Prickly and Slow-Solid anything except Armadillo. There are Hedgehogs and Tortoises in other places, of course (there are some in my garden);* but the real old and clever kind, with their scales lying lippety-lappety one over the other, like pine-cone scales, that lived on the banks of the turbid Amazon in the High and Far-Off Days, are always called Armadillos, because they were so clever.

So *that's* all right, Best Beloved. Do you see?

THIS is a picture of the whole story of the Jaguar and the Hedgehog and the Tortoise *and* the Armadillo all in a heap. It looks rather the same any way you turn it.* The Tortoise is in the middle, learning how to bend, and that is why the shelly plates on his back are so spread apart. He is standing on the Hedgehog, who is waiting to learn how to swim. The Hedgehog is a Japanesy Hedgehog, because I couldn't find our own Hedgehogs in the garden when I wanted to draw them. (It was daytime, and they had gone to bed under the dahlias.) Speckly Jaguar is looking over the edge, with his paddy-paw carefully tied up by his mother, because he pricked himself scooping the Hedgehog. He is much surprised to see what the Tortoise is doing, and his paw is hurting him. The snouty thing with the little eye that Speckly Jaguar is trying to climb over is the Armadillo that the Tortoise and the Hedgehog are going to turn into when they have finished bending and swimming. It is all a magic picture, and that is one of the reasons why I haven't drawn the Jaguar's whiskers. The other reason was that he was so young that his whiskers had not grown. The Jaguar's pet name with his Mummy was Doffles.

I'VE never sailed the Amazon,
   I've never reached Brazil;
But the *Don* and *Magdalena,**
   They can go there when they will!

      Yes, weekly from Southampton,
      Great steamers, white and gold,
      Go rolling down to Rio
      (Roll down—roll down to Rio!)
      And I'd like to roll to Rio
      Some day before I'm old!

I've never seen a Jaguar,
   Nor yet an Armadill—
O dilloing in his armour,
   And I s'pose I never will,

      Unless I go to Rio
      These wonders to behold—
      Roll down—roll down to Rio—
      Roll really down to Rio!
      Oh, I'd love to roll to Rio
      Some day before I'm old!

HOW THE FIRST LETTER
WAS WRITTEN

NCE upon a most early time was a Neolithic man. He was not a Jute or an Angle, or even a Dravidian, which he might well have been, Best Beloved, but never mind why. He was a Primitive, and he lived cavily in a Cave, and he wore very few clothes, and he couldn't read and he couldn't write and he didn't want to, and except when he was hungry he was quite happy. His name was Tegumai Bopsulai, and that means, 'Man-who-does-not-put-his-foot-forward-in-a-hurry'; but we, O Best Beloved, will call him Tegumai, for short. And his wife's name was Teshumai Tewindrow, and that means, 'Lady-who-asks-a-very-many-questions'; but we, O Best Beloved, will call her Teshumai, for short. And his little girl-daughter's name was Taffimai Metallumai, and that means, 'Small-person-without-any-manners-who-ought-to-be-spanked'; but I'm going to call her Taffy. And she was Tegumai Bopsulai's Best Beloved and her own Mummy's Best Beloved, and she was not spanked half as much as was good for her; and they were all three very happy. As soon as Taffy could run about she went everywhere with her Daddy Tegumai, and sometimes they would not come home to the Cave till they were hungry, and then Teshumai Tewindrow would say, 'Where in the world have you two been to, to get so shocking dirty? Really, my Tegumai, you're no better than my Taffy.'

Now attend and listen!

One day Tegumai Bopsulai went down through the beaver-swamp to the Wagai river to spear carp-fish for dinner, and Taffy went too. Tegumai's spear was made of wood with shark's teeth at the end, and before he had caught any fish at all he acciden-tally broke it clean across by jabbing it down too hard on the bottom of the river. They were miles and miles from home (of course they had their lunch with them in a little bag), and Tegumai had forgot-ten to bring any extra spears.

'Here's a pretty kettle of fish!' said Tegumai. 'It will take me half the day to mend this.'

'There's your big black spear at home,' said Taffy. 'Let me run back to the Cave and ask Mummy to give it me.'

'It's too far for your little fat legs,' said Tegumai.

'Besides, you might fall into the beaver-swamp and be drowned. We must make the best of a bad job.' He sat down and took out a little leather mendy-bag, full of reindeer-sinews and strips of leather, and lumps of bee's-wax and resin, and began to mend the spear. Taffy sat down too, with her toes in the water and her chin in her hand, and thought very hard. Then she said—

'I say, Daddy, it's an awful nuisance that you and I don't know how to write,* isn't it? If we did we could send a message for the new spear.'

'Taffy,' said Tegumai, 'how often have I told you not to use slang? "Awful" isn't a pretty word,—but it *would* be a convenience, now you mention it, if we could write home.'

Just then a Stranger-man came along the river, but he belonged to a far tribe, the Tewaras, and he did not understand one word of Tegumai's language. He stood on the bank and smiled at Taffy, because he had a little girl-daughter of his own at home. Tegumai drew a hank of deer-sinews from his mendy-bag and began to mend his spear.

'Come here,' said Taffy. 'Do you know where my Mummy lives?' And the Stranger-man said 'Um!'—being, as you know, a Tewara.

'Silly!' said Taffy, and she stamped her foot, because she saw a shoal of very big carp going up the river just when her Daddy couldn't use his spear.

'Don't bother grown-ups,' said Tegumai, so busy with his spear-mending that he did not turn round.*

'I aren't,' said Taffy. 'I only want him to do what I want him to do, and he won't understand.'

'Then don't bother me,' said Tegumai, and he went on pulling and straining at the deer-sinews with his mouth full of loose ends. The Stranger-man—a genuine Tewara he was—sat down on the grass, and Taffy showed him what her Daddy was doing. The Stranger-man thought, 'This is a very wonderful child. She stamps her foot at me and she makes faces. She must be the daughter of that noble Chief who is so great that he won't take any notice of me.' So he smiled more politely than ever.

'Now,' said Taffy, 'I want you to go to my Mummy, because your legs are longer than mine, and you won't fall into the beaver-swamp, and ask for Daddy's other spear—the one with the black handle that hangs over our fireplace.'

The Stranger-man (*and* he was a Tewara) thought, 'This is a very, very wonderful child. She waves her arms and she shouts at me, but I don't understand a word of what she says. But if I don't do what she wants, I greatly fear that that haughty Chief, Man-who-turns-his-back-on-callers, will be angry.' He got up and twisted a big flat piece of bark off a birch-tree and gave it to Taffy. He did this, Best Beloved, to show that his heart was as white as the birch-bark and that he meant no harm; but Taffy didn't quite understand.

'Oh!' said she. 'Now I see! You want my Mummy's living address? Of course I can't write, but I can draw pictures if I've anything sharp to scratch with. Please lend me the shark's tooth off your necklace.'

The Stranger-man (and *he* was a Tewara) didn't say anything, so Taffy put up her little hand and pulled at the beautiful bead and seed and shark-tooth necklace round his neck.

The Stranger-man (and he *was* a Tewara) thought, 'This is a very, very, very wonderful child. The shark's tooth on my necklace is a magic shark's tooth, and I was always told that if anybody touched it without my leave they would immediately swell up or burst. But this child doesn't swell up or burst, and that important Chief, Man-who-attends-strictly-to-his-business, who has not yet taken any notice of me at all, doesn't seem to be afraid that she will swell up or burst. I had better be more polite.'

So he gave Taffy the shark's tooth, and she lay down flat on her tummy with her legs in the air, like some people on the drawing-room floor when they want to draw pictures,* and she said, 'Now I'll draw you some beautiful pictures! You can look over my shoulder, but you mustn't joggle. First I'll draw Daddy fishing. It isn't very like him; but Mummy will know, because I've drawn his spear all broken. Well, now I'll draw the other spear that he wants, the black-handled spear. It looks as if it was sticking in Daddy's back, but that's because the shark's tooth slipped and this piece of bark isn't big enough. That's the spear I want you to fetch; so I'll draw a picture of me myself 'splaining to you. My hair doesn't stand up like I've drawn, but it's easier to draw that way. Now I'll draw you. *I* think you're very nice really, but I can't make you pretty in the picture, so you mustn't be 'fended. Are you 'fended?'

The Stranger-man (and he was *a* Tewara) smiled. He thought, 'There must be a big battle going to be fought somewhere, and this extraordinary child, who takes my magic shark's tooth but who does not swell up or burst, is telling me to call all the great Chief's tribe to help him. He *is* a great Chief, or he would have noticed me.'

'Look,' said Taffy, drawing very hard and rather scratchily, 'now I've drawn you, and I've put the spear that Daddy wants into your hand, just to remind you that you're to bring it. Now I'll show you how to find my Mummy's living-address. You go along till you come to two trees (those are trees), and then you go over a hill (that's a hill), and then you come into a beaver-swamp all full of beavers. I haven't put in all the beavers, because I can't draw beavers, but I've drawn their heads, and that's all you'll see of them when you cross the swamp. Mind you don't fall in! Then our Cave is just beyond the beaver-swamp. It isn't as high as the hills really, but I can't draw things very small. That's my Mummy outside. She is beautiful. She is the most beautifullest Mummy there ever was, but she won't be 'fended when she sees I've drawn her so plain. She'll be pleased of me because I can draw. Now, in case you forget, I've drawn the spear that Daddy wants *outside* our Cave. It's *inside* really, but you show the picture to my Mummy and she'll give it you. I've made her holding up her hands, because I know she'll be so pleased to see you. Isn't it a beautiful picture? And do you quite understand, or shall I 'splain again?'

The Stranger-man (and he was a *Tewara*) looked at the picture and nodded very hard. He said to himself, 'If I do not fetch this great Chief's tribe to help him, he will be slain by his enemies who are coming up on all sides with spears. Now I see why the great Chief pretended not to notice me! He feared that his enemies were hiding in the bushes and would see him deliver a message to me. Therefore he turned his back, and let the wise and wonderful child draw the terrible picture showing me his difficulties. I will away and get help for him from his tribe.' He did not even ask Taffy the road, but raced off into the bushes like the wind, with the birch-bark in his hand, and Taffy sat down most pleased.

Now this is the picture that Taffy had drawn for him!*

'What have you been doing, Taffy?' said Tegumai.
He had mended his spear and was carefully waving
it to and fro.

'It's a little berangement of my own, Daddy dear,'
said Taffy. 'If you won't ask me questions, you'll
know all about it in a little time, and you'll be
surprised. You don't know how surprised you'll
be, Daddy! Promise you'll be surprised.'

'Very well,' said Tegumai, and went on fishing.

The Stranger-man—did you know he was a
Tewara?—hurried away with the picture and ran
for some miles, till quite by accident he found
Teshumai Tewindrow at the door of her Cave,
talking to some other Neolithic ladies who had

come in to a Primitive lunch. Taffy was very like Teshumai, specially about the upper part of the face and the eyes, so the Stranger-man—always a pure Tewara—smiled politely and handed Teshumai the birch-bark. He had run hard, so that he panted, and his legs were scratched with brambles, but he still tried to be polite.

As soon as Teshumai saw the picture she screamed like anything and flew at the Stranger-man. The other Neolithic ladies at once knocked him down and sat on him in a long line of six, while Teshumai pulled his hair. 'It's as plain as the nose on this Stranger-man's face,' she said. 'He has stuck my Tegumai all full of spears, and frightened poor Taffy so that her hair stands all on end; and not content with that, he brings me a horrid picture of how it was done. Look!' She showed the picture to all the Neolithic ladies sitting patiently on the Stranger-man. 'Here is my Tegumai with his arm broken; here is a spear sticking into his back; here is a man with a spear ready to throw; here is another man throwing a spear from a Cave, and here are a whole pack of people' (they were Taffy's beavers really, but they did look rather like people) 'coming up behind Tegumai. Isn't it shocking!'

'Most shocking!' said the Neolithic ladies, and they filled the Stranger-man's hair with mud (at which he was surprised), and they beat upon the Reverberating Tribal Drums, and called together all the chiefs of the Tribe of Tegumai, with their Hetmans and Dolmans, all Neguses, Woons, and Akhoonds of the organisation, in addition to the Warlocks, Angekoks, Juju-men, Bonzes,* and the rest, who decided that before they chopped the Stranger-man's head off he should instantly lead them down to the river and show them where he had hidden poor Taffy.

By this time the Stranger-man (in spite of being a Tewara) was really annoyed. They had filled his hair quite solid with mud; they had rolled him up and down on knobby pebbles; they had sat upon him in a long line of six; they had thumped him and bumped him till he could hardly breathe; and though he did not understand their language, he was almost sure that the names the Neolithic ladies called him were not ladylike.* However, he said nothing till all the Tribe of Tegumai were assembled, and then he led them back to the bank of the Wagai river, and there they found Taffy making daisy-chains, and Tegumai carefully spearing small carp with his mended spear.

'Well, you *have* been quick!' said Taffy. 'But why did you bring so many people? Daddy dear, this is my surprise. *Are* you surprised, Daddy?'

'Very,' said Tegumai; 'but it has ruined all my fishing for the day. Why, the whole dear, kind, nice, clean, quiet Tribe is here, Taffy.'

And so they were. First of all walked Teshumai Tewindrow and the Neolithic ladies, tightly holding on to the Stranger-man, whose hair was full of mud (although he was a Tewara). Behind them came the Head Chief, the Vice-Chief, the Deputy and Assistant Chiefs (all armed to the upper teeth), the Hetmans and Heads of Hundreds, Platoffs with their Platoons, and Dolmans with their Detachments; Woons, Neguses, and Akhoonds ranking in the rear (still armed to the teeth). Behind them was the Tribe in hierarchical order, from owners of four caves* (one for each season), a private reindeer-run, and two salmon-leaps, to feudal and prognathous Villeins, semi-entitled to half a bearskin of winter nights, seven yards from the fire, and adscript serfs, holding the reversion of a scraped marrow-bone under heriot (Aren't those beautiful words, Best Beloved?). They were all there, prancing and shouting, and they frightened every fish for twenty miles, and Tegumai thanked them in a fluid Neolithic oration.

Then Teshumai Tewindrow ran down and kissed and hugged Taffy very much indeed; but the Head Chief of the Tribe of Tegumai took Tegumai by the top-knot feathers and shook him severely.

'Explain! Explain! Explain!' cried all the Tribe of Tegumai.

'Goodness' sakes alive!' said Tegumai. 'Let go of my top-knot. Can't a man break his carp-spear without the whole countryside descending on him? You're a very interfering people.'

'I don't believe you've brought my Daddy's

black-handled spear after all,' said Taffy. 'And what *are* you doing to my nice Stranger-man?'

They were thumping him by twos and threes and tens till his eyes turned round and round. He could only gasp and point at Taffy.*

'Where are the bad people who speared you, my darling?' said Teshumai Tewindrow.

'There weren't any,' said Tegumai. 'My only visitor this morning was the poor fellow that you are trying to choke. Aren't you well, or are you ill, O Tribe of Tegumai?'

'He came with a horrible picture,' said the Head Chief,—'a picture that showed you were full of spears.'

'Er—um—P'raps I'd better 'splain that I gave him that picture,' said Taffy, but she did not feel quite comfy.

'You!' said the Tribe of Tegumai all together. 'Small-person-with-no-manners-who-ought-to-be-spanked! You?'

'Taffy dear, I'm afraid we're in for a little trouble,' said her Daddy, and put his arm round her, so she didn't care.

'Explain! Explain! Explain!' said the Head Chief of the Tribe of Tegumai, and he hopped on one foot.

'I wanted the Stranger-man to fetch Daddy's spear, so I drawded it,' said Taffy. 'There wasn't lots of spears. There was only one spear. I drawded

it three times to make sure. I couldn't help it looking as if it stuck into Daddy's head—there wasn't
room on the birch-bark; and those things that
Mummy called bad people are my beavers. I
drawded them to show him the way through the
swamp; and I drawded Mummy at the mouth of
the Cave looking pleased because he is a nice
Stranger-man, and *I* think you are just the stupidest
people in the world,' said Taffy. 'He is a very nice
man. Why have you filled his hair with mud? Wash
him!'

Nobody said anything at all for a long time, till
the Head Chief laughed; then the Stranger-man
(who was at least a Tewara) laughed; then Tegumai
laughed till he fell down flat on the bank; then all
the Tribe laughed more and worse and louder. The
only people who did not laugh were Teshumai
Tewindrow and all the Neolithic ladies. They were
very polite to all their husbands, and said 'idiot!'
ever so often.

Then the Head Chief of the Tribe of Tegumai
cried and said and sang, 'O Small-person-without-
any-manners-who-ought-to-be-spanked, you've hit
upon a great invention!'

'I didn't intend to; I only wanted Daddy's black-
handled spear,' said Taffy.

'Never mind. It *is* a great invention, and some
day men will call it writing. At present it is only
pictures, and, as we have seen to-day, pictures are

THIS is the story of Taffimai Metallumai carved on an old tusk a very long time ago by the Ancient Peoples. If you read my story, or have it read to you, you can see how it is all told out on the tusk. The tusk was part of an old tribal trumpet that belonged to the Tribe of Tegumai. The pictures were scratched on it with a nail or something, and then the scratches were filled up with black wax, but all the dividing lines and the five little rounds at the bottom were filled with red wax. When it was new there was a sort of network of beads and shells and precious stones at one end of it; but now that has been broken and lost—all except the little bit that you see. The letters round the tusk are magic—Runic magic,*—and if you can read them you will find out something rather new. The tusk is of ivory—very yellow and scratched. It is two feet long and two feet round, and weighs eleven pounds nine ounces.

not always properly understood. But a time will come, O Babe of Tegumai, when we shall make letters—all twenty-six of 'em,—and when we shall be able to read as well as to write, and then we shall always say exactly what we mean without any mistakes. Let the Neolithic ladies wash the mud out of the stranger's hair!'

'I shall be glad of that,' said Taffy, 'because, after all, though you've brought every single other spear in the Tribe of Tegumai, you've forgotten my Daddy's black-handled spear.'

Then the Head Chief cried and said and sang, 'Taffy dear, the next time you write a picture-letter, you'd better send a man who can talk our language with it, to explain what it means. I don't mind it myself, because I am a Head Chief, but it's very bad for the rest of the Tribe of Tegumai, and, as you can see, it surprises the stranger.'*

Then they adopted the Stranger-man (a genuine Tewara of Tewar) into the Tribe of Tegumai, because he was a gentleman and did not make a fuss about the mud that the Neolithic ladies had put into his hair. But from that day to this (and I suppose it is all Taffy's fault), very few little girls have ever liked learning to read or write. Most of them prefer to draw pictures and play about with their Daddies—just like Taffy.

THERE runs a road by Merrow Down—*
  A grassy track to-day it is—
An hour out of Guildford town,
  Above the river Wey it is.

Here, when they heard the horse-bells ring,
  The ancient Britons dressed and rode
To watch the dark Phœnicians bring
  Their goods along the Western Road.

And here, or hereabouts, they met
  To hold their racial talks and such—
To barter beads for Whitby jet,
  And tin for gay shell torques and such.

But long and long before that time
  (When bison used to roam on it)
Did Taffy and her Daddy climb
  That down, and had their home on it.

Then beavers built in Broadstonebrook
  And made a swamp where Bramley stands;
And bears from Shere would come and look
  For Taffimai where Shamley stands.

The Wey, that Taffy called Wagai,
  Was more than six times bigger then;
And all the Tribe of Tegumai
  They cut a noble figure then!

HOW THE ALPHABET
WAS MADE

HE week after Taffimai Metallumai (we will still call her Taffy, Best Beloved) made that little mistake about her Daddy's spear and the Stranger-man and the picture-letter and all, she went carp-fishing again with her Daddy. Her Mummy wanted her to stay at home and help hang up hides to dry on the big drying-poles outside their Neolithic Cave, but Taffy slipped away down to her Daddy quite early, and they fished. Presently she began to giggle, and her Daddy said, 'Don't be silly, child.'

'But wasn't it inciting!' said Taffy. 'Don't you remember how the Head Chief puffed out his cheeks, and how funny the nice Stranger-man looked with the mud in his hair?'

'Well do I,' said Tegumai. 'I had to pay two

deerskins—soft ones with fringes—to the Stranger-man for the things we did to him.'

'*We* didn't do anything,' said Taffy. 'It was Mummy and the other Neolithic ladies—and the mud.'

'We won't talk about that,' said her Daddy. 'Let's have lunch.'

Taffy took a marrow-bone and sat mousy-quiet for ten whole minutes, while her Daddy scratched on pieces of birch-bark with a shark's tooth. Then she said, 'Daddy, I've thinked of a secret surprise. You make a noise—any sort of noise.'

'Ah!' said Tegumai. 'Will that do to begin with?'

'Yes,' said Taffy. 'You look just like a carp-fish with its mouth open. Say it again, please.'

'Ah! ah! ah!' said her Daddy. 'Don't be rude, my daughter.'

'I'm not meaning rude, really and truly,' said Taffy. 'It's part of my secret-surprise-think. *Do* say *ah*, Daddy, and keep your mouth open at the end, and lend me that tooth. I'm going to draw a carp-fish's mouth wide-open.'

'What for?' said her Daddy.

'Don't you see?' said Taffy, scratching away on the bark. 'That will be our little secret s'prise. When I draw a carp-fish with his mouth open in the smoke at the back of our Cave—if Mummy doesn't mind—it will remind you of that ah-noise. Then we can play that it was me jumped out of the dark and

s'prised you with that noise—same as I did in the
beaver-swamp last winter.'

'Really?' said her Daddy, in the voice that grown-
ups use when they are truly attending. 'Go on, Taffy.'

'Oh bother!' she said. 'I can't draw all of a carp-
fish, but I can draw something that
means a carp-fish's mouth. Don't you
know how they stand on their heads
rooting in the mud? Well, here's a pre-
tence carp-fish (we can play that the
rest of him is drawn). Here's just his mouth, and
that means *ah*.' And she drew this. (1.)

'That's not bad,' said Tegumai, and scratched on
his own piece of bark for himself; 'but you've forgotten the feeler that hangs across his mouth.'

'But I can't draw, Daddy.'

'You needn't draw anything of him except just
the opening of his mouth and the feeler
across. Then we'll know he's a carp-
fish, 'cause the perches and trouts
haven't got feelers. Look here, Taffy.'
And he drew this. (2.)

'Now I'll copy it,' said Taffy. 'Will you understand *this* when you see it?' And she
drew this. (3.)

'Perfectly,' said her Daddy. 'And I'll
be quite as s'prised when I see it anywhere, as if you had jumped out from
behind a tree and said "Ah!"'

'Now, make another noise,' said Taffy, very proud.

'Yah!' said her Daddy, very loud.

'H'm,' said Taffy. 'That's a mixy noise. The end part is *ah*-carp-fish-mouth; but what can we do about the front part? *Yer-yer-yer* and *ah! Ya!*'

'It's very like the carp-fish-mouth noise. Let's draw another bit of the carp-fish and join 'em,' said her Daddy. *He* was quite incited too.

'No. If they're joined, I'll forget. Draw it separate. Draw his tail. If he's standing on his head the tail will come first. 'Sides, I think I can draw tails easiest,' said Taffy.

'A good notion,' said Tegumai. 'Here's a carp-fish tail for the *yer*-noise.' And he drew this. (4.)

'I'll try now,' said Taffy. ''Member I can't draw like you, Daddy. Will it do if I just draw the split part of the tail, and a sticky-down line for where it joins?' And she drew this. (5.)

Her Daddy nodded, and his eyes were shiny bright with 'citement.

'That's beautiful,' she said. 'Now, make another noise, Daddy.'

'Oh!' said her Daddy, very loud.

'That's quite easy,' said Taffy. 'You make your mouth all round like an egg or a stone. So an egg or a stone will do for that.'

'You can't always find eggs or stones. We'll have to scratch a round something like one.' And he drew this. (6.)

'My gracious!' said Taffy, 'what a lot of noise-pictures we've made,—carp-mouth, carp-tail, and egg! Now, make another noise, Daddy.'

'Ssh!' said her Daddy, and frowned to himself, but Taffy was too incited to notice.

'That's quite easy,' she said, scratching on the bark.

'Eh, what?' said her Daddy. 'I meant I was thinking, and didn't want to be disturbed.'

'It's a noise, just the same. It's the noise a snake makes, Daddy, when it is thinking and doesn't want to be disturbed. Let's make the *ssh*-noise a snake. Will this do?' And she drew this. (7.)

'There,' she said. 'That's another s'prise-secret. When you draw a hissy-snake by the door of your little back-cave where you mend the spears, I'll know you're thinking hard; and I'll come in most mousy-quiet. And if you draw it on a tree by the river when you're fishing, I'll know you want me to walk most *most* mousy-quiet, so as not to shake the banks.'

'Perfectly true,' said Tegumai. 'And there's more in this game than you think. Taffy, dear, I've a notion that your Daddy's daughter has hit upon

the finest thing that there ever was since the Tribe
of Tegumai took to using shark's teeth instead of
flints for their spear-heads. I believe we've found
out *the* big secret of the world.'

'Why?' said Taffy, and her eyes shone too with
incitement.

'I'll show,' said her Daddy. 'What's water in the
Tegumai language?'

'*Ya*, of course, and it means river too—like Wagai-
ya—the Wagai river.'

'What is bad water that gives you fever if you
drink it—black water—swamp-water?'

'*Yo*, of course.'

'Now look,' said her Daddy. 'S'pose you saw
this scratched by the side of a pool
in the beaver-swamp?' And he drew
this. (8.)

'Carp-tail and round egg. Two
noises mixed! *Yo*, bad water,' said
Taffy. ''Course I wouldn't drink that water because
I'd know you said it was bad.'

'But I needn't be near the water at all. I might be
miles away, hunting, and still——'

'And *still* it would be just the same as if you
stood there and said, "G'way, Taffy, or you'll get
fever." All that in a carp-fish-tail and a round egg!
O Daddy, we must tell Mummy, quick!' and Taffy
danced all round him.

'Not yet,' said Tegumai; 'not till we've gone a

little further. Let's see. *Yo* is bad water, but *so* is food cooked on the fire, isn't it?' And he drew this. (9.)

'Yes. Snake and egg,' said Taffy. 'So that means dinner's ready. If you saw that scratched on a tree you'd know it was time to come to the Cave. So'd I.'

'My Winkie!' said Tegumai. 'That's true too. But wait a minute. I see a difficulty. *So* means "come and have dinner," but *sho* means the drying-poles where we hang our hides.'

'Horrid old drying-poles!' said Taffy. 'I hate helping to hang heavy, hot, hairy hides on them. If you drew the snake and egg, and I thought it meant dinner, and I came in from the wood and found that it meant I was to help Mummy hang the hides on the drying-poles, what *would* I do?'

'You'd be cross. So'd Mummy. We must make a new picture for *sho*. We must draw a spotty snake that hisses *sh-sh*, and we'll play that the plain snake only hisses *ssss*.'

'I couldn't be sure how to put in the spots,' said Taffy. 'And p'raps if *you* were in a hurry you might leave them out, and I'd think it was *so* when it was *sho*, and then Mummy would catch me just the same. *No!* I think we'd better draw a picture of the horrid high drying-poles their very selves, and make *quite* sure. I'll put 'em in just after the hissy-snake. Look!' And she drew this. (10.)

'P'raps that's safest. It's very like our drying-poles, anyhow,' said her Daddy, laughing. 'Now I'll make a new noise with a snake and drying-pole sound in it. I'll say *shi*. That's Tegumai for spear, Taffy.' And he laughed.

'Don't make fun of me,' said Taffy, as she thought of her picture-letter and the mud in the Stranger-man's hair. '*You* draw it, Daddy.'

'We won't have beavers or hills this time, eh?' said her Daddy. 'I'll just draw a straight line for my spear.' And he drew this. (11.)

'Even Mummy couldn't mistake that for me being killed.'

'*Please* don't, Daddy. It makes me uncomfy. Do some more noises. We're getting on beautifully.'

'Er-hm!' said Tegumai, looking up. 'We'll say *shu*. That means sky.'

Taffy drew the snake and the drying-pole. Then she stopped. 'We must make a new picture for that end sound, mustn't we?'

'*Shu-shu-u-u-u!*' said her Daddy. 'Why, it's just like the round-egg-sound made thin.'

'Then s'pose we draw a thin round egg, and pre- tend it's a frog that hasn't eaten anything for years.'

'N-no,' said her Daddy. 'If we drew that in a hurry we might mistake it for the round egg itself. *Shu-shu-shu! I'll* tell you what we'll do. We'll open a little hole at the end of the round egg to show how the O-noise runs out all thin, *ooo—oo—oo*. Like this.' And he drew this. (12.)

'Oh, that's lovely! Much better than a thin frog. Go on,' said Taffy, using her shark's tooth.

Her Daddy went on drawing, and his hand shook with incitement. He went on till he had drawn this. (13.)

'Don't look up, Taffy,' he said. 'Try if you can make out what that means in the Tegumai language. If you can, we've found the Secret.'

'Snake—pole—broken-egg—carp-tail and carp-mouth,' said Taffy. '*Shu-ya*. Sky-water (rain).' Just then a drop fell on her hand, for the day had clouded over. 'Why, Daddy, it's raining. Was *that* what you meant to tell me?'

'Of course,' said her Daddy. 'And I told it you without saying a word, didn't I?'

'Well, I *think* I would have known it in a minute, but that raindrop made me quite sure. I'll always remember now. *Shu-ya* means rain, or "it is going to rain." Why, Daddy!' She got up and danced round him. 'S'pose you went out before I was awake, and drawed *shu-ya* in the smoke on the wall, I'd know it was going to rain and I'd take my beaver-skin hood. Wouldn't Mummy be surprised!'

Tegumai got up and danced. (Daddies didn't mind

doing those things in those days.) 'More than that! More than that!' he said. 'S'pose I wanted to tell you it wasn't going to rain much and you must come down to the river, what would we draw? Say the words in Tegumai-talk first.'

'*Shu-ya-las, ya maru.* (Sky-water ending. River come to.) *What* a lot of new sounds! *I* don't see how we can draw them.'

'But I do—but I do!' said Tegumai. 'Just attend a minute, Taffy, and we won't do any more to-day. We've got *shu-ya* all right, haven't we? but this *las* is a teaser. *La-la-la!*' and he waved his shark-tooth.

'There's the hissy-snake at the end and the carp-mouth before the snake—*as-as-as*. We only want *la-la*,' said Taffy.

'I know it, but we have to make *la-la*. And we're the first people in all the world who've ever tried to do it, Taffimai!'

'Well,' said Taffy, yawning, for she was rather tired. '*Las* means breaking or finishing as well as ending, doesn't it?'

'So it does,' said Tegumai. '*Yo-las* means that there's no water in the tank for Mummy to cook with—just when I'm going hunting, too.'

'And *shi-las* means that your spear is broken. If I'd only thought of *that* instead of drawing silly beaver-pictures for the Stranger!'

'*La! La! La!*' said Tegumai, waving his stick and frowning. 'Oh bother!'

'I could have drawn *shi* quite easily,' Taffy went on. 'Then I'd have drawn your spear all broken— this way!' And she drew. (14.)

'The very thing,' said Tegumai. 'That's *la* all over.

It isn't like any of the other marks, either.' And he drew this. (15.)

'Now for *ya*. Oh, we've done that before. Now for *maru*. *Mum-mum-mum*. *Mum* shuts one's mouth up, doesn't it? We'll draw a shut mouth like this.' And he drew. (16.)

'Then the carp-mouth open. That makes *Ma-ma-ma!* But what about this *rrrrr*-thing, Taffy?'

'It sounds all rough and edgy, like your shark-tooth saw when you're cutting out a plank for the canoe,' said Taffy.

'You mean all sharp at the edges, like this?' said Tegumai. And he drew. (17.)

''Xactly,' said Taffy. 'But we don't want all those teeth: only put two.'

'I'll only put in one,' said Tegumai. 'If this game of ours is going to be what I think it will, the easier we make our sound-pictures the better for everybody.' And he drew. (18.)

'*Now* we've got it,' said Tegumai, standing on one leg. 'I'll draw 'em all in a string
like fish.'

       18

'Hadn't we better put a little bit of stick
or something between each word, so's they won't
rub up against each other and jostle, same as if they
were carps?'

'Oh, I'll leave a space for that,' said her Daddy.
And very incitedly he drew them all without stopping, on a big new bit of birch-bark. (19.)

'*Shu-ya-las ya-maru*,' said Taffy, reading it out
sound by sound.

'That's enough for to-day,' said Tegumai. 'Besides, you're getting tired, Taffy. Never mind, dear.

19

We'll finish it all to-morrow, and then we'll be remembered for years and years after the biggest trees
you can see are all chopped up for firewood.'

So they went home, and all that evening Tegumai
sat on one side of the fire and Taffy on the other,
drawing *ya's* and *yo's* and *shu's* and *shi's* in the
smoke on the wall and giggling together till her
Mummy said, 'Really, Tegumai, you're worse than
my Taffy.'

'Please don't mind,' said Taffy. 'It's only our

secret-s'prise, Mummy dear, and we'll tell you all about it the very minute it's done; but *please* don't ask me what it is now, or else I'll have to tell.'

So her Mummy most carefully didn't; and bright and early next morning Tegumai went down to the river to think about new sound-pictures, and when Taffy got up she saw *Ya-las* (water is ending or running out) chalked on the side of the big stone water-tank, outside the Cave.

'Um,' said Taffy. 'These picture-sounds are rather a bother! Daddy's just as good as come here himself and told me to get more water for Mummy to cook with.' She went to the spring at the back of the house and filled the tank from a bark bucket, and then she ran down to the river and pulled her Daddy's left ear—the one that belonged to her to pull when she was good.

'Now come along and we'll draw all the left-over sound-pictures,' said her Daddy, and they had a most inciting day of it, and a beautiful lunch in the middle, and two games of romps. When they came to T, Taffy said that as her name, and her Daddy's, and her Mummy's all began with that sound, they should draw a sort of family group of themselves holding hands. That was all very well to draw once or twice; but when it came to drawing it six or seven times, Taffy and Tegumai drew it scratchier and scratchier, till at last the T-sound was only a thin long Tegumai with his arms out to hold Taffy and Teshumai. You can see from these three pictures partly how it happened. (20, 21, 22.)

Many of the other pictures were much too beautiful to begin with, especially before lunch; but as they were drawn over and over again on birch-

bark, they became plainer and easier, till at last even Tegumai said he could find no fault with them. They turned the hissy-snake the other way round for the Z-sound, to show it was hissing backwards in a soft and gentle way (23); and they just made a

twiddle for E, because it came into the pictures so often (24); and they drew pictures of the sacred Beaver of the Tegumais for the B-sound (25, 26, 27, 28); and because it was a nasty, nosy noise, they just drew noses for the N-sound, till they were tired (29); and they drew a picture of the big lake-pike's mouth for the greedy Ga-sound (30); and they drew the pike's mouth again with a spear

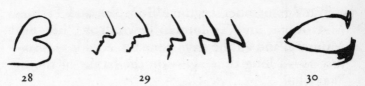

28   29   30

behind it for the scratchy, hurty Ka-sound (31);
and they drew pictures of a little bit of the winding
Wagai river for the nice windy-windy Wa-sound
(32, 33); and so on and so forth and so following
till they had done and drawn all the sound-pictures

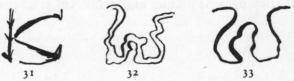

31   32   33

that they wanted, and there was the Alphabet, all
complete.

And after thousands and thousands and thousands of years, and after Hieroglyphics, and
Demotics, and Nilotics, and Cryptics, and Cufics,
and Runics, and Dorics, and Ionics, and all sorts of
other ricks and tricks (because the Woons, and the
Neguses, and the Akhoonds, and the Repositories
of Tradition would never leave a good thing alone
when they saw it), the fine old easy, understand-
able Alphabet—A, B, C, D, E, and the rest of 'em—
got back into its proper shape again for all Best
Beloveds to learn when they are old enough.

But *I* remember Tegumai Bopsulai, and Taffimai Metallumai and Teshumai Tewindrow, her dear Mummy, and all the days gone by. And it was so— just so—a long time ago—on the banks of the big Wagai!

ONE of the first things that Tegumai Bopsulai did after Taffy and he had made the Alphabet was to make a magic Alphabet-necklace of all the letters, so that it could be put in the Temple of Tegumai and kept for ever and ever.* All the Tribe of Tegumai brought their most precious beads and beautiful things, and Taffy and Tegumai spent five whole years getting the necklace in order. This is a picture of the magic Alphabet-necklace. The string was made of the finest and strongest reindeer-sinew, bound round with thin copper wire.

Beginning at the top, the first bead is an old silver one that belonged to the Head Priest of the Tribe of Tegumai; then come three black mussel-pearls; next is a clay bead (blue and grey); next a nubbly gold bead sent as a present by a tribe who got it from Africa (but it must have been Indian really); the next is a long flat-sided glass bead from Africa (the Tribe of Tegumai took it in a fight); then come two clay beads (white and green), with dots on one, and dots and bands on the other; next are three rather chipped amber beads; then three clay beads (red and white), two with dots, and the big one in the middle with a toothed pattern. Then the letters begin, and between each letter is a little whitish clay bead with the letter repeated small. Here are the letters:—

A is scratched on a tooth—an elk-tush, I think.
B is the Sacred Beaver of Tegumai on a bit of old ivory.
C is a pearly oyster-shell—inside front.
D must be a sort of mussel-shell—outside front.
E is a twist of silver wire.
F is broken, but what remains of it is a bit of stag's horn.
G is painted black on a piece of wood. (The bead after G is a small shell, and not a clay bead. I don't know why they did that.)
H is a kind of big brown cowrie-shell.
I is the inside part of a long shell ground down by hand. (It took Tegumai three months to grind it down.)
J is a fish-hook in mother-of-pearl.
L is the broken spear in silver. (K ought to follow J, of course; but the necklace was broken once and they mended it wrong.)
K is a thin slice of bone scratched and rubbed in black.
M is on a pale grey shell.

N is a piece of what is called porphyry with a nose scratched on it. (Tegumai spent five months polishing this stone.)

O is a piece of oyster-shell with a hole in the middle.

P and Q are missing. They were lost, a long time ago, in a great war, and the tribe mended the necklace with the dried rattles of a rattlesnake, but no one ever found P and Q. That is how the saying began, 'You must mind your P's and Q's.'*

R is, of course, just a shark's tooth.

S is a little silver snake.

T is the end of a small bone, polished brown and shiny.

U is another piece of oyster-shell.

W is a twisty piece of mother-of-pearl that they found inside a big mother-of-pearl shell, and sawed off with a wire dipped in sand and water. It took Taffy a month and a half to polish it and drill the holes.

X is silver wire joined in the middle with a raw garnet. (Taffy found the garnet.)

Y is the carp's tail in ivory.

Z is a bell-shaped piece of agate marked with Z-shaped stripes. They made the Z-snake out of one of the stripes by picking out the soft stone and rubbing in red sand and bee's-wax. Just in the mouth of the bell you see the clay bead repeating the Z-letter.

These are all the letters.

The next bead is a small round greeny lump of copper ore; the next is a lump of rough turquoise; the next is a rough gold nugget (what they call water-gold); the next is a melon-shaped clay bead (white with green spots). Then come four flat ivory pieces, with dots on them rather like dominoes; then come three stone beads, very badly worn; then two soft iron beads with rust-holes at the edges (they must have been magic, because they look very common); and last is a very very old African bead, like glass—blue, red, white, black, and yellow. Then comes the loop to slip over the big silver button at the other end, and that is all.

I have copied the necklace very carefully. It weighs one pound seven and a half ounces. The black squiggle behind is only put in to make the beads and things look better.

OF all the Tribe of Tegumai
  Who cut that figure, none remain,—
On Merrow Down the cuckoos cry—
  The silence and the sun remain.

But as the faithful years return
  And hearts unwounded sing again,
Comes Taffy dancing through the fern
  To lead the Surrey spring again.

Her brows are bound with bracken-fronds,
  And golden elf-locks fly above;
Her eyes are bright as diamonds
  And bluer than the skies above.

In mocassins and deer-skin cloak,
  Unfearing, free and fair she flits,
And lights her little damp-wood smoke
  To show her Daddy where she flits.

For far—oh, very far behind,
  So far she cannot call to him,
Comes Tegumai alone to find
  The daughter that was all to him.

THE CRAB THAT PLAYED
WITH THE SEA

EFORE the High and Far-Off Times, O my Best Beloved, came the Time of the Very Beginnings; and that was in the days when the Eldest Magician was getting Things ready. First he got the Earth ready; then he got the Sea ready; and then he told all the Animals that they could come out and play. And the Animals said, 'O Eldest Magician, what shall we play at?' and he said, 'I will show you.' He took the Elephant—All-the-Elephant-there-was—and said, 'Play at being an Elephant,' and All-the-Elephant-there-was played. He took the Beaver—All-the-Beaver-there-was—and said, 'Play at being a Beaver,' and All-the-Beaver-there-was played. He took the Cow—All-the-Cow-there-was—and said, 'Play at being a Cow,' and

All-the-Cow-there-was played. He took the Turtle—All-the-Turtle-there-was—and said, 'Play at being a Turtle,' and All-the-Turtle-there-was played. One by one he took all the beasts and birds and fishes and told them what to play at.

But towards evening, when people and things grow restless and tired, there came up the Man (With his own little girl-daughter?)—Yes, with his own best-beloved little girl-daughter sitting upon his shoulder, and he said, 'What is this play, Eldest Magician?' And the Eldest Magician said, 'Ho, Son of Adam, this is the play of the Very Beginning; but you are too wise for this play.' And the Man saluted and said, 'Yes, I am too wise for this play; but see that you make all the Animals obedient to me.'

Now, while the two were talking together, Pau Amma the Crab, who was next in the game, scuttled off sideways and stepped into the sea, saying to himself, 'I will play my play alone in the deep waters, and I will never be obedient to this son of Adam.' Nobody saw him go away except the little girl-daughter where she leaned on the Man's shoulder. And the play went on till there were no more Animals left without orders; and the Eldest Magician wiped the fine dust off his hands and walked about the world to see how the Animals were playing.

He went North, Best Beloved, and he found All-the-Elephant-there-was digging with his tusks and stamping with his feet in the nice new clean earth that had been made ready for him.

'*Kun?*' said All-the-Elephant-there-was, meaning, 'Is this right?'

'*Payah kun,*' said the Eldest Magician, meaning, 'That is quite right'; and he breathed upon the great rocks and lumps of earth that All-the-Elephant-there-was had thrown up, and they became the great Himalayan Mountains, and you can look them out on the map.

He went East, and he found All-the-Cow-there-was feeding in the field that had been made ready for her, and she licked her tongue round a whole forest at a time, and swallowed it and sat down to chew her cud.

'*Kun?*' said All-the-Cow-there-was.

'*Payah kun,*' said the Eldest Magician; and he breathed upon the bare patch where she had eaten, and upon the place where she had sat down, and one became the great Indian Desert, and the other became the Desert of Sahara, and you can look them out on the map.

He went West, and he found All-the-Beaver-there-was making a beaver-dam across the mouths of broad rivers that had been got ready for him.

'*Kun?*' said All-the-Beaver-there-was.

'*Payah kun,*' said the Eldest Magician; and he breathed upon the fallen trees and the still water, ·

THIS is a picture of Pau Amma the Crab running away while the Eldest Magician was talking to the Man and his Little Girl Daughter. The Eldest Magician is sitting on his magic throne, wrapped up in his Magic Cloud. The three flowers in front of him are the three Magic Flowers.* On the top of the hill you can see All-the-Elephant-there-was, and All-the-Cow-there-was, and All-the-Turtle-there-was going off to play as the Eldest Magician told them. The Cow has a hump, because she was All-the-Cow-there-was; so she had to have all there was for all the cows that were made afterwards. Under the hill there are Animals who have been taught the game they were to play. You can see All-the-Tiger-there-was smiling at All-the-Bones-there-were, and you can see All-the-Elk-there-was, and All-the-Parrot-there-was, and All-the-Bunnies-there-were on the hill. The other Animals are on the other side of the hill, so I haven't drawn them. The little house up the hill is All-the-House-there-was. The Eldest Magician made it to show the Man how to make houses when he wanted to. The Snake round that spiky hill is All-the-Snake-there-was, and he is talking to All-the-Monkey-there-was, and the Monkey is being rude to the Snake, and the Snake is being rude to the Monkey. The Man is very busy talking to the Eldest Magician. The Little Girl Daughter is looking at Pau Amma as he runs away. That humpy thing in the water in front is Pau Amma. He wasn't a common Crab in those days. He was a King Crab. That is why he looks different. The thing that looks like bricks that the Man is standing in, is the Big Miz-Maze. When the Man has done talking with the Eldest Magician he will walk in the Big Miz-Maze, because he has to. The mark on the stone under the Man's foot is a magic mark;* and down underneath I have drawn the three Magic Flowers all mixed up with the Magic Cloud. All this picture is Big Medicine and Strong Magic.

and they became the Everglades in Florida, and you may look them out on the map.

Then he went South and found All-the-Turtle-there-was scratching with his flippers in the sand that had been got ready for him, and the sand and the rocks whirled through the air and fell far off into the sea.

'*Kun?*' said All-the-Turtle-there-was.

'*Payah kun*,' said the Eldest Magician; and he breathed upon the sand and the rocks, where they had fallen in the sea, and they became the most beautiful islands of Borneo, Celebes, Sumatra, Java, and the rest of the Malay Archipelago, and you can look *them* out on the map!

By and by the Eldest Magician met the Man on the banks of the Perak River, and said, 'Ho! Son of Adam, are all the Animals obedient to you?'

'Yes,' said the Man.

'Is all the Earth obedient to you?'

'Yes,' said the Man.

'Is all the Sea obedient to you?'

'No,' said the Man. 'Once a day and once a night the Sea runs up the Perak River and drives the sweet-water back into the forest, so that my house is made wet; once a day and once a night it runs down the river and draws all the water after it, so that there is nothing left but mud, and my canoe is upset. Is that the play you told it to play?'

'No,' said the Eldest Magician. 'That is a new and a bad play.'

'Look!' said the Man, and as he spoke the great Sea came up the mouth of the Perak River, driving the river backwards till it overflowed all the dark forests for miles and miles, and flooded the Man's house.

'This is wrong. Launch your canoe and we will find out who is playing with the Sea,' said the Eldest Magician. They stepped into the canoe; the little girl-daughter came with them; and the Man took his *kris*—a curving, wavy dagger with a blade like a flame,—and they pushed out on the Perak River. Then the Sea began to run back and back, and the canoe was sucked out of the mouth of the Perak River, past Selangor, past Malacca, past Singapore, out and out to the Island of Bintang, as though it had been pulled by a string.

Then the Eldest Magician stood up and shouted, 'Ho! beasts, birds, and fishes, that I took between my hands at the Very Beginning and taught the play that you should play, which one of you is playing with the Sea?'

Then all the beasts, birds, and fishes said together, 'Eldest Magician, we play the plays that you taught us to play—we and our children's children. But not one of us plays with the Sea.'

Then the Moon rose big and full over the water, and the Eldest Magician said to the hunchbacked old man who sits in the Moon spinning a fishing-line with which he hopes one day to catch the world, 'Ho! Fisher of the Moon, are you playing with the Sea?'

'No,' said the Fisherman, 'I am spinning a line with which I shall some day catch the world; but I do not play with the Sea.' And he went on spinning his line.

Now there is also a Rat up in the Moon who always bites the old Fisherman's line as fast as it is made, and the Eldest Magician said to him, 'Ho! Rat of the Moon, are *you* playing with the Sea?'

And the Rat said, 'I am too busy biting through the line that this old Fisherman is spinning. I do not play with the Sea.' And he went on biting the line.

Then the little girl-daughter put up her little soft brown arms with the beautiful white shell bracelets and said, 'O Eldest Magician! when my father here talked to you at the Very Beginning, and I leaned upon his shoulder while the beasts were being taught their plays, one beast went away naughtily into the Sea before you had taught him his play.'

And the Eldest Magician said, 'How wise are little children who see and are silent! What was that beast like?'

And the little girl-daughter said, 'He was round and he was flat; and his eyes grew upon stalks; and he walked sideways like this; and he was covered with strong armour upon his back.'

And the Eldest Magician said, 'How wise are little children who speak truth! Now I know where Pau Amma went. Give me the paddle!'

So he took the paddle; but there was no need to paddle, for the water flowed steadily past all the islands till they came to the place called Pusat Tasek—the Heart of the Sea—where the great hollow is that leads down to the heart of the world, and in that hollow grows the Wonderful Tree, Pauh Janggi, that bears the magic twin-nuts. Then the Eldest Magician slid his arm up to the shoulder through the deep warm water, and under the roots of the Wonderful Tree he touched the broad back of Pau Amma the Crab. And Pau Amma settled down at the touch, and all the Sea rose up as water rises in a basin when you put your hand into it.

'Ah!' said the Eldest Magician. 'Now I know who has been playing with the Sea'; and he called out, 'What are you doing, Pau Amma?'

And Pau Amma, deep down below, answered, 'Once a day and once a night I go out to look for my food. Once a day and once a night I return. Leave me alone.'

Then the Eldest Magician said, 'Listen, Pau Amma. When you go out from your cave the waters of the Sea pour down into Pusat Tasek, and all the beaches of all the islands are left bare, and the little fish die, and Raja Moyang Kaban, the King of the Elephants, his legs are made muddy. When you come back and sit in Pusat Tasek, the waters of the Sea rise, and half the little islands are drowned, and the Man's house is flooded, and Raja Abdullah,* the King of the Crocodiles, his mouth is filled with the salt water.'

Then Pau Amma, deep down below, laughed and said, 'I did not know I was so important. Henceforward I will go out seven times a day, and the waters shall never be still.'

And the Eldest Magician said, 'I cannot make you play the play you were meant to play, Pau Amma, because you escaped me at the Very Beginning; but if you are not afraid, come up and we will talk about it.'

'I am not afraid,' said Pau Amma, and he rose to the top of the sea in the moonlight. There was nobody in the world so big as Pau Amma—for he was the King Crab of all Crabs. Not a common Crab, but a King Crab. One side of his great shell touched the beach at Sarawak; the other touched the beach at Pahang; and he was taller than the smoke of three volcanoes! As he rose up through the branches of the Wonderful Tree he tore off one of the great twin-fruits—the magic double-kernelled nuts that make people young,—and the little girl-daughter saw it bobbing alongside the canoe, and pulled it in and began to pick out the soft eyes of it with her little golden scissors.

'Now,' said the Magician, 'make a Magic, Pau Amma, to show that you are really important.'

Pau Amma rolled his eyes and waved his legs, but he could only stir up the Sea, because, though he was a King Crab, he was nothing more than a Crab, and the Eldest Magician laughed.

'You are not so important after all, Pau Amma,' he said. 'Now, let *me* try,' and he made a Magic with his left hand—with just the little finger of his left hand—and—lo and behold, Best Beloved, Pau Amma's hard, blue-green-black shell fell off him as a husk falls off a cocoa-nut, and Pau Amma was left all soft—soft as the little crabs that you sometimes find on the beach, Best Beloved.

'Indeed, you are very important,' said the Eldest Magician. 'Shall I ask the Man here to cut you with his *kris*? Shall I send for Raja Moyang Kaban, the King of the Elephants, to pierce you with his tusks? or shall I call Raja Abdullah, the King of the Crocodiles, to bite you?'

And Pau Amma said, 'I am ashamed! Give me back my hard shell and let me go back to Pusat Tasek, and I will only stir out once a day and once a night to get my food.'

And the Eldest Magician said, 'No, Pau Amma, I will *not* give you back your shell, for you will grow bigger and prouder and stronger, and perhaps you will forget your promise, and you will play with the Sea once more.'

Then Pau Amma said, 'What shall I do? I am so big that I can only hide in Pusat Tasek, and if I go anywhere else, all soft as I am now, the sharks and the dogfish will eat me. And if I go to Pusat Tasek,

THIS is the picture of Pau Amma* the Crab rising out of the sea as tall as the smoke of three volcanoes. I haven't drawn the three volcanoes, because Pau Amma was so big. Pau Amma is trying to make a Magic, but he is only a silly old King Crab, and so he can't do anything. You can see he is all legs and claws and empty hollow shell. The canoe is the canoe that the Man and the Girl Daughter and the Eldest Magician sailed from the Perak River in. The Sea is all black and bobbly, because Pau Amma has just risen up out of Pusat Tasek. Pusat Tasek is underneath, so I haven't drawn it. The Man is waving his curvy *kris*-knife at Pau Amma. The Little Girl Daughter is sitting quietly in the middle of the canoe. She knows she is quite safe with her Daddy. The Eldest Magician is standing up at the other end of the canoe beginning to make a Magic. He has left his magic throne on the beach, and he has taken off his clothes so as not to get wet, and he has left the Magic Cloud behind too, so as not to tip the boat over. The thing that looks like another little canoe outside the real canoe is called an outrigger. It is a piece of wood tied to sticks, and it prevents the canoe from being tipped over. The canoe is made out of one piece of wood, and there is a paddle at one end of it.

all soft as I am now, though I may be safe, I can never stir out to get my food, and so I shall die.' Then he waved his legs and lamented.

'Listen, Pau Amma,' said the Eldest Magician. 'I cannot make you play the play you were meant to play, because you escaped me at the Very Beginning; but if you choose, I can make every stone and every hole and every bunch of weed in all the seas a safe Pusat Tasek for you and your children for always.'

Then Pau Amma said, 'That is good, but I do not choose yet. Look! there is that Man who talked to you at the Very Beginning. If he had not taken up your attention I should not have grown tired of waiting and run away, and all this would never have happened. What will *he* do for me?'

And the Man said, 'If you choose, I will make a Magic, so that both the deep water and the dry ground will be a home for you and your children— so that you shall be able to hide both on the land and in the sea.'

And Pau Amma said, 'I do not choose yet. Look! there is that girl who saw me running away at the Very Beginning. If she had spoken then, the Eldest Magician would have called me back, and all this would never have happened. What will *she* do for me?'

And the little girl-daughter said, 'This is a good nut that I am eating. If you choose, I will make a

Magic and I will give you this pair of scissors, very sharp and strong, so that you and your children can eat cocoa-nuts like this all day long when you come up from the Sea to the land; or you can dig a Pusat Tasek for yourself with the scissors that belong to you when there is no stone or hole near by; and when the earth is too hard, by the help of these same scissors you can run up a tree.'

And Pau Amma said, 'I do not choose yet, for, all soft as I am, these gifts would not help me. Give me back my shell, O Eldest Magician, and then I will play your play.'

And the Eldest Magician said, 'I will give it back, Pau Amma, for eleven months of the year; but on the twelfth month of every year it shall grow soft again, to remind you and all your children that I can make magics, and to keep you humble, Pau Amma; for I see that if you can run both under the water and on land, you will grow too bold; and if you can climb trees and crack nuts and dig holes with your scissors, you will grow too greedy, Pau Amma.'

Then Pau Amma thought a little and said, 'I have made my choice. I will take all the gifts.'

Then the Eldest Magician made a Magic with the right hand, with all five fingers of his right hand, and lo and behold, Best Beloved, Pau Amma grew smaller and smaller and smaller, till at last there was only a little green crab swimming in the water alongside the canoe, crying in a very small voice, 'Give me the scissors!'

And the girl-daughter picked him up on the palm of her little brown hand, and sat him in the bottom of the canoe and gave him her scissors, and he waved them in his little arms, and opened them and shut them and snapped them, and said, 'I can eat nuts. I can crack shells. I can dig holes. I can climb trees. I can breathe in the dry air, and I can find a safe Pusat Tasek under every stone. I did not know I was so important. *Kun?*' (Is this right?)

'*Payah kun,*' said the Eldest Magician, and he laughed and gave him his blessing; and little Pau Amma scuttled over the side of the canoe into the water; and he was so tiny that he could have hidden under the shadow of a dry leaf on land or of a dead shell at the bottom of the sea.

'Was that well done?' said the Eldest Magician.

'Yes,' said the Man. 'But now we must go back to Perak, and that is a weary way to paddle. If we had waited till Pau Amma had gone out of Pusat Tasek and come home, the water would have carried us there by itself.'

'You are lazy,' said the Eldest Magician. 'So your children shall be lazy. They shall be the laziest people in the world. They shall be called the Malazy—the lazy people'; and he held up his finger to the Moon and said, 'O Fisherman, here is this Man too lazy to row home. Pull his canoe home with your line, Fisherman.'

'No,' said the Man. 'If I am to be lazy all my days, let the Sea work for me twice a day for ever. That will save paddling.'

And the Eldest Magician laughed and said, '*Payah kun*' (That is right).

And the Rat of the Moon stopped biting the line; and the Fisherman let his line down till it touched the Sea, and he pulled the whole deep Sea along, past the Island of Bintang, past Singapore, past Malacca, past Selangor, till the canoe whirled into the mouth of the Perak River again.

'*Kun?*' said the Fisherman of the Moon.

'*Payah kun*,' said the Eldest Magician. 'See now that you pull the Sea twice a day and twice a night for ever, so that the Malazy fishermen may be saved paddling. But be careful not to do it too hard, or I shall make a Magic on you as I did to Pau Amma.'

Then they all went up the Perak River and went to bed, Best Beloved.

Now listen and attend!

From that day to this the Moon has always pulled the Sea up and down and made what we call the tides. Sometimes the Fisher of the Sea pulls a little too hard, and then we get spring-tides; and sometimes he pulls a little too softly, and then we get what are called neap-tides; but nearly always he is careful, because of the Eldest Magician.

And Pau Amma? You can see when you go to the beach, how all Pau Amma's babies make little Pusat Taseks for themselves under every stone and bunch of weed on the sands; you can see them waving their little scissors; and in some parts of the world they truly live on the dry land and run up the palm-trees and eat cocoa-nuts, exactly as the girl-daughter promised. But once a year all Pau Ammas must shake off their hard armour and be soft—to remind them of what the Eldest Magician could do. And so it isn't fair to kill or hunt Pau Amma's babies just because old Pau Amma was stupidly rude a very long time ago.

Oh yes! And Pau Amma's babies hate being taken out of their little Pusat Taseks and brought home in pickle-bottles. That is why they nip you with their scissors, and it serves you right!

CHINA-GOING P. and O.'s*
Pass Pau Amma's playground close,
And his Pusat Tasek lies
Near the track of most B.I.'s.
N.Y.K. and N.D.L.
Know Pau Amma's home as well
As the Fisher of the Sea knows
'Bens,' M.M.'s, and Rubattinos.
But (and this is rather queer)
A.T.L.'s can *not* come here;
O. and O. and D.O.A.
Must go round another way.
Orient, Anchor, Bibby, Hall,
Never go that way at all.
U.C.S. would have a fit
If it found itself on it.
And if 'Beavers' took their cargoes
To Penang instead of Lagos,
Or a fat Shaw-Savill bore
Passengers to Singapore,
Or a White Star were to try a
Little trip to Sourabaya,
Or a B.S.A. went on
Past Natal to Cheribon,
Then great Mr Lloyds* would come
With a wire* and drag them home!

You'll know what my riddle means
When you've eaten mangosteens.

Or if you can't wait till then, ask them to let you have
the outside page of the *Times*;* turn over to page 2, where
it is marked 'Shipping' on the top left hand; then take the
Atlas (and that is the finest picture-book in the world) and
see how the names of the places that the steamers go to fit
into the names of the places on the map. Any steamer-
kiddy ought to be able to do that; but if you can't read, ask
some one to show it you.

THE CAT THAT WALKED BY HIMSELF

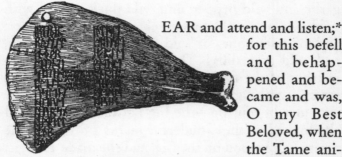

HEAR and attend and listen;* for this befell and behappened and became and was, O my Best Beloved, when the Tame animals were wild. The Dog was wild, and the Horse was wild, and the Cow was wild, and the Sheep was wild, and the Pig was wild—as wild as wild could be—and they walked in the Wet Wild Woods by their wild lones. But the wildest of all the wild animals was the Cat. He walked by himself, and all places were alike to him.

Of course the Man was wild too. He was dreadfully wild. He didn't even begin to be tame till he met the Woman, and she told him that she did not like living in his wild ways. She picked out a nice dry Cave, instead of a heap of wet leaves, to lie down in; and she strewed clean sand on the floor; and she lit a nice fire of wood at the back of the

Cave; and she hung a dried wild-horse skin, tail-down, across the opening of the Cave; and she said, 'Wipe your feet, dear, when you come in, and now we'll keep house.'

That night, Best Beloved, they ate wild sheep roasted on the hot stones, and flavoured with wild garlic and wild pepper; and wild duck stuffed with wild rice and wild fenugreek and wild coriander; and marrow-bones of wild oxen; and wild cherries, and wild grenadillas. Then the Man went to sleep in front of the fire ever so happy; but the Woman sat up, combing her hair. She took the bone of the shoulder of mutton—the big flat blade-bone—and she looked at the wonderful marks on it, and she threw more wood on the fire, and she made a Magic. She made the First Singing Magic in the world.

Out in the Wet Wild Woods all the wild animals gathered together where they could see the light of the fire a long way off, and they wondered what it meant.

Then Wild Horse stamped with his wild foot and said, 'O my Friends and O my Enemies, why have the Man and the Woman made that great light in that great Cave, and what harm will it do us?'

Wild Dog lifted up his wild nose and smelled the smell of the roast mutton, and said, 'I will go up and see and look, and say; for I think it is good. Cat, come with me.'

'Nenni!'* said the Cat. 'I am the Cat who walks

by himself, and all places are alike to me. I will not come.'

'Then we can never be friends again,' said Wild Dog, and he trotted off to the Cave. But when he had gone a little way the Cat said to himself, 'All places are alike to me. Why should I not go too and see and look and come away at my own liking?' So he slipped after Wild Dog softly, very softly, and hid himself where he could hear everything.

When Wild Dog reached the mouth of the Cave he lifted up the dried horse-skin with his nose and sniffed the beautiful smell of the roast mutton, and the Woman, looking at the blade-bone, heard him, and laughed, and said, 'Here comes the first. Wild Thing out of the Wild Woods, what do you want?'

Wild Dog said, 'O my Enemy and Wife of my Enemy, what is this that smells so good in the Wild Woods?'

Then the Woman picked up a roasted mutton-bone and threw it to Wild Dog, and said, 'Wild Thing out of the Wild Woods, taste and try.' Wild Dog gnawed the bone, and it was more delicious than anything he had ever tasted, and he said, 'O my Enemy and Wife of my Enemy, give me another.'

The Woman said, 'Wild Thing out of the Wild Woods, help my Man to hunt through the day and guard this Cave at night, and I will give you as many roast bones as you need.'

THIS is the picture of the Cave where the Man and the Woman lived first of all. It was really a very nice Cave, and much warmer than it looks. The Man had a canoe. It is on the edge of the river, being soaked in water to make it swell up. The tattery-looking thing across the river is the Man's salmon-net to catch salmon with. There are nice clean stones leading up from the river to the mouth of the Cave, so that the Man and the Woman could go down for water without getting sand between their toes. The things like black-beetles far down the beach are really trunks of dead trees that floated down the river from the Wet Wild Woods on the other bank. The Man and the Woman used to drag them out and dry them and cut them up for firewood. I haven't drawn the horse-hide curtain at the mouth of the Cave, because the Woman has just taken it down to be cleaned. All those little smudges on the sand between the Cave and the river are the marks of the Woman's feet and the Man's feet.

The Man and the Woman are both inside the Cave eating their dinner. They went to another cosier Cave when the Baby came, because the Baby used to crawl down to the river and fall in, and the Dog had to pull him out.

'Ah!' said the Cat, listening. 'This is a very wise Woman, but she is not so wise as I am.'

Wild Dog crawled into the Cave and laid his head on the Woman's lap, and said, 'O my Friend and Wife of my Friend, I will help your Man to hunt through the day, and at night I will guard your Cave.'

'Ah!' said the Cat, listening. 'That is a very foolish Dog.' And he went back through the Wet Wild Woods waving his wild tail, and walking by his wild lone. But he never told anybody.

When the Man waked up he said, 'What is Wild Dog doing here?' And the Woman said, 'His name is not Wild Dog any more, but the First Friend, because he will be our friend for always and always and always. Take him with you when you go hunting.'

Next night the Woman cut great green armfuls of fresh grass from the water-meadows, and dried it before the fire, so that it smelt like new-mown hay, and she sat at the mouth of the Cave and plaited a halter out of horse-hide, and she looked at the shoulder-of-mutton bone—at the big broad blade-bone—and she made a Magic. She made the Second Singing Magic in the world.

Out in the Wild Woods all the wild animals wondered what had happened to Wild Dog, and at last Wild Horse stamped with his foot and said, 'I will go and see and say why Wild Dog has not returned. Cat, come with me.'

'Nenni!' said the Cat. 'I am the Cat who walks by himself, and all places are alike to me. I will not come.' But all the same he followed Wild Horse softly, very softly, and hid himself where he could hear everything.

When the Woman heard Wild Horse tripping and stumbling on his long mane, she laughed and said, 'Here comes the second. Wild Thing out of the Wild Woods, what do you want?'

Wild Horse said, 'O my Enemy and Wife of my Enemy, where is Wild Dog?'

The Woman laughed, and picked up the blade-bone and looked at it, and said, 'Wild Thing out of the Wild Woods, you did not come here for Wild Dog, but for the sake of this good grass.'

And Wild Horse, tripping and stumbling on his long mane, said, 'That is true; give it me to eat.'

The Woman said, 'Wild Thing out of the Wild Woods, bend your wild head and wear what I give you, and you shall eat the wonderful grass three times a day.'

'Ah,' said the Cat, listening, 'this is a clever Woman, but she is not so clever as I am.'

Wild Horse bent his wild head, and the Woman slipped the plaited hide halter over it, and Wild Horse breathed on the Woman's feet and said, 'O my Mistress, and Wife of my Master, I will be your servant for the sake of the wonderful grass.'

'Ah,' said the Cat, listening, 'that is a very foolish

THIS is the picture of the Cat* that Walked by Himself, walking by his wild lone through the Wet Wild Woods and waving his wild tail. There is nothing else in the picture except some toadstools. They had to grow there because the woods were so wet. The lumpy thing on the low branch isn't a bird. It is moss that grew there because the Wild Woods were so wet.

Underneath the truly picture is a picture of the cosy Cave that the Man and the Woman went to after the Baby came. It was their summer Cave, and they planted wheat in front of it. The Man is riding on the Horse to find the Cow and bring her back to the Cave to be milked. He is holding up his hand to call the Dog, who has swum across to the other side of the river, looking for rabbits.

Horse.' And he went back through the Wet Wild Woods, waving his wild tail and walking by his wild lone. But he never told anybody.

When the Man and the Dog came back from hunting, the Man said, 'What is Wild Horse doing here?' And the Woman said, 'His name is not Wild Horse any more, but the First Servant, because he will carry us from place to place for always and always and always. Ride on his back when you go hunting.'

Next day, holding her wild head high that her wild horns should not catch in the wild trees, Wild Cow came up to the Cave, and the Cat followed, and hid himself just the same as before; and everything happened just the same as before; and the Cat said the same things as before; and when Wild Cow had promised to give her milk to the Woman every day in exchange for the wonderful grass, the Cat went back through the Wet Wild Woods waving his wild tail and walking by his wild lone, just the same as before. But he never told anybody. And when the Man and the Horse and the Dog came home from hunting and asked the same questions same as before, the Woman said, 'Her name is not Wild Cow any more, but the Giver of Good Food. She will give us the warm white milk for always and always and always, and I will take care of her while you and the First Friend and the First Servant go hunting.'

Next day the Cat waited to see if any other Wild

Thing would go up to the Cave, but no one moved
in the Wet Wild Woods, so the Cat walked there
by himself; and he saw the Woman milking the
Cow, and he saw the light of the fire in the Cave,
and he smelt the smell of the warm white milk.

Cat said, 'O my Enemy and Wife of my Enemy,
where did Wild Cow go?'

The Woman laughed and said, 'Wild Thing out
of the Wild Woods, go back to the Woods again,
for I have braided up my hair, and I have put away
the magic blade-bone, and we have no more need
of either friends or servants in our Cave.'

Cat said, 'I am not a friend, and I am not a servant. I am the Cat who walks by himself, and I wish
to come into your Cave.'

Woman said, 'Then why did you not come with
First Friend on the first night?'

Cat grew very angry and said, 'Has Wild Dog
told tales of me?'

Then the Woman laughed and said, 'You are the
Cat who walks by himself, and all places are alike
to you. You are neither a friend nor a servant. You
have said it yourself. Go away and walk by yourself in all places alike.'

Then Cat pretended to be sorry and said, 'Must
I never come into the Cave? Must I never sit by the
warm fire? Must I never drink the warm white milk?
You are very wise and very beautiful. You should
not be cruel even to a Cat.'

Woman said, 'I knew I was wise, but I did not

know I was beautiful. So I will make a bargain with you. If ever I say one word in your praise, you may come into the Cave.'

'And if you say two words in my praise?' said the Cat.

'I never shall,' said the Woman, 'but if I say two words in your praise, you may sit by the fire in the Cave.'

'And if you say three words?' said the Cat.

'I never shall,' said the Woman, 'but if I say three words in your praise, you may drink the warm white milk three times a day for always and always and always.'

Then the Cat arched his back and said, 'Now let the Curtain at the mouth of the Cave, and the Fire at the back of the Cave, and the Milk-pots that stand beside the Fire, remember what my Enemy and the Wife of my Enemy has said.' And he went away through the Wet Wild Woods waving his wild tail and walking by his wild lone.

That night when the Man and the Horse and the Dog came home from hunting, the Woman did not tell them of the bargain that she had made with the Cat, because she was afraid that they might not like it.

Cat went far and far away and hid himself in the Wet Wild Woods by his wild lone for a long time till the Woman forgot all about him. Only the Bat —the little upside-down Bat—that hung inside

the Cave knew where Cat hid; and every evening
Bat would fly to Cat with news of what was
happening.

One evening Bat said, 'There is a Baby in the
Cave. He is new and pink and fat and small, and
the Woman is very fond of him.'

'Ah,' said the Cat, listening, 'but what is the Baby
fond of?'

'He is fond of things that are soft and tickle,' said
the Bat. 'He is fond of warm things to hold in his
arms when he goes to sleep. He is fond of being
played with. He is fond of all those things.'

'Ah,' said the Cat, listening, 'then my time has
come.'

Next night Cat walked through the Wet Wild
Woods and hid very near the Cave till morning-
time, and Man and Dog and Horse went hunting.
The Woman was busy cooking that morning, and
the Baby cried and interrupted. So she carried him
outside the Cave and gave him a handful of pebbles
to play with. But still the Baby cried.

Then the Cat put out his paddy paw and patted
the Baby on the cheek, and it cooed; and the Cat
rubbed against its fat knees and tickled it under its
fat chin with his tail. And the Baby laughed; and
the Woman heard him and smiled.

Then the Bat—the little upside-down Bat—that
hung in the mouth of the Cave said, 'O my Hostess
and Wife of my Host and Mother of my Host's

Son, a Wild Thing from the Wild Woods is most
beautifully playing with your Baby.'

'A blessing on that Wild Thing whoever he may
be,' said the Woman, straightening her back, 'for I
was a busy woman this morning and he has done
me a service.'

That very minute and second, Best Beloved, the
dried horse-skin Curtain that was stretched tail-
down at the mouth of the Cave fell down—
woosh!—because it remembered the bargain she had
made with the Cat; and when the Woman went to
pick it up—lo and behold!—the Cat was sitting
quite comfy inside the Cave.

'O my Enemy and Wife of my Enemy and
Mother of my Enemy,' said the Cat, 'it is I: for you
have spoken a word in my praise, and now I can sit
within the Cave for always and always and always.
But still I am the Cat who walks by himself, and all
places are alike to me.'

The Woman was very angry, and shut her lips
tight and took up her spinning-wheel and began to
spin.

But the Baby cried because the Cat had gone
away, and the Woman could not hush it, for it struggled and kicked and grew black in the face.

'O my Enemy and Wife of my Enemy and
Mother of my Enemy,' said the Cat, 'take a strand
of the thread that you are spinning and tie it to
your spinning-whorl and drag it along the floor,

and I will show you a Magic that shall make your Baby laugh as loudly as he is now crying.'

'I will do so,' said the Woman, 'because I am at my wits' end; but I will not thank you for it.'

She tied the thread to the little clay spindle-whorl and drew it across the floor, and the Cat ran after it and patted it with his paws and rolled head over heels, and tossed it backward over his shoulder and chased it between his hind-legs and pretended to lose it, and pounced down upon it again, till the Baby laughed as loudly as it had been crying, and scrambled after the Cat and frolicked all over the Cave till it grew tired and settled down to sleep with the Cat in its arms.

'Now,' said Cat, 'I will sing the Baby a song that shall keep him asleep for an hour.' And he began to purr, loud and low, low and loud, till the Baby fell fast asleep. The Woman smiled as she looked down upon the two of them, and said, 'That was wonderfully done. No question but you are very clever, O Cat.'

That very minute and second, Best Beloved, the smoke of the Fire at the back of the Cave came down in clouds from the roof—*puff!*—because it remembered the bargain she had made with the Cat; and when it had cleared away—lo and behold!— the Cat was sitting quite comfy close to the fire.

'O my Enemy and Wife of my Enemy and Mother of my Enemy,' said the Cat; 'it is I: for you have spoken a second word in my praise, and now I can sit by the warm fire at the back of the Cave for always and always and always. But still I am the Cat who walks by himself, and all places are alike to me.'

Then the Woman was very very angry, and let down her hair and put more wood on the fire and brought out the broad blade-bone of the shoulder of mutton and began to make a Magic that should prevent her from saying a third word in praise of the Cat. It was not a Singing Magic, Best Beloved, it was a Still Magic; and by and by the Cave grew so still that a little wee-wee mouse crept out of a corner and ran across the floor.

'O my Enemy and Wife of my Enemy and Mother of my Enemy,' said the Cat, 'is that little mouse part of your Magic?'

'Ouh! Chee! No indeed!' said the Woman, and she dropped the blade-bone and jumped upon the footstool in front of the fire and braided up her hair very quick for fear that the mouse should run up it.

'Ah,' said the Cat, watching, 'then the mouse will do me no harm if I eat it?'

'No,' said the Woman, braiding up her hair, 'eat it quickly and I will ever be grateful to you.'

Cat made one jump and caught the little mouse, and the Woman said, 'A hundred thanks. Even the First Friend is not quick enough to catch little mice as you have done. You must be very wise.'

That very moment and second, O Best Beloved, the Milk-pot that stood by the fire cracked in two pieces—*ffft!*—because it remembered the bargain she had made with the Cat; and when the Woman jumped down from the footstool—lo and behold!— the Cat was lapping up the warm white milk that lay in one of the broken pieces.

'O my Enemy and Wife of my Enemy and Mother of my Enemy,' said the Cat, 'it is I: for you have spoken three words in my praise, and now I can drink the warm white milk three times a day for always and always and always. But *still* I am the Cat who walks by himself, and all places are alike to me.'

Then the Woman laughed and set the Cat a bowl of the warm white milk and said, 'O Cat, you are as clever as a man, but remember that your bargain was not made with the Man or the Dog, and I do not know what they will do when they come home.'

'What is that to me?' said the Cat. 'If I have my place in the Cave by the fire and my warm white milk three times a day I do not care what the Man or the Dog can do.'

That evening when the Man and the Dog came into the Cave, the Woman told them all the story of the bargain, while the Cat sat by the fire and smiled. Then the Man said, 'Yes, but he has not made a bargain, with *me* or with all proper Men after me.' Then he took off his two leather boots and he took up his little stone axe (that makes three) and he fetched a piece of wood and a hatchet (that is five altogether), and he set them out in a row and he said, 'Now we will make *our* bargain. If you do not catch mice when you are in the Cave for always and always and always, I will throw these five things at you whenever I see you, and so shall all proper Men do after me.'

'Ah,' said the Woman, listening, 'this is a very clever Cat, but he is not so clever as my Man.'

The Cat counted the five things (and they looked very knobby) and he said, 'I will catch mice when I am in the Cave for always and always and always; but *still* I am the Cat who walks by himself, and all places are alike to me.'

'Not when I am near,' said the Man. 'If you had not said that last I would have put all these things away for always and always and always; but now I am going to throw my two boots and my little stone axe (that makes three) at you whenever I meet you. And so shall all proper Men do after me!'

Then the Dog said, 'Wait a minute. He has not made a bargain with *me* or with all proper Dogs after me.'* And he showed his teeth and said, 'If you are not kind to the Baby while I am in the Cave for always and always and always, I will hunt you till I catch you, and when I catch you I will bite you. And so shall all proper Dogs do after me.'

'Ah,' said the Woman, listening, 'this is a very clever Cat, but he is not so clever as the Dog.'

Cat counted the Dog's teeth (and they looked very pointed) and he said, 'I will be kind to the Baby while I am in the Cave, as long as he does not pull my tail too hard, for always and always and always. But *still* I am the Cat that walks by himself, and all places are alike to me!'

'Not when I am near,' said the Dog. 'If you had not said that last I would have shut my mouth for always and always and always; but *now* I am going to hunt you up a tree whenever I meet you. And so shall all proper Dogs do after me.'

Then the Man threw his two boots and his little stone axe (that makes three) at the Cat, and the Cat ran out of the Cave and the Dog chased him up a tree; and from that day to this, Best Beloved, three proper Men out of five will always throw things at a Cat whenever they meet him, and all proper Dogs will chase him up a tree. But the Cat keeps his side of the bargain too. He will kill mice, and he will be kind to Babies when he is in the house, just as long as they do not pull his tail too hard. But when he has done that, and between times, and when the moon gets up and night comes,* he is the Cat that walks by himself, and all places are alike to him. Then he goes out to the Wet Wild Woods or up the Wet Wild Trees or on the Wet Wild Roofs, waving his wild tail and walking by his wild lone.*

Pussy can sit by the fire and sing,
    Pussy can climb a tree,
Or play with a silly old cork and string
    To 'muse herself, not me.
But I like *Binkie* my dog, because
    He knows how to behave;
So, *Binkie's* the same as the First Friend was,
    And I am the Man in the Cave.

Pussy will play man-Friday till
    It's time to wet her paw
And make her walk on the window-sill
    (For the footprint Crusoe saw);
Then she fluffles her tail and mews,
    And scratches and won't attend.
But *Binkie* will play whatever I choose,
    And he is my true First Friend.

Pussy will rub my knees with her head
    Pretending she loves me hard;
But the very minute I go to my bed
    Pussy runs out in the yard,
And there she stays till the morning-light;
    So I know it is only pretend;
But *Binkie*, he snores at my feet all night,
    And he is my Firstest Friend!

THE BUTTERFLY THAT STAMPED

HIS, O my Best Beloved, is a story—a new and a wonderful story—a story quite different from the other stories— a story about The Most Wise Sovereign Suleiman-bin-Daoud* —Solomon the Son of David.

There are three hundred and fifty-five stories about Suleiman-bin-Daoud; but this is not one of them. It is not the story of the Lapwing who found the Water; or the Hoopoe who shaded Suleiman-bin-Daoud from the heat. It is not the story of the Glass Pavement, or the Ruby with the Crooked Hole, or the Gold Bars of Balkis.* It is the story of the Butterfly that Stamped.

Now attend all over again and listen!

Suleiman-bin-Daoud was wise. He understood what the beasts said, what the birds said, what the fishes said, and what the insects said. He understood what the rocks said deep under the earth when they bowed in towards each other and groaned; and he understood what the trees said when they rustled in the middle of the morning. He understood everything, from the bishop on the bench to the hyssop on the wall;* and Balkis, his Head Queen, the Most Beautiful Queen Balkis, was nearly as wise as he was.

Suleiman-bin-Daoud was strong. Upon the third finger of his right hand he wore a ring. When he turned it once, Afrits and Djinns came out of the earth to do whatever he told them. When he turned it twice, Fairies came down from the sky to do whatever he told them; and when he turned it three times, the very great angel Azrael of the Sword* came dressed as a water-carrier, and told him the news of the three worlds,—Above—Below—and Here.

And yet Suleiman-bin-Daoud was not proud. He very seldom showed off, and when he did he was sorry for it. Once he tried to feed all the animals in all the world in one day, but when the food was ready an Animal came out of the deep sea and ate it up in three mouthfuls. Suleiman-bin-Daoud was very surprised and said, 'O Animal, who are you?' And the Animal said, 'O King, live for ever! I am the smallest of thirty thousand brothers, and our home is at the bottom of the sea. We heard that you were going to feed all the animals in all the

world, and my brothers sent me to ask when dinner would be ready.' Suleiman-bin-Daoud was more
surprised than ever and said, 'O Animal, you have
eaten all the dinner that I made ready for all the
animals in the world.' And the Animal said, 'O
King, live for ever, but do you really call *that* a
dinner? Where I come from we each eat twice as
much as that between meals.' Then Suleiman-bin-
Daoud fell flat on his face and said, 'O Animal! I
gave that dinner to show what a great and rich king
I was, and not because I really wanted to be kind
to the animals. Now I am ashamed, and it serves
me right.' Suleiman-bin-Daoud was a really truly
wise man, Best Beloved. After that he never forgot
that it was silly to show off; and now the real story
part of my story begins.

He married ever so many wives. He married nine
hundred and ninety-nine wives,* besides the Most
Beautiful Balkis; and they all lived in a great golden
palace in the middle of a lovely garden with
fountains. He didn't really want nine hundred and
ninety-nine wives, but in those days everybody
married ever so many wives, and of course the King
had to marry ever so many more just to show that
he was the King.

Some of the wives were nice, but some were simply horrid, and the horrid ones quarrelled with the
nice ones and made them horrid too, and then they
would all quarrel with Suleiman-bin-Daoud, and

THIS is the picture of the Animal* that came out of the sea and ate up all the food that Suleiman-bin-Daoud had made ready for all the animals in all the world. He was really quite a nice Animal, and his Mummy was very fond of him and of his twenty-nine thousand nine hundred and ninety-nine other brothers that lived at the bottom of the sea. You know that he was the smallest of them all, and so his name was Small Porgies. He ate up all those boxes and packets and bales and things that had been got ready for all the animals, without ever once taking off the lids or untying the strings, and it did not hurt him at all. The sticky-up masts behind the boxes of food belong to Suleiman-bin-Daoud's ships. They were busy bringing more food when Small Porgies came ashore. He did not eat the ships. They stopped unloading the foods and instantly sailed away to sea till Small Porgies had quite finished eating. You can see some of the ships beginning to sail away by Small Porgies' shoulder. I have not drawn Suleiman-bin-Daoud, but he is just outside the picture, very much astonished. The bundle hanging from the mast of the ship in the corner is really a package of wet dates for parrots to eat. I don't know the names of the ships. That is all there is in that picture.

that was horrid for him. But Balkis the Most Beautiful never quarrelled with Suleiman-bin-Daoud. She loved him too much. She sat in her rooms in the Golden Palace, or walked in the Palace garden, and was truly sorry for him.

Of course if he had chosen to turn his ring on his finger and call up the Djinns and the Afrits they would have magicked all those nine hundred and ninety-nine quarrelsome wives into white mules of the desert or greyhounds or pomegranate seeds; but Suleiman-bin-Daoud thought that that would be showing off. So, when they quarrelled too much, he only walked by himself in one part of the beautiful Palace gardens and wished he had never been born.

One day, when they had quarrelled for three weeks—all nine hundred and ninety-nine wives together—Suleiman-bin-Daoud went out for peace and quiet as usual; and among the orange-trees he met Balkis the Most Beautiful, very sorrowful because Suleiman-bin-Daoud was so worried. And she said to him, 'O my Lord and Light of my Eyes, turn the ring upon your finger and show these Queens of Egypt and Mesopotamia and Persia and China that you are the great and terrible King.' But Suleiman-bin-Daoud shook his head and said, 'O my Lady and Delight of my Life, remember the Animal that came out of the sea and made me ashamed before all the animals in all the world because I showed off. Now, if I showed off before these Queens of Persia and Egypt and Abyssinia and China, merely because they worry me, I might be made even more ashamed than I have been.'

And Balkis the Most Beautiful said, 'O my Lord and Treasure of my Soul, what will you do?'

And Suleiman-bin-Daoud said, 'O my Lady and Content of my Heart, I shall continue to endure my fate at the hands of these nine hundred and ninety-nine Queens who vex me with their continual quarrelling.'

So he went on between the lilies and the loquats and the roses and the cannas and the heavy-scented ginger-plants that grew in the garden, till he came to the great camphor-tree that was called the Camphor Tree of Suleiman-bin-Daoud. But Balkis hid among the tall irises and the spotted bamboos and the red lilies behind the camphor-tree, so as to be near her own true love, Suleiman-bin-Daoud.

Presently two Butterflies flew under the tree, quarrelling.

Suleiman-bin-Daoud heard one say to the other, 'I wonder at your presumption in talking like this to me. Don't you know that if I stamped with my foot all Suleiman-bin-Daoud's Palace and this garden here would immediately vanish in a clap of thunder?'

Then Suleiman-bin-Daoud forgot his nine hundred and ninety-nine bothersome wives, and laughed, till the camphor-tree shook, at the Butterfly's boast. And he held out his finger and said, 'Little man, come here.'

The Butterfly was dreadfully frightened, but he managed to fly up to the hand of Suleiman-bin-Daoud, and clung there, fanning himself. Suleiman-bin-Daoud bent his head and whispered very softly, 'Little man, you know that all your stamping wouldn't bend one blade of grass. What made you tell that awful fib to your wife?—for doubtless she is your wife.'

The Butterfly looked at Suleiman-bin-Daoud and saw the most wise King's eyes twinkle like stars on a frosty night, and he picked up his courage with both wings, and he put his head on one side and said, 'O King, live for ever. She *is* my wife; and you know what wives are like.'

Suleiman-bin-Daoud smiled in his beard and said, 'Yes, *I* know, little brother.'

'One must keep them in order somehow,' said the Butterfly, 'and she has been quarrelling with me all the morning. I said that to quiet her.'

And Suleiman-bin-Daoud said, 'May it quiet her. Go back to your wife, little brother, and let me hear what you say.'

Back flew the Butterfly to his wife, who was all of a twitter behind a leaf, and she said, 'He heard you! Suleiman-bin-Daoud himself heard you!'

'Heard me!' said the Butterfly. 'Of course he did. I meant him to hear me.'

'And what did he say? Oh, what did he say?'

'Well,' said the Butterfly, fanning himself most

importantly, 'between you and me, my dear—of
course I don't blame him, because his Palace must
have cost a great deal and the oranges are just ripen-
ing,—he asked me not to stamp, and I promised I
wouldn't.'

'Gracious!' said his wife, and sat quite quiet; but
Suleiman-bin-Daoud laughed till the tears ran down
his face at the impudence of the bad little Butterfly.

Balkis the Most Beautiful stood up behind the
tree among the red lilies and smiled to herself, for
she had heard all this talk. She thought, 'If I am
wise I can yet save my Lord from the persecutions
of these quarrelsome Queens,' and she held out her
finger and whispered softly to the Butterfly's Wife,
'Little woman, come here.' Up flew the Butterfly's
Wife, very frightened, and clung to Balkis's white
hand.

Balkis bent her beautiful head down and whispered, 'Little woman, do you believe what your
husband has just said?'

The Butterfly's Wife looked at Balkis, and saw
the Most Beautiful Queen's eyes shining like deep
pools with starlight on them, and she picked up her
courage with both wings and said, 'O Queen, be
lovely for ever. *You* know what men-folk are like.'

And the Queen Balkis, the Wise Balkis of Sheba,
put her hand to her lips to hide a smile and said,
'Little sister, *I* know.'

'They get angry,' said the Butterfly's Wife,

fanning herself quickly, 'over nothing at all, but we must humour them, O Queen. They never mean half they say. If it pleases my husband to believe that I believe he can make Suleiman-bin-Daoud's Palace disappear by stamping his foot, I'm sure *I* don't care. He'll forget all about it to-morrow.'

'Little sister,' said Balkis, 'you are quite right; but next time he begins to boast, take him at his word. Ask him to stamp, and see what will happen. *We* know what men-folk are like, don't we? He'll be very much ashamed.'

Away flew the Butterfly's Wife to her husband, and in five minutes they were quarrelling worse than ever.

'Remember!' said the Butterfly. 'Remember what I can do if I stamp my foot.'

'I don't believe you one little bit,' said the Butterfly's Wife. 'I should very much like to see it done. Suppose you stamp now.'

'I promised Suleiman-bin-Daoud that I wouldn't,' said the Butterfly, 'and I don't want to break my promise.'

'It wouldn't matter if you did,' said his wife. 'You couldn't bend a blade of grass with your stamping. I dare you to do it,' she said. 'Stamp! Stamp! Stamp!'

Suleiman-bin-Daoud, sitting under the camphor-tree, heard every word of this, and he laughed as he had never laughed in his life before. He forgot all about his Queens; he forgot about the Animal that came out of the sea; he forgot about showing off. He just laughed with joy, and Balkis, on the other side of the tree, smiled because her own true love was so joyful.

Presently the Butterfly, very hot and puffy, came whirling back under the shadow of the camphor-tree and said to Suleiman, 'She wants me to stamp! She wants to see what will happen, O Suleiman-bin-Daoud! You know I can't do it, and now she'll never believe a word I say. She'll laugh at me to the end of my days!'

'No, little brother,' said Suleiman-bin-Daoud, 'she will never laugh at you again,' and he turned the ring on his finger—just for the little Butterfly's sake, not for the sake of showing off,—and, lo and behold, four huge Djinns* came out of the earth!

'Slaves,' said Suleiman-bin-Daoud, 'when this gentleman on my finger' (that was where the impudent Butterfly was sitting) 'stamps his left front forefoot you will make my Palace and these gardens disappear in a clap of thunder. When he stamps again you will bring them back carefully.'

'Now, little brother,' he said, 'go back to your wife and stamp all you've a mind to.'

Away flew the Butterfly to his wife, who was crying, 'I dare you to do it! I dare you to do it! Stamp! Stamp now! Stamp!' Balkis saw the four vast Djinns stoop down to the four corners of the gardens with the Palace in the middle, and she clapped her hands softly and said, 'At last Suleiman-bin-Daoud will do for the sake of a Butterfly what he ought to have done long ago for his own sake, and the quarrelsome Queens will be frightened!'

Then the Butterfly stamped. The Djinns jerked the Palace and the gardens a thousand miles into the air: there was a most awful thunder-clap, and everything grew inky-black. The Butterfly's Wife fluttered about in the dark, crying, 'Oh, I'll be good! I'm so sorry I spoke! Only bring the gardens back, my dear darling husband, and I'll never contradict again.'

The Butterfly was nearly as frightened as his wife, and Suleiman-bin-Daoud laughed so much that it was several minutes before he found breath enough to whisper to the Butterfly, 'Stamp again, little brother. Give me back my Palace, most great magician.'

'Yes, give him back his Palace,' said the Butterfly's Wife, still flying about in the dark like a moth. 'Give him back his Palace, and don't let's have any more horrid magic.'

'Well, my dear,' said the Butterfly as bravely as he could, 'you see what your nagging has led to. Of course it doesn't make any difference to *me*—I'm used to this kind of thing—but as a favour to you and to Suleiman-bin-Daoud I don't mind putting things right.'

So he stamped once more, and that instant the

Djinns let down the Palace and the gardens, without even a bump. The sun shone on the dark-green orange-leaves; the fountains played among the pink Egyptian lilies; the birds went on singing; and the Butterfly's Wife lay on her side under the camphor-tree waggling her wings and panting, 'Oh, I'll be good! I'll be good!'

Suleiman-bin-Daoud could hardly speak for laughing. He leaned back all weak and hiccoughy, and shook his finger at the Butterfly and said, 'O great wizard, what is the sense of returning to me my Palace if at the same time you slay me with mirth!'

Then came a terrible noise, for all the nine hundred and ninety-nine Queens ran out of the Palace shrieking and shouting and calling for their babies. They hurried down the great marble steps below the fountain, one hundred abreast, and the Most Wise Balkis went statelily forward to meet them and said, 'What is your trouble, O Queens?'

They stood on the marble steps one hundred abreast and shouted, '*What* is our trouble? We were living peacefully in our golden Palace, as is our custom, when upon a sudden the Palace disappeared, and we were left sitting in a thick and noisome darkness; and it thundered, and Djinns and Afrits moved about in the darkness! *That* is our trouble, O Head Queen, and we are most extremely troubled on account of that trouble, for it was a troublesome trouble, unlike any trouble we have known.'

THIS is the picture of the four gull-winged Djinns lifting up Suleiman-bin-Daoud's Palace the very minute after the Butterfly had stamped. The Palace and the gardens and everything came up in one piece like a board, and they left a big hole in the ground all full of dust and smoke. If you look in the corner, close to the thing that looks like a lion, you will see Suleiman-bin-Daoud with his magic stick and the two Butterflies behind him. The thing that looks like a lion is really a lion carved in stone, and the thing that looks like a milk-can is really a piece of a temple or a house or something. Suleiman-bin-Daoud stood there so as to be out of the way of the dust and the smoke when the Djinns lifted up the Palace. I don't know the Djinns' names. They were servants of Suleiman-bin-Daoud's magic ring, and they changed about every day. They were just common gull-winged Djinns.

The thing at the bottom is a picture of a very friendly Djinn called Akraig. He used to feed the little fishes in the sea three times a day, and his wings were made of pure copper. I put him in to show you what a nice Djinn is like. He did not help to lift the Palace. He was busy feeding little fishes in the Arabian Sea when it happened.

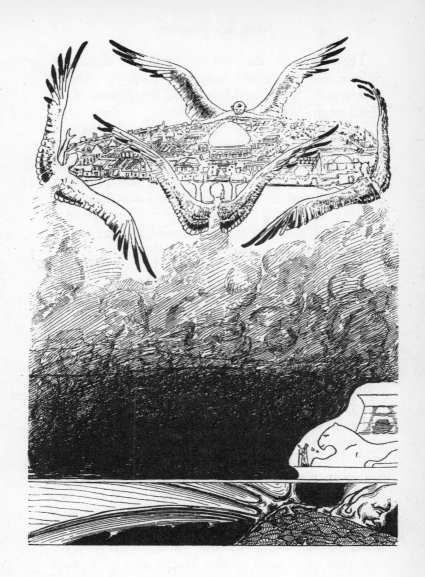

Then Balkis the Most Beautiful Queen—
Suleiman-bin-Daoud's Very Best Beloved—Queen
that was of Sheba and Sabie and the Rivers of the
Gold of the South—from the Desert of Zinn to the
Towers of Zimbabwe—Balkis, almost as wise as
the Most Wise Suleiman-bin-Daoud himself, said,
'It is nothing, O Queens! A Butterfly has made
complaint against his wife because she quarrelled
with him, and it has pleased our Lord Suleiman-
bin-Daoud to teach her a lesson in low-speaking
and humbleness, for that is counted a virtue among
the wives of the butterflies.'

Then up and spoke an Egyptian Queen—the
daughter of a Pharaoh—and she said, 'Our Palace
cannot be plucked up by the roots like a leek for
the sake of a little insect. No! Suleiman-bin-Daoud
must be dead, and what we heard and saw was the
earth thundering and darkening at the news.'

Then Balkis beckoned that bold Queen without
looking at her, and said to her and to the others,
'Come and see.'

They came down the marble steps, one hundred
abreast, and beneath his camphor-tree, still weak
with laughing, they saw the Most Wise King
Suleiman-bin-Daoud rocking back and forth with a
Butterfly on either hand, and they heard him say,
'O wife of my brother in the air, remember after
this to please your husband in all things, lest he be
provoked to stamp his foot yet again; for he has
said that he is used to this Magic, and he is most

eminently a great magician—one who steals away the very Palace of Suleiman-bin-Daoud himself. Go in peace, little folk!' And he kissed them on the wings, and they flew away.

Then all the Queens except Balkis—the Most Beautiful and Splendid Balkis, who stood apart smiling—fell flat on their faces, for they said, 'If these things are done when a Butterfly is displeased with his wife, what shall be done to us who have vexed our King with our loud-speaking and open quarrelling through many days?'

Then they put their veils over their heads, and they put their hands over their mouths, and they tiptoed back to the Palace most mousy-quiet.

Then Balkis—the Most Beautiful and Excellent Balkis—went forward through the red lilies into the shade of the camphor-tree and laid her hand upon Suleiman-bin-Daoud's shoulder and said, 'O my Lord and Treasure of my Soul, rejoice, for we have taught the Queens of Egypt and Ethiopia and Abyssinia and Persia and India and China with a great and a memorable teaching.'

And Suleiman-bin-Daoud, still looking after the Butterflies where they played in the sunlight, said, 'O my Lady and Jewel of my Felicity, when did this happen? For I have been jesting with a Butterfly ever since I came into the garden.' And he told Balkis what he had done.

Balkis—the Tender and Most Lovely Balkis—said, 'O my Lord and Regent of my Existence, I hid behind the camphor-tree and saw it all. It was I who told the Butterfly's Wife to ask the Butterfly to stamp, because I hoped that for the sake of the jest my Lord would make some great Magic and that the Queens would see it and be frightened.' And she told him what the Queens had said and seen and thought.

Then Suleiman-bin-Daoud rose up from his seat under the camphor-tree, and stretched his arms and rejoiced and said, 'O my Lady and Sweetener of my Days, know that if I had made a Magic against my Queens for the sake of pride or anger, as I made that feast for all the animals, I should certainly have been put to shame. But by means of your wisdom I made the Magic for the sake of a jest and for the sake of a little Butterfly, and—behold—it has also delivered me from the vexations of my vexatious wives! Tell me, therefore, O my Lady and Heart of my Heart, how did you come to be so wise?'

And Balkis the Queen, beautiful and tall, looked up into Suleiman-bin-Daoud's eyes and put her head a little on one side, just like the Butterfly, and said, 'First, O my Lord, because I loved you; and secondly, O my Lord, because I know what women-folk are.'

Then they went up to the Palace and lived happily ever afterwards.

But wasn't it clever of Balkis?

THERE was never a Queen like Balkis,
  From here to the wide world's end;
But Balkis talked to a butterfly
  As you would talk to a friend.

There was never a King like Solomon,
  Not since the world began;
But Solomon talked to a butterfly
  As a man would talk to a man.

She was Queen of Sabæa—
  And *he* was Asia's Lord—
But they both of 'em talked to butterflies
  When they took their walks abroad!

APPENDIX A

THE TABU TALE

 HE most important thing about Tegumai Bopsulai and his dear daughter, Taffimai Metallumai, was the Tabus of Tegumai, which were all Bopsulai.

Listen and attend, and remember, O Best Beloved; because *we* know about Tabus, you and I.

When Taffimai Metallumai (but you can still call her Taffy) went out into the woods hunting with Tegumai, she never kept still. She kept very unstill. She danced among dead leaves, she did. She snapped dry branches off, she did. She slid down banks and pits, she did—quarries and pits of sand, she did. She splashed through swamps and bogs, she did; and she made a horrible noise!

So all the animals that they hunted—squirrels, beavers, otters, badgers, and deer, and the rabbits—knew when Taffy and her Daddy were coming, and ran away.

Then Taffy said: 'I'm awfully sorry, Daddy, dear.'

Then Tegumai said: 'What's the use of being sorry? The squirrels have gone, and the beavers have dived, the deer have jumped, and the rabbits are deep in their buries. You ought to be beaten, O Daughter of Tegumai, and I would, too, if I didn't happen to love you.' Just then he saw a squirrel kinking and prinking round the trunk of an ash-tree, and he said: 'H'sh! There's our lunch, Taffy, if you'll only keep quiet.'

Taffy said: 'Where? Where? Show me! Show!' She said it in a raspy-gaspy whisper that would have frightened a steam-cow, and she skittered about in the bracken, being a 'citable child; and the squirrel flicked his tail and went off in large, free, loopy-leps to about the middle of Sussex before he ever stopped.

Tegumai was severely angry. He stood quite still, making up his mind whether it would be better to boil Taffy, or skin Taffy, or tattoo Taffy, or cut her hair, or send her to bed for one night without being kissed; and while he was thinking, the Head Chief of the Tribe of Tegumai came through the woods all in his eagle-feathers.

He was the Head Chief of the High and the Low and the Middle Medicine for the whole Tribe of Tegumai, and he and Taffy were rather friends.

He said to Tegumai: 'What is the matter, O Chiefest of Bopsulai? You look angry.'

'I *am* angry,' said Tegumai, and he told the Head Chief all about Taffy's very unstillness in the woods; and about the way she frightened the game; and about her falling into swamps because she would look behind her when she ran; and about her falling out of trees because she wouldn't take good hold on both sides of her; and about her getting her legs all greeny with duckweed from ponds and places, and bringing it sploshing into the cave.

The Head Chief shook his head till the eagle-feathers and the little shells on his forehead rattled, and then he said: 'Well, well! I'll see about it later. I wanted to talk to you, O Tegumai, on serious business.'

'Talk away, O Head Chief,' said Tegumai; and they both sat down politely.

'Observe and take notice, O Tegumai,' said the Head Chief. 'The Tribe of Tegumai have been fishing the Wagai river ever so long and ever so much too much. 'Consequence is, there's hardly any carp of any size left in it, and even the little carps are going away.'

'Quite so, O Tegumai,' said the Head Chief. 'What do you think of putting the Big Tribal Tabu on it, so as to stop every one from fishing there for six months?'

'That's a good plan, O Head Chief,' said Tegumai. 'But what will the consequence be if any of our people break the tabu?'

"Consequence will be, O Tegumai,' said the Head Chief, 'that we will make them understand it with sticks and stinging-nettles and dobs of mud; and if *that* doesn't teach them, we'll draw fine, freehand tribal patterns on their backs with the cutty edges of mussel-shells. Come along with me, O Tegumai, and we will proclaim the Tribal Tabu on the Wagai river.'

Then they went up to the Head Chief's head house, where all the Tribal Magic of Tegumai belonged; and they brought out the Big Tribal Tabu-pole,* made of wood, with the image of the Tribal Beaver of Tegumai and the other animals carved on top, and all the tribal Tabu-marks carved underneath.

Then they called up the Tribe of Tegumai with the Big Tribal Horn that roars and blores, and the Middle Tribal Conch that squeaks and squawks, and the Little Tribal Drum that taps and raps.

They made a lovely noise, and Taffy was allowed to beat the Little Tribal Drum, because she was rather friends with the Head Chief.

When all the Tribe had come together in front of the Head Chief's house, the Head Chief stood up and said and sang: 'O Tribe of Tegumai! The Wagai river has been fished too much, and the carp fish are getting frightened. Nobody must fish in the Wagai river for six months. It is tabu both sides and the middle; on all islands and mud-banks. It is tabu to bring a fishing-spear nearer than ten man-strides to the bank of the river. It is tabu, it is tabu, it is most specially tabu, O Tribe of Tegumai! It is tabu for this month and next month and next month and next month and next month and next month. Now go and put up the Tabu-pole by the river, and don't let anybody pretend that they haven't understood!'

Then the Tribe of Tegumai shouted, and put up the Tabu-pole by the banks of the Wagai river, and swiftly they ran down both banks (half the Tribe on one side and half on the other), and chased away all the small boys who hadn't attended the meeting because they were looking for crayfish in the river; and then they all praised the Head Chief and Tegumai Bopsulai.

Tegumai went home after this, but Taffy stayed with the Head Chief, because they were rather friends. She was very much surprised. She had never seen a tabu put on anything before, and she said to the Head Chief: 'What does tabu mean azactly?'

The Head Chief said: 'Tabu doesn't mean anything till you break it, O Only Daughter of Tegumai; but when you break it, it means sticks and stinging-nettles and fine, freehand, tribal patterns drawn on your back with the cutty edges of mussel-shells.'

Then Taffy said: 'Could I have a tabu of my own—a little small tabu to play with?'

THIS is a picture of the Tribal Totem Pole after it was put up on the banks of the Wagai river. That fat thing at the top is the Tribal Beaver of the Tribe of Tegumai. It is carved from lime-wood, and though you can't see the nails, it is nailed on to the rest of the pole, which is all in one piece. Below the Beaver are four birds—two ducks, one of them looking at an egg, a sparrow-bird, and a bird whose name I don't know. Below them is a Rabbit, below the Rabbit a Weasel, below the Weasel a Fox or a Dog (I am not quite sure which), and below the Dog two Fishes. On the other side of the pole is an Otter, a Badger, a Bison, and a Wild Horse. The rope that steadies the pole is looped round next to the Fishes. This shows that the Tabu is a Fish Tabu. If the Head Chief wanted to tabu the tribe killing Rabbits or Duck, he would have put the rope next to the Rabbit or the Duck carving; and so on with the other animals and birds.

The two black figures below the rope are meant for the Bad Man who didn't keep Tabu, and so grew all knobby and uncomfy, and the Good Man who kept Tabu and grew fat and round. They are painted on the pole with a paint made from oak-apples and pounded-up pieces of iron. At the very bottom of the pole (but there was not room to put it in the picture) are six copper rings to show that the Tabu was to last for six months.

You will see that there is nobody at all in the woods and hills behind. That is because the Tabu is a Strong Tabu and nobody would break it.

Then the Head Chief said: 'I'll give you a little tabu of your own, just because you made up that picture-writing which will one day grow into the A B C.' (You remember how Taffy and Tegumai made up the Alphabet? That was why she and the Head Chief were rather friends.)

He took off one of his magic necklaces—he had twenty-two of them—and it was made of bits of pink coral, and he said: 'If you put this necklace on anything that belongs to you your own self, no one can touch that thing until you take the necklace off. It will only work inside your own cave; and if you have left anything of yours lying about where you shouldn't, the tabu won't work till you have put that thing back in its proper place.'

'Thank you very much indeed,' said Taffy. 'Now, what d'you truly s'pose it will do to my Daddy?'

'I'm not quite sure,' said the Head Chief. 'He may throw himself down on the floor and shout, or he may have cramps, or he may just flop, or he may take Three Sorrowful Steps and say sorrowful words, and then you can pull his hair three times if you like.'

'And what will it do to my Mummy?' said Taffy.

'There aren't any tabus on people's Mummies,' said the Head Chief.

'Why not?' said Taffy.

'Because if there were tabus on people's Mummies, people's Mummies could put tabus on breakfasts, and dinners, and teas, and that would be very bad for the Tribe. Long and long ago the Tribe decided not to have tabus on people's Mummies anywhere—for anything.'

'Well,' said Taffy, 'do you know if my Daddy has any tabus of his own that will work on me—s'posin' I broke a tabu by accident?'

'You *don't* mean to say,' said the Head Chief, 'that your Daddy has never put any tabus on you yet?'

'No,' said Taffy; 'he only says "Don't," and gets angry.'

'Ah! I suppose he thought you were a kiddy,' said the Head Chief. 'Now, if you show him that you've a real tabu of your own, I shouldn't be surprised if he put several real tabus on you.'

'Thank you,' said Taffy; 'but I have a little garden of my very own outside the cave, and if you don't mind I should like you to make this tabu-necklace work so that if I hang it up on the wild roses in front of the garden, and people go inside, they won't be able to come out till they have said they are sorry.'

'Oh, certainly, certainly,' said the Head Chief. 'Of course you can tabu your very own garden.'

'Thank you,' said Taffy; 'and now I will go home and see if this tabu truly works.'

When she got back to the cave, it was nearly time for dinner; and when she came to the door,

Teshumai Tewindrow, her dear Mummy, instead of saying: 'Where have you been, Taffy?' said: 'O Daughter of Tegumai! come in and eat,' same as if she had been a grown-up person. That was because she saw a tabu-necklace on Taffy's neck.

Her Daddy was sitting in front of the fire waiting for dinner, and he said the very same thing, and Taffy felt *most* important.

She looked all round the cave to see that her own things (her private mendy-bag of otter-skin, with the shark's teeth and the bone needles and the deer-sinew thread; her mud-shoes of birch-bark; her spear and her throwing-stick and her lunch-basket) were all in their proper places, and then she slipped off her tabu-necklace quite quickly and hung it over the handle of the little wooden water-bucket that she used to draw water with.

Then her Mummy said to Tegumai, her Daddy, quite accidental: 'O Tegumai! won't you get us some fresh drinking-water for dinner?'

'Certainly,' said Tegumai, and he jumped up and lifted Taffy's bucket with the tabu-necklace on it. Next minute he fell down flat on the floor and shouted; then he curled himself up and rolled round the cave; then he stood up and flopped several times.

'My dear,' said Teshumai Tewindrow, 'it looks to me as if you had rather broken somebody's tabu somehow. Does it hurt?'

'Horribly,' said Tegumai. He took three sorrowful

steps and put his head on one side, and shouted: 'I broke tabu! I broke tabu! I broke tabu!'

'Taffy, dear, that must be your tabu,' said Teshumai Tewindrow. 'You'd better pull his hair three times, or he will have to go on shouting till evening; and you know what Daddy is like when he once begins.'

Tegumai stooped down, and Taffy pulled his hair three times; and he wiped his face, and said: 'My Tribal Word! That's a dreadful strong tabu of yours, Taffy. Where did you get it from?'

'The Head Chief gave it me. He told me you'd have cramps and flops if you broke it,' said Taffy.

'He was quite right. But he didn't tell you anything about Sign-tabus, did he?'

'No,' said Taffy. 'He said that if I showed you I had a real tabu of my own, you'd most likely put some real tabus on me.'

'Quite right, my only daughter dear,' said Tegumai. 'I'll give you some tabus that will simply a-maze you—stinging-nettle-tabus, sign-tabus, black and white tabus—dozens of tabus. Now attend to me. Do you know what this means?'

Tegumai skiffled his forefinger in the air snaky-fashion. 'That's tabu on wriggling when you're eating your dinner. It is an important tabu, and if you break it you'll have cramps—same as I did—or else I'll have to tattoo you all over.'

Taffy sat quite still through dinner, and then

Tegumai held up his right hand in front of him, the fingers close together. 'That's the Still Tabu, Taffy. Whenever I do that, you must stop *as* you are whatever you're doing. If you are sewing, you must stop with the needle half-way through the deer-skin. If you're walking, you stop on one foot. If you're climbing, you stop on one branch. You don't move again until you see me go like this.'

Tegumai put up his right hand and waved it in front of his face two or three times. 'That's the sign for Carry On. You can go on with whatever you are doing when you see me make *that*.'

'Aren't there any necklaces for that tabu?' said Taffy.

'Yes. There is a red and black necklace, of course, but how can I come tramping through the fern to give you a Still-Tabu necklace every time I see a deer or a rabbit and want you to be quiet?' said Tegumai. 'I thought you were a better hunter than that. Why, I might have to shoot an arrow over your head the minute after I had put Still Tabu on you.'

'But how would I know what you were shooting at?' said Taffy.

'Watch my hand,' said Tegumai. 'You know the three little jumps a deer gives before he starts to run off—like this?' He looped his forefinger three times in the air, and Taffy nodded. 'When you see me do that, you'll know we've found a deer. A little jiggle of the forefinger means a rabbit.'

'Yes. Rabbits run like that,' said Taffy, and jig-
gled her forefinger the same way.

'Squirrel's a long, climby-up twist in the air. Like
this!'

'Same as squirrels kinking round trees. *I* see,' said
Taffy.

'Otter's a long, smooth, straight wave in the air—
like this.'

'Same as otters swimming in a pool. *I* see,' said
Taffy.

'And beaver's just as if I was smacking somebody with my open hand.'

'Same as beavers' tails smacking on the water
when they are frightened. *I* see.'

'Those aren't tabus. Those are just signs to show
you what I am hunting. The Still Tabu is *the* thing
you must watch, because it's a big tabu.'

'I can put the Still Tabu on, too,' said Teshumai
Tewindrow, who was sewing deerskins together. 'I
can put it on you, Taffy, when you get too rowdy
going to bed.'

'What happens if I break it?' said Taffy.

'You can't break a tabu except by accident.'

'But s'pose I *did*,' said Taffy.

'You'd lose your own tabu-necklace. You'd have
to take it back to the Head Chief, and you'd just be
called Taffy again, and not Daughter of Tegumai.
Or perhaps we'd change your name to Tabumai
Skellumzulai—the Bad Thing, who can't Keep a

Tabu—and very likely you wouldn't be kissed for a day and night.'

'Umm!' said Taffy. 'I don't think tabus are fun at all.'

'Well, take your tabu-necklace back to the Head Chief, and say you want to be a kiddy again, O Only Daughter of Tegumai!' said her Daddy.

'No,' said Taffy. 'Tell me more about tabus. Can't I have some more of my own—my very own— strong tabus that give people Tribal Fits?'

'No,' said her Daddy. 'You aren't old enough to be allowed to give people Tribal Fits. That pink necklace will do quite well for you.'

'Then tell me more about tabus,' said Taffy.

'But I am sleepy, daughter dear. I'll just put tabu on any one talking to me till the sun gets behind that hill, and we'll go out in the evening and see if we can catch rabbits. Ask Mummy about the other tabus. It's a great comfort that you are a tabu-girl, because now I shan't have to tell you anything more than once.'

Taffy talked quietly to her Mummy till the sun was in the right position. Then she waked Tegumai, and they got all their hunting things ready and went out into the woods. But just as she passed her little garden outside the cave, Taffy took off her tabu-necklace and hung it on a rose-bush. Her garden-border was only marked with white stones, but she called the rose the real gate into it, and all the Tribe knew it.

'Who do you s'pose you'll catch?' said Tegumai.

'Wait and see till we come back,' said Taffy. 'The Head Chief said that any one who breaks that tabu will have to stay in my garden till I let him out.'

They went along through the woods and crossed the Wagai river on a fallen tree, and they climbed up to the top of a big bare hill where there were plenty of rabbits in the fern.

'Remember you're a tabu-girl now,' said Tegumai, when Taffy began to skitter about and ask questions instead of hunting for rabbits; and he made the Still Tabu sign, and Taffy stopped as if she had been all turned into solid stone. She was stooping to tie up a shoestring, and she stayed still with her hand on the string (*We* know that kind of tabu, don't we, Best Beloved?) only she looked hard at her Daddy, which you always must do when the Still Tabu is on. Presently, when he had walked a long way off, he turned round and made the Carry On sign. So she walked forward quietly through the bracken, always looking at her Daddy, and a rabbit jumped up in front of her. She was just going to throw her stick when she saw Tegumai make the Still Tabu sign, and she stopped with her mouth half open and her throwing-stick in her hand. The rabbit ran towards Tegumai, and Tegumai caught it. Then he came across the fern and kissed her and said: 'That is what I call a superior girl-daughter. It's some pleasure to hunt with you now, Taffy.'

A little while afterwards, a rabbit jumped up

where Tegumai could not see it, but Taffy could, and she knew it was coming towards her if Tegumai did not frighten it; so she held up her hand, made the Rabbit Sign (so as he should know that she wasn't in fun), and she put the Still Tabu on her own Daddy! She did—indeed she did, Best Beloved!

Tegumai stopped with one foot half lifted to climb over an old tree-trunk. The rabbit ran past Taffy, and Taffy killed it with her throwing-stick; but she was so excited that she forgot to take off the Still Tabu for quite two minutes, and all that time Tegumai stood on one leg, not daring to put his other foot down. Then he came and kissed her and threw her up in the air, and put her on his shoulder and danced and said: 'My Tribal Word and Testimony! This is what I call having a daughter that *is* a daughter, O Only Daughter of Tegumai!' And Taffy was most tremensely and wonderhugely pleased.

It was almost dark when they went home. They had five rabbits and two squirrels, as well as a water-rat. Taffy wanted the water-rat's skin for a shell-purse. (People had to kill water-rats in those days because they couldn't buy purses, but *we* know that water-rats are just as much tabu, these particular days, for you and me as anything else that is alive.)

'I think I've kept you out a little too late,' said Tegumai, when they were near home, 'and Mummy won't be pleased with us. Run home, Taffy! You can see the cave-fire from here.'

Taffy ran along, and that very minute Tegumai heard something crackle in the bushes, and a big, lean, grey wolf jumped out and began to trot quietly after Taffy.

Now, all the Tegumai people hated wolves and killed them whenever they could, and Tegumai had never seen one so close to his cave before.

He hurried after Taffy, but the wolf heard him and jumped back into the bushes. Those wolves were afraid of grown-ups, but they used to try to catch the children of the Tribe. Taffy was swinging the water-rat and singing to herself—her Daddy had taken off all tabus—so she didn't notice anything.

There was a little meadow close to the cave, and by the mouth of the cave Taffy saw a tall man standing in her rose-garden, but it was too dark to make out properly.

'I do believe my tabu-necklace has truly caught somebody,' she said, and she was just running up to look when she heard her Daddy say: 'Still, Taffy! Still Tabu till I take it off!'

She stopped where she was—the water-rat in one hand and the throwing-stick in the other—only turning her head towards her Daddy to be ready for the Carry On sign.

It was the longest Still Tabu she had had put

upon her all that day. Tegumai had stepped back close to the wood and was holding his stone throwing-hatchet in one hand, and with the other he was making the Still Tabu sign.

Then she thought she saw something black creeping sideways at her across the grass. It came nearer and nearer, then it moved back a little and then it crawled closer.

Then she heard her Daddy's stone throwing-hatchet whirr past her shoulder just like a partridge, and at the same time another hatchet whirred out from her rose-garden; and there was a howl, and a big grey wolf lay kicking on the grass, quite dead.

Then Tegumai picked her up and kissed her seven times and said: 'My Tribal Word and Tegumai Testimony, Taffy, but you *are* a daughter to be proud of! Did you know what it was?'

'I'm not sure,' said Taffy, 'but I think I guessed it was a wolf. I knew you wouldn't let it hurt me.'

'Good girl,' said Tegumai, and he stooped over the wolf and picked up both hatchets. 'Why, here's the Head Chief's hatchet!' he said, and he held up the Head Chief's magic throwing-hatchet, with the big greenstone head.

'Yes,' said the Head Chief from inside Taffy's rose-garden, 'and I'd be very much obliged if you would bring it back to me. I came to call on you this afternoon, and accidentally I stepped into Taffy's garden before I saw her tabu-necklace on the rose-tree. So, of course, I had to wait till Taffy came back to let me out.'

Then the Head Chief all in his feathers and shells took the Three Sorrowful Steps with his head on one side, and said: 'I broke tabu! I broke tabu! I broke tabu!' and bowed solemnly and statelily before Taffy, till his tall eagle-head feathers nearly touched the ground, and he said and sang: 'O Daughter of Tegumai, I saw everything that happened. You are a true tabu-girl. I am very pleased at you. At first I wasn't pleased, because I had to wait in your garden since six o'clock, and I know you only put tabu on your garden for fun.'

'No, not fun,' said Taffy. 'I truly wanted to see if my tabu would catch anybody; but I didn't know that a little tabu like mine would work on a big Head Chief like you, O Head Chief.'

'I told you it worked. I gave it you myself,' said the Head Chief. 'Of course it would work. But I don't mind. I want to tell you, Taffy, my dear, that I wouldn't have minded staying in your garden from twelve o'clock instead of only six o'clock, to see how beautifully you kept that last Still Tabu that your Daddy put on you. I give you my Chiefly Word, Taffy, that a great many men in the Tribe wouldn't have kept that tabu as you kept it, with that wolf crawling up to you across the grass.'

'What are you going to do with the wolfskin, O Head Chief?' said Tegumai, because any animal that

the Head Chief threw his hatchet at belonged to
the Head Chief by the Tribal Custom of Tegumai.

'I am going to give it to Taffy, of course, for a
winter cloak, and I'll make her a magic necklace of
her very own out of the teeth and claws,' said the
Head Chief; 'and I am going to have the story of
Taffy and the Still Tabu painted on wood on the
Tribal Tabu-Count, so that all the girl-daughters of
the Tribe can see and know and remember and
understand.'

Then they all three went into the cave, and
Teshumai Tewindrow gave them a most beautiful
supper, and the Head Chief took off his eagle-head
feathers and all his necklaces; and when it was time
for Taffy to go to bed in her own little cave,
Tegumai and the Head Chief came in to say good-
night, and they romped all round the cave, and
dragged Taffy over the floor on a deerskin (same as
some people are dragged about on a hearthrug),
and they finished by throwing the otter-skin cush-
ions about and knocking down a lot of old spears
and fishing-rods that were hung on the walls. At
last things grew so rowdy that Teshumai Tewindrow
came in and said: 'Still! Still Tabu on every one of
you! How do you ever expect that child to go to
sleep?' And they said the really good-night and
Taffy went to sleep.

After that, what happened? Oh, Taffy learned all
the tabus just like some people we know. She learned

the White Shark Tabu, which made her eat up her dinner instead of playing with it (and that goes with a green and white necklace, you know); she learned the Grown-Up Tabu, which prevented her from talking when Neolithic ladies came to call (and, you know, a blue and white necklace goes with that); she learned the Owl Tabu, which prevented her staring at strangers (and a black and blue necklace goes with that); she learned the Open Hand Tabu (and we know a white necklace goes with that) which prevented her snapping and snarling when people borrowed things that belonged to her; and she learned five other tabus.

But the chief thing she learned, and the one that she never broke, not even by accident, was the Still Tabu.

That was why she was taken everywhere that her Daddy went.

THIS is the picture that the Head Chief made of Taffy keeping the Still Tabu. It is done in the Head-Chiefly style of the Tribe of Tegumai, and it is full of Tabu meanings and signs. The wolf is lying under what is meant to be a Tabu tree. He is made squarely because that was the Head-Chiefly way of drawing. All that wavy curly stuff underneath him is the Tabu way of drawing grass, and below the grass is a thing like a piece of stone wall, which is the Tabu way of drawing earth. Taffy is always drawn in outline—quite white. You will see her over to the right, keeping the Still Tabu very hard. I do not know why they did not draw the water-rat that she was carrying, but I think it was because it wouldn't look pretty in the picture. Tegumai is standing over at the left, throwing his hatchet at the wolf. He is dressed in a cloak embroidered with the Sacred Beaver of the Tribe all turned into a pattern—to show that he belonged to the Tribe of Tegumai. He has a quiver with two arrows and a bow stuck into it, to show that he is hunting. He is making the Still Tabu sign with his left hand. Up above in the right-hand corner you will see the Head Chief standing in Taffy's garden, throwing his axe at the wolf. It is not a portrait of the Head Chief, but a sort of picture-writing of all the Head Chief there was. The square cap and the feathers behind show that it is a Head Chief, and the Sacred Beaver drawn on the edge of his cloak shows that he is the Head Chief of the Tegumais. There is no face, because the face of a Head Chief does not matter.

The Double-Headed Beaver right in the middle of Taffy's garden shows that there is a Tabu on the garden; which is why the Head Chief couldn't get out. The black door to the left is supposed to be the door into Taffy's cave, and those step-things behind are hills and rocks drawn in the Tabu way. The curly things under the eight roses in pots are the Tabu way of drawing short grass and turf.

This is a picture that really ought to be coloured, because half the meaning is lost without the colours.

HAM AND THE PORCUPINE

WHEN All the Animals lived in Big Nursery, before it was time to go into the Ark, Big Nurse had to brush their hair. She told them to stand still while she did it or it might be the worse for them. So they stood still. The Lion stood still and had his hair brushed into a splendid mane with a blob at the tip of his tail. The Horse stood still, and had his hair brushed into a beautiful mane and a noble tail. The Cow stood still and had her horns polished, too. The Bear stood still and got a Lick and a Promise. They *all* stood still, except one Animal, and he wouldn't. He wiggled and kicked sideways at Big Nurse.

Big Nurse told him, over and over again, that he would not make anything by behaving so. But he said he wasn't going to stand still for anyone, and he wanted his hair to grow all over him. So, at last, Big Nurse washed her hands of him and said: 'On-your-own-head-be-it-and-all-over-you!' *So*, that Animal went away, and his hair grew and grew—on his own head it was and all over him—all the while that they were waiting to go into the Ark.

And the more it grew, the longer, the harder, the harsher, and the pricklier it grew, till, at last, it was all long spines and jabby quills. On his own head it was and all over him, and particularly on his tail! So they called him Porcupine and stood him in the corner till the Ark was ready.

Then they all went into the Ark, two by two; but not one wanted to go in with Porcupine on account of his spines, except one small brother of his called Hedgehog who always stood still to have his hair brushed (*he* wore it short), and Porcupine hated him.

Their cabin was on the orlop-deck—the lowest—which was reserved for the Nocturnal Mammalia, such as Bats, Badgers, Lemurs, Bandicoots and Myoptics at large. Noah's second son, Ham,* was in charge there, because he matched the decorations; being dark-complexioned but very wise.

When the lunch-gong sounded, Ham went down with a basketful of potatoes, carrots, small fruits, grapes, onions and green corn for their lunches.

The first Animal that he found was the small Hedgehog Brother, having the time of his life among the blackbeetles. He said to Ham, 'I doubt if I would go near Porcupine this morning. The motion has upset him and he's a little fretful.'

Ham said: 'Dunno anything about that. My job is to feed 'em.' So he went into Porcupine's cabin, where Porcupine was taking up all the room in the world in his bunk, and his quills rattling like a loose window in a taxi.

Ham gave him three sweet potatoes, six inches of sugarcane, and two green corn-cobs. When he had finished, Ham said: 'Don't you ever say "thank-you" for anything?' 'Yes,' said Porcupine. 'This is my way of saying it.' And he swung round and slapped and swished with his tail sideways at Ham's bare right leg and made it bleed from the ankle to the knee.

Ham hopped up on deck, with his foot in his hand, and found Father Noah at the wheel.

'What do *you* want on the bridge at this hour of high noon?' said Noah.

Ham said, 'I want a large tin of Ararat biscuits.'*

'For what and what for?' said Noah.

'Because something on the orlop-deck thinks it can teach a nigger something about porcupines,' said Ham. 'I want to show him.'

'Then why waste biscuits?' said Noah.

'Law!' said Ham. 'I only done ask for the largest lid offen the largest box of Ararat biscuits on the boat.'

'Speak to your Mother,' said Noah. 'She issues the stores.'

So Ham's Mother, Mrs Noah, gave him the largest lid off the very largest box of Ararat biscuits in the Ark as well as some biscuits for himself; and Ham went down to the orlop-deck with the box-lid held low in his dark right hand, so that it covered his dark right leg from the knee to the ankle.

'Here's something I forgot,' said Ham and he held out an Ararat biscuit to Porcupine, and Porcupine ate it quick.

'Now say "Thank-you,"' said Ham.

'I will,' said Porcupine, and he whipped round, *swish*, with his wicked tail and hit the biscuit-tin. And *that* did him no good.

'Try again,' said Ham, and Porcupine swished and slapped with his tail harder than ever.

'Try again,' said Ham. This time the Porcupine swished so hard that his quill-ends jarred on his skin inside him, and some of the quills broke off short.

Then Ham sat down on the other bunk and said, 'Listen! Just because a man looks a little sunburned and talks a little chuffy, don't think you can be fretful with him. I am Ham! The minute that this Dhow touches Mount Ararat, I shall be Emperor of Africa from the Bayuda Bend* to the Bight of Benin, and from the Bight of Benin to Dar-es-Salam, and from Dar-es-Salam to the Drakensberg, and from the Drakensberg to where the Two Seas meet round the same Cape. I shall be Sultan of Sultans, Paramount Chief of all Indunas, Medicine Men, and Rain-doctors, and specially of the Wunungiri*— the Porcupine People—who are waiting for you. *You* will belong to me! You will live in holes and burrows and old diggings all up and down Africa;

and if ever I hear of you being fretful again I will tell my Wunungiri, and they will come down after you underground, and pull you out backwards. I—amm—Hamm!'

Porcupine was so frightened at this that he stopped rattling his quills under the bunk and lay quite still.

Then the small Hedgehog Brother who was under the bunk too, having the time of his life among the blackbeetles there, said: 'This doesn't look rosy for me. After all, I'm his brother in a way of speaking, and I suppose I shall have to go along with him underground, and *I* can't dig for nuts!'

'Not in the least,' said Ham. 'On his own head it was and all over him, just as Big Nurse said. But *you* stood still to have your hair brushed. Besides, you aren't in my caravan. As soon as this old buggalow (he meant the Ark) touches Ararat, I go South and East with my little lot—Elephants and Lions and things—*and* Porcupig—and scatter 'em over Africa. You'll go North and West with one or other of my Brothers (I've forgotten which), and you'll fetch up in a comfy little place called England—all among gardens and box-borders and slugs, where people will be glad to see you. And you will be a lucky little fellow always.'

'Thank you, Sir,' said the small Hedgehog Brother. 'But what about my living underground? That isn't my line of country.'

'Not the least need,' said Ham. And he touched the small Hedgehog Brother with his foot, and Hedgehog curled up—which he had never done before.

'Now you'll be able to pick up your own dry-leaf-bedding on your own prickles so as you can lie warm in a hedge from October till April if you like. Nobody will bother you except the gipsies;* and you'll be no treat to any dog.'

'Thank you, Sir,' said small Hedgehog Brother, and he uncurled himself and went after more blackbeetles.

And it all happened just as Ham said.

*   *   *

I don't know how the keepers at the Zoo feed Porcupine *but*, from that day to this, every keeper that *I* have ever seen feed a porcupine in Africa, takes care to have the lid of a biscuit-box held low in front of his right leg so that Porcupine can't get in a swish with his tail at it, after he has had his lunch.

Palaver done set!* Go and have your hair brushed!

EXPLANATORY NOTES

AUTHOR'S PREFACE. Published with the first story in *SN*, XXV/2 (Dec. 1897), 89, under the title 'The "Just-So" Stories'; it was never collected.

1 *Blue Skalallatoot stories*: all that survives of these is a map and a letter (*KJ* (Mar. 1968), 6–8). Of the Orvin Silvester Woodsey stories nothing is known.

HOW THE WHALE GOT HIS THROAT. First published *SN* as 'How the Whale got his Tiny Throat', Dec. 1897. The obvious source is the book of Jonah, chs. 2–3, but RK has also used the alternative account in MM, vol. ii. Further details may have come from two episodes in *The Surprising Adventures of Baron Munchausen* (1786) (see below).

On the knife forming the initial 'I', there are the initials 'RK' between the screws that join hilt and blade. On the blade is inscribed 'Holfen Tromsoe 1847'. Other Nordic references in the book are the runic characters in the 'First Letter' illustration and the 'Cat' initial. Cf. also the 'Kangaroo' initial.

4 *latitude Fifty North, longitude Forty West*: roughly 550 miles east-north-east of St John's, Newfoundland, a deep-water area between the Grand Banks (scene of RK's *Captains Courageous*) and the Mid-Atlantic Ridge. In *SN* the bearing is '41.42 and 26.36', without specifying 'north' and 'west', the last figure being '37' a few lines further on; according to RG, this would be an unlikely place for whales.

suspenders: a US term; the English equivalent is braces.

infinite-resource-and-sagacity: the epithet suggests a deliberate echo of Homer and that other resourceful shipwrecked mariner, hero of the *Odyssey*.

5 *stepped and he lepped*: three phrases, including this one, were added in the book version. In the *Munchausen* story (ch. viii) the Baron is swallowed by a large fish: 'I played my pranks, such as tumbling, hop, step and jump, etc., but nothing seemed to disturb him so much as the quick motion of my feet in dancing the hornpipe . . .'.

natal-shore: Homer's Odysseus also longs for his island home.

6 *picture of the Whale*: in *SOM*, 128–9, RK describes how on a trip to England (in the summer of 1894 or 1895) he saw from the ship 'a whale, who submerged just in time to clear us, and looked up into my face with an unforgettable little eye the size of a bullock's. . . . When I was illustrating *Just So Stories*, I remembered and strove after that eye.'

jaws-of-a-gaff: on a gaff-rigged sailing vessel, the upper edge of the quadrilateral mainsail is attached to a spar, the gaff. Its jaws are a fitting at the forward end; this fastens round the mast, allowing the other end to swing free as the sail is adjusted to catch the wind.

8 *up the beach*: MM, ii. 117: 'the fish approached the shore by
divine command, where it ejected [Jonah] like an infant
wrapped in swaddling clothes.'

Change here ... Fitchburg Road: railway stations in New
Hampshire and Massachusetts in RK's time. He and Josephine
may have heard them in a station announcement at Beaver
Falls or South Vernon, junctions respectively north and south
of Brattleboro. From Beaver Falls the Fitchburg Railroad ran
south-east via Keene to Boston, connecting at Ayer with a
line to Nashua. At South Vernon the Central Vermont met
the New London and Ashuelot Railroads; the latter ran north-
east via Ashuelot and Winchester to Keene.

there it stuck: in *Munchausen* ch. xvii a whale has swallowed
several ships. When it opens its mouth, the Baron frees their
crews by propping up two masts to prevent its jaws closing.

Sloka: verse form of the Sanskrit epics.

10 *shadow-pictures*: these and their surrounding patterns resemble the carvings of the South Pacific Islands.

HOW THE CAMEL GOT HIS HUMP. First published *SN*,
Jan. 1898. For some probable sources see Introduction, p.
xxiv–xxv. AT lists a category of tales (p. 24, no. 9), 'The
Unjust Partner: the bear works, the idle fox cheats him'.

13 *he was a Howler himself*: this phrase not in *SN*, here or later.

14 *punchayet*: literally a 'council of five'; a village council in
India.

15 *My long and bubbling friend*: not in *SN*; nor is the phrase
'Bubbles, I want you to work'.

16 *picture of the Djinn*: the figures in this drawing recall some
of William Harvey's engravings in E. W. Lane's *Arabian
Nights' Entertainment*, ed. E. Stanley Poole (London: Chatto
& Windus, 1883; Murray, 1859).

The symbol of an egg is associated with the creation of the
world in many cultures, including Finnish, Egyptian, and
Hindu.

20 *Noah's Ark*: the style of this lower drawing has a Japanese
look. The background of the ark forms a capital A, making

the first example of the 'ARK-A' phonetic rebus that signs several drawings later in the book.

One of RK's early projects for *St Nicholas* (never published) was a story about a little boy who tried to make a Noah's Ark on an Indian pond, but could not control the animals and had to be rescued before he was drowned (letter to Mary Mapes Dodge, 15 Oct. 1892: Thomas Pinney (ed.), *The Letters of Rudyard Kipling* (London: Macmillan, 1990), ii. 62). His tentative title for a book of animal fables (including material used in *The Jungle Book*) was 'Noah's Ark Tales' (letter to Mrs Dodge, 24 Nov. 1892: ibid. 72). At 18 months Josephine Kipling was given a Noah's Ark which became a favourite toy (letter to Louisa Baldwin, 15 June 1894: ibid. 130). See also the border to the drawing of the elephant and crocodile.

HOW THE RHINOCEROS GOT HIS SKIN. First published *SN*, Feb. 1898, introduced by: 'Now this is the last tale and it tells how the Rhinoceros got his wrinkly skin.' The idea of a merchant on an 'uninhabited island' that is mysteriously connected to an exotic hinterland probably comes from E. W. Lane's *Arabian Nights* ch. xx, which describes the seven voyages of es-Sindibad (Sinbad). Rhinoceroses occur in one such place in the Second Voyage, while Socotra is mentioned in Lane's note 38 to this chapter. The consumption of unattended food, with perilous consequences, can be found in e.g. *Goldilocks and the Three Bears*. AT lists a folk-tale category (pp. 129, 139, and 144), 'Clothes stolen while bathing'.

The initial imitates Mexican art. The main figure's bird costume is Mayan, and its flanking animals are probably jaguars (cf. 'The Beginning of the Armadilloes'). The elongated figure around the top may be intended for the plumed serpent Quetzalcoatl: both this and the jaguar were important religious symbols. The rectangular eyes and the figure's boots resemble Zuni figures from New Mexico.

23 *Parsee*: descendant of refugees who settled in India after the Arab invasion of Persia in the 7th–8th centuries. Followers of the sage Zoroaster, they worship God in the forms of light and fire. The founder of the Bombay School of Art, where

RK's father was employed at the time of his birth, was a rich Parsee called Sir Jamsetjee Jeejeebhoy.

24 *Socotra*: Socotra is an island in the Indian Ocean, off the Horn of Africa. Mazandaran is a province of Iran.

26 *one of Pharaoh's chariots*: the words on the wheel read 'ptian Army No. 17633'. There are also some hieroglyphics. See Exod. 14: 25: 'and took off their [the Egyptians'] chariot wheels'.

Pestonjee Bomonjee: this was the name of a real Parsee (later a well-known artist) who was one of RK's father's students in Bombay (*KJ* (Mar. 1938), 24).

30 *Orotavo . . . Sonaput*: these are not thought to be real names, but echo places in India, Madagascar, and Tenerife. There follows in *SN*: 'where all small people—beginning to breathe slowly and evenly—must inevitably also accompany him—in order to arrive easily and unknowingly—at the enormous battlements of the luxurious city of Uninterrupted Slumber.' (See also the poem 'The City of Sleep' in 'The Brushwood Boy', *The Day's Work*.)

31 *Cape Gardafui*: extreme point of the Horn of Africa. Socotra Island and its group lie to the east of it. Ships sailing to Bombay would leave them to starboard on emerging from the Gulf of Aden into the Indian Ocean.

P. and O.: the Peninsular and Oriental Steamship Co. took British functionaries to and from India by way of the Suez Canal and the Red Sea (see RK's poem 'The Exiles' Line').

HOW THE LEOPARD GOT HIS SPOTS. First published *LHJ*, Oct. 1901, as part of a series advertised as a world exclusive (ignoring the publication of the first three stories in *SN*). The title 'Just So Stories' was not mentioned. Nelson Doubleday, son of RK's US publisher, claimed to have suggested the story's theme (see Introduction, p. xx), which is also a biblical text (see note to p. 43 below). Written 30 Mar. 1900 (CK), but perhaps started earlier (see Introduction, p. xx). Some minor changes in the book version suggest that the stories were Americanized for *LHJ*; other small changes expand passages that children may have found puzzling.

F. Posselt, *The Fables of the Veld* (Oxford University Press, 1929), 12, has a traditional African tale in which the leopard is given his spots by the guinea-fowl as a reward for guarding her nest. Finding it safe on her return, 'she marked his skin'.

The marks on the knife in the initial resemble Urdu writing, but do not appear to spell anything.

33 *High Veldt*: *RG* defines this as a plateau including 'most of Basutoland, the Orange Free State and the Southern Transvaal'.

35 *Baviaan*: the name means 'baboon' in Dutch.

grown-up: phrase in parentheses is not in *LHJ*.

36 *drawn him from a statue*: the drawing recalls Egyptian statuary, also perhaps Lockwood Kipling's illustrations to *Kim*, which were photographed from low-relief terracotta plaques (Lockwood had trained as an architectural sculptor). Thoth, god of wisdom in Egyptian mythology, was sometimes depicted as a baboon.

Hebric: none of these inscriptions spell anything in the scripts they imitate. They are mostly shaped to give the visual impression 'Baviaan' or 'this is wise Baviaan'. The marks on the sash resemble Coptic, derived from ancient Egyptian. The upper inscription on the plinth looks like Cuneiform, a form of writing found in ancient Persian and Babylonic inscriptions. The two inscriptions following imitate Bengali and Burmese scripts, and the next gives an impression of Hebrew. The lowest line is thought to be picture-writing invented by RK.

38 *Say that quickly aloud ... the forest must have been*: sentence in parentheses not in *LHJ*. 'Sprottled and spottled' in its description was also added to the book version.

39 *O you person without any form*: instead of this in *LHJ*: 'This is much too serious for dumb-crambo. (He meant he wouldn't eat him up, Best Beloved.)' Subsequent references to 'any form' have also been added in the book.

43 *for a nigger*: these words are not in *LHJ*.

Can the Ethiopian ... the Leopard his spots?: quoted from Jer. 13: 23.

44 *Sambo*: see Helen Bannerman's *Little Black Sambo* (1899: illustrated by the author), a now-controversial children's classic of the period. It was set not in Africa but in South India.

Find-the-Cat: puzzle-pictures, often including animals, were popular in the last half of the 19th century. The precise one referred to here has not been identified. The forest resembles the 'gloomy wood' in Gustave Doré's illustration to Dante, *The Vision of Hell* (trans. H. F. Cary, 1871), Canto I, l. 2.

THE ELEPHANT'S CHILD. First published in *LHJ*, Apr. 1900. Said to be inspired by the same child's letter as the Leopard story (see Introduction, p. xx). CK dates its writing as 18 Aug. 1899. On 16 Oct. 1899 RK revised *Just So Stories* begun in August.

The Ramayana of Tulsi Dass, trans F. S. Growse (N.W. Provinces and Oudh Government Press), Bk. I, p. 21 n., records this legend of an elephant: 'An alligator had seized him by the foot while bathing, and though he struggled desperately for 2000 years, he was unable to escape his enemy . . .'. Finally he realizes 'that god alone could save him'. RK owned the second edition, of 1880.

AT lists as folk-tale archetypes the quest; the defeat of a monster in its lair; and specifically (p. 186, no. 517) 'The Boy who Learned Many Things', who is driven out by his family and, because he understands the speech of birds, achieves greatness and comes back to triumph over them. Several tales in George McCall Theal, *Kaffir Folklore: Or, a Selection from the Traditional Tales Current among the People Living on the Eastern Border of the Cape Colony* (London: Sonnenschein, 1882), involve quest journeys to a river.

The initial 'I' is an Islamic-style design. Its square shape suggests the tiles of William de Morgan, whose studio RK was taken to visit as a boy (*SOM* 22). The peacock is a character in MM's account (vol. i) of the Eden myth, parodied in RK's 'The Enemies to Each Other' (*Debits and Credits*).

48 *Kolokolo Bird*: 'cluck-cluck bird'? In E. Jacottet, *Contes populaires des Basutos* (Paris: Leroux, 1895), 211, the hen is sent on a mission that makes possible a happy ending. She precedes her message with: 'Kokolokoloko!'

48 *great grey-green, greasy . . . fever-trees*: this description of the
river is rather long for a Homeric epithet; but does one hear
behind its rhythm the beat of African drums? See also
Rabelais, Bk. I, ch. 1, where Gargantua's genealogy is found
in 'un gros, gras, grand, gris, joli, petit, moisi livret, plus,
mais non mieux sentant que les roses' ('a big, fat, great, grey,
pretty, little, mouldy booklet, more strongly, but not better
smelling than roses)'. RK greatly respected Rabelais: see
'The Last of the Stories' (1889; collected in *Abaft the Funnel*
and *Uncollected Prose*, Sussex and Burwash edns.). *Acacia
xanthophloea* is a large deciduous thorn-tree, known as the
'fever-tree' because it grows in marshy places and was erro-
neously believed to carry malarial infection.

49 *little short red kind*: this and other descriptions in parentheses in this sentence are not in *LHJ*.

Khama's country: now Botswana.

53 *hijjus*: hideous(ly).

56 *Elephant's Child*: it has been pointed out that the elephant
resembles an Indian, not an African one.

59 *nobody spanked anybody any more*: in *LHJ*, 'everything
started fair'.

62 *I keep six honest serving-men*: Mrs Bambridge, RK's surviv-
ing daughter, said that this was 'her' poem, adding that as a
little girl she used to be known in the family as 'Elsie Why'.
RG suggests as its origin a medieval Latin epigram in the
Register of Daniel Rough, Clerk of Romney [Kent] in the
14th century:

Si sapiens fore vis sex servus qui tibi mando
Quid dicas et ubi, de quo, cur, quomodo, quando.

If you wish to be wise I commend to you six servants,
Ask what, where, about what, why, how, when.

THE SING-SONG OF OLD MAN KANGAROO. First published *LHJ*, June 1900. Perhaps begun in Aug. 1899 (see Introduction, p. xx). Not mentioned in CK. AT (p. 24) describes
a type of tale called 'The False Beauty-Doctor: the trickster
pretends to make the dupe beautiful and injures him'.

Possible sources include K. Langloh Parker, *Australian Legendary Tales* (1896), 'Bohra the Kangaroo', in which a four-legged kangaroo 'like a dog' is transformed by joining a tribal dance round a fire while the women sing. See also Baldwin Spencer and F. J. Gillen, *The Native Tribes of Central Australia* (London: Macmillan, 1899), 193–6, in which a totemic kangaroo is pursued by a dingo pack across Australia, magically returning to life each time they catch him—his bones and tail becoming features of the landscape. There is an account of the story being chanted by the Kangaroo tribe (p. 205), and the phrase 'old man kangaroo' is also used (p. 201). The initial 'N' recalls the Northern Lights; behind it is the constellation of the Plough or Great Bear.

63 *Little God Nqa*: in *LHJ* it is Nqa who has a 'bath in the salt-pan': Nqong has a 'roost in the Blue Gums'. No such gods as Nqa, Nquing, and Nqong occur in Spencer and Gillen, *Native Tribes*. *RG* suggests that they derive from 'Qong', a Melanesian god of Night, and 'Quing', a Bushman hunter, both mentioned in Andrew Lang's *Myth, Ritual and Religion* (1887); the first suggestion seems more plausible than the second, but neither is wholly convincing.

65 *ti-trees*: more usually spelt 'tea-tree'—an evergreen flowering shrub.

Tropics of Capricorn and Cancer: the tropic of Capricorn runs across Australia. The tropic of Cancer does not.

Wollgong River: an invented name.

Flinders: there is a range of mountains called Flinders in South Australia, but *RG* considers this reference to be to the Flinders river in Queensland.

66 *picture of Old Man Kangaroo*: this and the next are the only illustrations in which the figures cast shadows.

68 *Darling Downs*: a region in south Queensland.

69 *Old Scratch*: the devil.

70 *thing with the letters on it*: the letters read 'Patent Fed. Govt. Aus.' (Federal Government of Australia). The frame round Nqong's clock resembles Maori carvings.

73 *Warrigaborrigarooma*: an invented name.

THE BEGINNING OF THE ARMADILLOES. First published *LHJ*, May 1900. Perhaps begun in 1899 (see Introduction), but not mentioned in CK.

RK would not visit Brazil until 1927, but one of his earliest literary passions (*SOM* 9) was *Robinson Crusoe*, who was wrecked on an island off the coast of 'the Brazils'. Possible sources include Charles Darwin, *The Voyage of the 'Beagle'* (1839), which describes (ch. vi) the armadillo's method of curling up against enemies. Oliver Goldsmith's *A History of the Earth and Animated Nature* (1774), vol. ii, bk. vi, places its description just after 'Animals of the Hedgehog, or Prickly kind'. Both these works are in RK's study. In *Jataka*, Bk. XXII, no. 543 (Bhuridatta-Jataka), a tortoise escapes a king who wishes to kill it by persuading him to put it into water; *SOM* 141 and *Kim*, ch. ix both mention *Jataka*. RK also read Aphra Behn, *Oroonoko* (c. 1688) (letter to H. S. Canby, 9 Oct. 1909, Yale), which refers to the animal's 'armour'.

AT lists (p. 49, no. 122G) as an Indian oral tale: 'Wash me before Eating: Turtle tells jackal he must be soaked in water to soften his shell'; the jackal drops the turtle into water, whereupon it swims away. Edward Steere, *Swahili Tales as told by Natives of Zanzibar* (SPCK, 1889), gives (p. 373) a similar story about a lion and a tortoise.

78 *marked in red*: the route of the explorers, and the signatures to the scrolls at top and bottom of the drawing, were in red in the first edition. The route is the double line marked with arrows.

are told about in writing: the scroll at the bottom of the map reads (*sic*):

YE MANIE MOUTHES OF YE AMAZONS RIVER. This was ye whollie desprate essaie and venture of ye Gyant Shipp Sir Mat Vows hys fitting—which conceive in ranke follie engendured evil. Of ye fifty-seven advturers wh leaved Bristol—Ap. 17. 1503 returned no more than eleven to yt towne and these in such case yt ye verie swine had cause rather for to mock them in streetes (their bellies being at ye least filled) and their skinnes unslitted than to envie them their state of grace as mere men. Ye tracke of our

wavering and lamentable vyage towards ye E Indies—now
a vission far removed is set downe in red [as the arrows
were in the first edn.].

                         Lancelot Mayhew A M

The other writings read, taken anticlockwise from the left-
hand bottom corner of the map (following the arrows):

And here as near as maybe ye sterne came ashoar.
Here was oure 1st Camp after yt shee broke apeeces 19 of
us onlie.
Here did wee all take ye Othe to Sir Mtw Vowse wh. J.
Hanper hee broke.
River yt we called Rumbullion River on ye second night
Sir M Vowse here broacht all ye rumbullion for good cawse.
And so by pirogues across much mud.
Much fever in ye airs heere.
Here is onlie Mud and Crabbes.
Batts Hill.
Littel river of ye Tsluci.
Tsluci, a meer village.
A great field of corne, wh Nick Dyer wd trompe and
misuse being then dronke.
Wee were pressed here.
Here was buried N. Dyer, a prophane man but a stoute
sailor (of an arrow).
Here we burned ye pinnace.
IMOXATLAN a vaste towne of ye Indians where we were
all lovinglie held for 5 (five) days.
Here is all hie forest with Monkies.
Wee wente by ye River-banke to avoide ye forest but soe
did not avoid ye fever.
Heere do they mine Gold.
Ye mines wh. we were forbid to see.
Here are hid the Idols of Imoxatlan.
For meddling with a Pagod wh. hee conceived to be pure
Golde Sam Batts of ye Gyant (Sir M. Vowse his venture)
was so handled by ye thinges Preestes yt hee dyed in III
daies.

S. Batts hys grave hee was borne over ye maine River in a pirogue ye Indians hoistinge but soone dyed.

A Pagod wh wee founde upon a tower on a hill & ye Indians burned offerents[?] before.

Here is more forest.

[In large scroll at top of map:] All heere is starke unknowne: our Indians reniginge guidance for yt they wer afearde of Divvels and wee sicklie and few did perfors turne backe to ye Coaste agen after all these peynes wel-persuaded yt Here is no coming att ye Indies at least by lande Lancet. Mayhew.

Sir Matt. Vowse having put on hys back & front pieces after cleansing of 'em brighte was here worshipt as a Pagod by divers sillie Indians.

A greate citie whence wee were beet. Oure 1st assault itt was for takinge and halinge forth Indians for guides and came neere to be our ende so we carrie East by Northe with yt wee had.

Wee took four pirogues upon ye shore, our need justifying.

Here liveth Armourdilla or Hog-in-harnesse.

Jno. Hanper—a mutineer [over drawing of a hanged man] alsoe for stealing of ye stores before.

Fort Towne and Palisadoe of ye Chief Imoxotlanchuatl.

Fields and gardens of ye Indiens.

All here is an evil & stinking Marsh or Quagg, yt goes west ye Indians affirme 314 Spanish Leeagues.

Rivers out of ye marsh of Ilolotiputl.

Ye 2nd pirogue got so far seeking a waie out but came back nothing further except wee count the fever. Four sicke.

Here are horned Birdes and have also crownes.

Nat Thomas his grave (of a calenture).

Matheusec—a guinea-man yt trod on a serpente was left here to his owne drugges and ye Mercie.

Here is all rough reede—a man highe.

Here is a Jaguyar like to a great Catt.

Here is found Pekkary, a littel feerce pigg, and with him Tapyr, ye lesser Elephant.

Here by God's great Mercy the Royal Tiger was careened and we took up.

This seems to be an invented story in imitation of Hakluyt, of whose *Voyages* (1598–1600) RK owned a set.

84 *a regular whale*: in *LHJ*, 'a Gangetic Porpoise'.

87 *there are some in my garden*: this phrase not in *LHJ*; the hedgehog is not native in the USA. The tortoises were presumably pets in the garden at Rottingdean.

88 *any way you turn it*: Nora Crook (*Kipling's Myths of Love and Death*, London: Macmillan, 1989) suggests (pls. 7 and 8) that this drawing owes something to Blake's 'Behemoth and Leviathan', in *The Book of Job* (1825).

90 *Don and Magdalena*: steamships of the Royal Mail Packet Company. They were 'white and gold' because at that time they had white hulls and buff upperworks.

HOW THE FIRST LETTER WAS WRITTEN. First published in *LHJ*, Dec. 1901. CK gives the title 'Neolithic Ladies' to something written on 19 Sept. 1900. In *LHJ* 'Teshumai' is 'Tashumai' throughout, and the 'Tewara' is a 'Tewarra'. Many other small alterations have been made in the book version.

The markings on the hull of the ark in the initial are the Plimsoll lines, indicating the appropriate water levels when the ship was fully (but safely) loaded in summer and in winter. The flag carries the initials of Noah and his sons Shem, Ham, and Japhet (Gen. 7).

93 *it's an awful nuisance . . . write*: instead of this in *LHJ*, 'it's a bother that there isn't anyone that we could send with a message for the new spear'.

94 *did not turn round*: after this in *LHJ*, 'to look at the Stranger-Man, even though the Stranger-Man was unquestionably a Tewarra'.

95 *to draw pictures*: after this in *LHJ*, 'but she didn't stick her tongue out'.

97 *Now this is the picture . . . for him!*: this sentence not in *LHJ*. There is a version of Taffy's drawing there, but it is much simpler than the one in the book.

100 *Hetmans . . . Bonzes*: many of these are nonsense words; the rest are rulers, priests, military leaders, and magicians from different parts of the world.

100 *They had filled ... not ladylike*: of this passage, only 'they had sat upon him in a long line of six' is in *LHJ*.

101 *four caves*: in *LHJ*, 'four graduated glacial vernal oestuffy and fungeriferous caves'.

102 *They were thumping him ... point at Taffy*: this passage not in *LHJ*.

104 *Runic magic*: the runes on the left side of the tusk read (*sic*):

> This is the stori of Taffimai all ritten out on an old tusk. If u begin at the top left hand corner and go on to the right u can see for urself the things as tha happened.

On the right side:

> The reason that I spell it queerli is because there are not enugh letters in the Runic alphabet for all the ourds that I ouant to use to u o Belofed.

The part below the tusk is given in *RG*:

> This is the identical tusk on ouch the tale of Taffimai ous ritten and etched by the author.

Runes were supposed to have magic properties: in the Icelandic *Egil's Saga*, an ignorant would-be lover makes his beloved ill by putting a misspelt love rune in her bed. The male figures on the tusk appear North American; the principal female figure looks like a cartoon portrait of Mrs Kipling.

106 *Then the Head Chief ... surprises the stranger*: this paragraph not in *LHJ*.

107 *Merrow Down*: Merrow was a village near Guildford in Surrey (now a suburb). RK's friend John St Loe Strachey lived at Merrow Down. Bramley, Shere, and Shamley [Green] are all place-names in the same area, as is the river Wey, a tributary of the Thames.

HOW THE ALPHABET WAS MADE. No previous publication. Date of writing in CK 11 Sept. 1900.

125 *kept for ever and ever*: a reproduction of the necklace was made by Spinks, the London jewellers, and presented to RK by Sir Percy and Lady Bates in 1932. It is on exhibition at Bateman's, RK's home in Sussex, now the property of the National Trust.

126 *mind your P's and Q's*: be very careful. Brewer's *Dictionary of Phrase and Fable* (Cassell, 1895) suggests that 18th-century French dancing teachers would tell their pupils to mind their 'pieds' (feet) and 'queues' (wigs). RK owned a Brewer.

THE CRAB THAT PLAYED WITH THE SEA. First published in *PM*, Aug. 1902, as 'The Crab that made the Tides'. Dated 4 Dec. 1901 in CK. A letter to W. W. Skeat of 5 Jan. 1935, quoted in *RG*, 1677, acknowledges the story's debt to him: 'You sent me, years ago, your *Malay Magic* out of which I took ("pinched" is another word for it) my tale of "The Crab that played with the Tides", and used your Eldest Magician, including the phrase *Kun, Paya Kun*; the Rat; the Pusat Tasek, etc. etc. . . .'.

132 *three Magic Flowers*: the Magician's pose resembles the Hindu god Vishnu, holding three (Tibetan) lotus blossoms. The lotus symbolizes the birth of a divine being in Egyptian, Hindu, and Buddhist mythology.

a magic mark: the swastika was part of RK's logo, accompanying an elephant's head with a lotus-flower held in its trunk. This was designed by his father, after the traditional Hindu merchant's sign, drawn on account books to bring good luck. When Hitler came to power in Germany RK had the swastika removed from the covers of his books.

137 *Raja Moyang Kaban . . . Raja Abdullah*: not mentioned in *PM*.

140 *picture of Pau Amma*: the white outlines on a black ground, often used by Beardsley, may here be meant to recall the shadow-puppets and shadow-scenery of the Wayang theatre of Malaya and Indonesia. Also typical of both countries is the batik method of printing cloth, in which the pattern is painted with wax so that it remains pale when the cloth is dyed.

147 *P. and O.'s*: ships of the Peninsular and Oriental Steamship
Co. Other shipping companies mentioned in this poem are:
British India Line; Nippon Yusen Kaisha (Japan Shipping
Co.); Norddeutscher Lloyd (North German Lloyd); Ben Line
Steamers Ltd. of Edinburgh; Compagnie des Messageries
Maritimes; Navigazione Generale Italiana (Societe Reunite
Ficcio Rubattino); Atlantic Transport Line; Oregon and
Oriental Line; Deutsche Ost Afrika Line; Union Castle
Steamship Co.; the Elder Dempster Co.'s Beaver service to
W. Africa; British and S. American Steamship Navigation
Co.

Mr Lloyds: Lloyd's insurance market.

wire: this plays on the double meaning, telegram or towing
hawser.

outside page of the Times: shipping news was regularly published in the position described.

THE CAT THAT WALKED BY HIMSELF. First published *LHJ*,
July 1902. CK gives the date of writing as 23 Jan. 1902. The
characters' menu of 'wild rice and wild grenadillas' suggests
an American setting, while it is hard to resist seeing the tree-
lined road past the Naulakha gates, covered in snow, in the
cat drawing. Carrington (*KJ* (Dec. 1982), 14) called this story
'Rudyard's gentle satire on Carrie, his wife'.

There were cats, perhaps semi-wild, at Naulakha (letter to
Ripley Hitchcock, 13 Nov. 1894: Pinney (ed.), *Letters*, ii.
159). On 1 Dec. 1894 RK gave his wife a Persian (CK). There
is no record of cats at Rottingdean until just over a year
before the story was written, when Carrie was given another
Persian (CK). *KJ* (Oct. 1952), 10, quotes a 'legend' (origin
unspecified) that a cat visited the Christ-child in the manger.
The baby was wakeful, and neither his mother, the ox, the
donkey, nor the dog could soothe him—but the cat purred
him to sleep. Rosalind Meyer (*KJ* (Sept. 1985), 55) sees the
truly domesticated animals as RK the husband, the cat being
the part of him that his wife could not tame.

The marks on the capital H have been decoded as runes
that read (*sic*):

I Rudyard Kipling dreu this but because there was no mutton bone in the house I faked the anatomi from memori. R. K.

On the crosspiece of the 'H' they read: 'I also urote all the plais ascribed by Mrs Gallup' [*RG*]. Mrs Gallup, in *The Bilateral Cipher of Francis Bacon* (1900), ascribed Shakespeare's plays to Bacon. She based her ideas on an alleged code concealed in variations in the print of the early editions. RK mocks the Baconians in a Shakespeare parody, 'The Marred Drives of Windsor', as part of 'The Muse among the Motors' (*Definitive Verse*); and also in the story 'The Propagation of Knowledge' (*Debits and Credits*).

149 *Hear and attend and listen*: this phrase not in *LHJ*.

150 '*Nenni!*': an old French negative that resembles the mild protest of a cat whose owner has displeased it.

156 *picture of the Cat*: the upper section of this drawing was used on the dust-jacket of the first edn. This and 'Baviaan' are the only two drawings without shading.

166 *or with all proper Dogs after me*: this phrase not in *LHJ*, where the next sentence reads: 'And he sat down and growled dreadfully and showed his teeth . . .'.

167 *and when the moon gets up and night comes*: not in *LHJ*.

Then he goes . . . wild lone: this sentence not in *LHJ*. Instead: 'and if you look out at nights you can see him, waving his wild tail and walking by his wild lone—just the same as before'.

THE BUTTERFLY THAT STAMPED. First published *LHJ*, Oct. 1902. Written 4 Mar. 1902 (CK). Principal sources for the story are the Bible and the Koran, Surah 27. In the Bible the Queen of Sheba does not marry Solomon but 'went to her own country'. Additional details, including the name Balkis, come from MM. None of these include the butterfly. CK says it was originally a firefly. The story of Solomon's feast for the animals, and his humbling by a sea-monster which ate all the food provided, is told in MM, ii. 79–80.

The letters on King Solomon's sash in the initial read H T W S S T K S. According to *RG*, this is a Masonic reference to 'the Mark Mason's song which begins, "Hiram, the Widow's Son, sent to King Solomon the great Key Stone". The eight letters are well known in Scottish Freemasonry.' Solomon is also wearing a bracelet with Masonic emblems, 'the square and compasses'. The building of the temple at Jerusalem under King Solomon, with help from King Huram of Tyre (2 Chron. 2 ff.), is an important source of Masonic symbolism. Solomon's chair is part of 'The Ceremony of Installation for the Master and Officers of a Masonic Lodge' (*The Textbook of Freemasonry* (London: Reeves & Turner, 1874), 193). The signature RK is at the foot of the tree.

169 *Suleiman-bin-Daoud*: Muslim form of Solomon-ben-David.

Lapwing ... Gold Bars of Balkis: the lapwing, the hoopoe, and the glass pavement are in the Koran, Surah 27; the ruby comes from MM, ii. 83–5. The bars are the 'gold talents' the Queen of Sheba gives Solomon in 1 Kgs. 10: 10 and 2 Chron. 9: 9.

170 *hyssop on the wall*: 1 Kgs. 4: 33. Solomon's understanding of birds is mentioned in the Koran, Surah 27, where he also converses with an ant (see also MM, ii).

Azrael of the Sword: Muslim angel of death.

171 *nine hundred and ninety-nine wives*: in 1 Kgs. 11: 3, 'he had seven hundred wives ... and three hundred concubines'.

172 *picture of the Animal*: this is the only drawing with such a heavy black outline round it.

179 *Djinns*: in *LHJ* (here and hereafter) 'Afrits'.

APPENDIX A: THE TABU TALE. First published in *Collier's Weekly*, 29 Aug. 1903, and in *Windsor Magazine*, Sept. 1903. Collected only in Scribner's Outward Bound edn. of *Just So Stories* (vol. 20) and in Sussex and Burwash edns., *Land and Sea Tales*, vols. xvi and xiv respectively. CK recorded that a children's story 'modelled on the totem tales' was written 11 Oct. 1898. In *SOM*, p. 123, RK mentions a visit to the native American collections in the Smithsonian, Washington, DC.

There is a full account of tabus in different communities of the world in vol. i, ch. ii of J. G. Frazer, *The Golden Bough* (1890).

192 *Tribal Tabu-pole*: in *Windsor Magazine*, 'painted red, twelve foot long and a foot thick. . .'.

APPENDIX B: HAM AND THE PORCUPINE. Uncollected: published in *The Princess Elizabeth Gift Book in aid of The Princess Elizabeth of York Hospital for Children* (London: Hodder & Stoughton, 1935), and in a US copyright edition, Doubleday Doran, Oct. 1935. Written summer 1935, inspired by a child's letter asking how the hedgehog got his prickles (*KJ*, Sept. 1980).

214 *Ham*: according to legend, Ham was the ancestor of the African peoples.

215 *Ararat biscuits*: *RG* suggests that this is a pun on 'arrowroot biscuits', a well-known brand made by Jacobs of Reading.

216 *Bayuda Bend*: a curve in the River Nile north of Khartoum.

Wunungiri: this word has not been identified as belonging to any African language.

218 *gipsies*: they were said to eat hedgehogs baked in a layer of clay with which, when cooked, the prickles came off.

Palaver done set!: 'this meeting is closed.'

JANE AUSTEN	**Emma**
	Mansfield Park
	Persuasion
	Pride and Prejudice
	Sense and Sensibility
MRS BEETON	**Book of Household Management**
LADY ELIZABETH BRADDON	**Lady Audley's Secret**
ANNE BRONTË	**The Tenant of Wildfell Hall**
CHARLOTTE BRONTË	**Jane Eyre**
	Shirley
	Villette
EMILY BRONTË	**Wuthering Heights**
SAMUEL TAYLOR COLERIDGE	**The Major Works**
WILKIE COLLINS	**The Moonstone**
	No Name
	The Woman in White
CHARLES DARWIN	**The Origin of Species**
CHARLES DICKENS	**The Adventures of Oliver Twist**
	Bleak House
	David Copperfield
	Great Expectations
	Nicholas Nickleby
	The Old Curiosity Shop
	Our Mutual Friend
	The Pickwick Papers
	A Tale of Two Cities
GEORGE DU MAURIER	**Trilby**
MARIA EDGEWORTH	**Castle Rackrent**

A SELECTION OF   OXFORD WORLD'S CLASSICS

American Literature

British and Irish Literature

Children's Literature

Classics and Ancient Literature

Colonial Literature

Eastern Literature

European Literature

History

Medieval Literature

Oxford English Drama

Poetry

Philosophy

Politics

Religion

The Oxford Shakespeare

A complete list of Oxford Paperbacks, including Oxford World's Classics, Oxford Shakespeare, Oxford Drama, and Oxford Paperback Reference, is available in the UK from the Academic Division Publicity Department, Oxford University Press, Great Clarendon Street, Oxford OX2 6DP.

In the USA, complete lists are available from the Paperbacks Marketing Manager, Oxford University Press, 198 Madison Avenue, New York, NY 10016.

Oxford Paperbacks are available from all good bookshops. In case of difficulty, customers in the UK can order direct from Oxford University Press Bookshop, Freepost, 116 High Street, Oxford OX1 4BR, enclosing full payment. Please add 10 per cent of published price for postage and packing.